I0645724

MALAFORMED REALITIES

VOLUME FOUR

THOMAS M. MALAFARINA

HELLBENDER BOOKS

an imprint of Sunbury Press, Inc.
Mechanicsburg, PA USA

an imprint of Sunbury Press, Inc.
Mechanicsburg, PA USA

NOTE: This is a work of fiction. Names, characters, places and incidents are the product of the author's imagination or are used fictitiously, and any resemblance to actual persons, living or dead, business establishments, events or locales is entirely coincidental.

Copyright © 2021 by Thomas M. Malafarina.
Cover Copyright © 2021 by Sunbury Press, Inc.

Sunbury Press supports copyright. Copyright fuels creativity, encourages diverse voices, promotes free speech, and creates a vibrant culture. Thank you for buying an authorized edition of this book and for complying with copyright laws. Except for the quotation of short passages for the purpose of criticism and review, no part of this publication may be reproduced, scanned, or distributed in any form without permission. You are supporting writers and allowing Sunbury Press to continue to publish books for every reader. For information contact Sunbury Press, Inc., Subsidiary Rights Dept., PO Box 548, Boiling Springs, PA 17007 USA or legal@sunburypress.com.

For information about special discounts for bulk purchases, please contact Sunbury Press Orders Dept. at (855) 338-8359 or orders@sunburypress.com.

To request one of our authors for speaking engagements or book signings, please contact Sunbury Press Publicity Dept. at publicity@sunburypress.com.

FIRST HELLBENDER BOOKS EDITION: January 2021

Set in Adobe Garamond | Interior design by Crystal Devine | Cover design by Lawrence Knorr | Edited by Lawrence Knorr.

Publisher's Cataloging-in-Publication Data
Names: Malafarina, Thomas M., author.
Title: Malformed realities / Thomas M. Malafarina.
Description: First trade paperback edition. | Mechanicsburg, PA : Hellbender Books, 2021.
Summary: Thomas Malafarina strikes again with 28 spine-tingling tales of horror.
Identifiers: ISBN 978-1-620064-74-0 (softcover).
Subjects: FICTION / Horror | FICTION / Short Stories (single author).

Product of the United States of America
0 1 1 2 3 5 8 13 21 34 55

Continue the Enlightenment!

This book is dedicated to
my wonderful wife, JoAnne,
without whom none of these
books could be possible. Thanks
as always for your love,
patience, and support.

CONTENTS

INTRODUCTION

Malaformed Realities Volume 1 started several years ago as an idea to get some of my many short stories out to the public. It provided a venue for me to showcase my growing collection of more than one hundred such stories. We had already published *13 Deadly Endings* and *Ghost Shadows,* which were also short story collections. Since that time, we've published *Malaformed Realities Volumes 2 and 3.* And now, as the stories continue to flow from my slightly off-center brain onto paper, we have for your reading pleasure *Malaformed Realities Volume 4.*

And what a collection it is. There are some old stories and some brand-new ones, all of them tailored for the Malaformed series. There's horror, suspense, twists, turns, and of course, just the right amount of gore to keep all of you Malcontents happy (If you're unfamiliar with my work, a Malcontent is someone who really enjoys reading my brand of horror).

So please sit back, turn the lights down low and enjoy the many twisted tales you'll find in *Malaformed Realities Volume 4.*

THOMAS M. MALAFARINA
2020

A FEW IMPERFECTIONS

"There is a kind of beauty in imperfection."
—Conrad Hall

"Things are beautiful if you love them."
—Jean Anouilh

"In our world of readily available cosmetic surgery,
it's possible that an attractive couple could end up having
an ugly baby and not understand why."
—Thomas M. Malafarina

The young, wealthy couple drove along the winding country road at a speed much faster than they should have been. Even though their Lexus LS 460, with its $80,000 price tag, was equipped to handle the curves, they were still traveling at too high a speed. This was probably the result of the intense discussion inside the vehicle, one that was rapidly degenerating into a full-blown argument.

"What in the hell are we supposed to do, Stephen?" Angela said, genuinely concerned.

"What do you mean?" Stephen asked, feigning ignorance, yet knowing exactly what she was talking about. It was all she had been talking about since they got in the car after leaving the hospital. Tucked away in the back seat of the sedan, safely secured in his car seat, their newborn baby boy Stephen Thurston Wellington III cooed to himself, oblivious to the conversation taking place in the front of the car or that he was the subject of that conversation.

"You know exactly what I mean. What are we going to do about the baby and his . . . his appearance?"

"Angela, please. I don't understand what you're getting so upset about. He's only two days old for God's sake." Stephen said, trying to look at the situation rationally and trying simultaneously to calm his wife down. However, he knew his effort was likely wasted since once Angela got an idea in her head, nothing could stop her from venting.

"But he's, he's hideous Stephen. There, I've finally said it aloud. And don't tell me you haven't been thinking the same thing. I saw the way you looked at him."

"Jesus, Angela. That's an incredibly horrible and thoughtless thing to say about your own child. My God! How could you even think such a thing, let alone express it?"

"I know, and I feel terrible saying it, but for Christ's sake Stephen. Somebody has to address the ugly elephant in the room. You have to agree with me, Stephen. He's, he's heinous."

"Now I wouldn't say anything as drastic as that, Angela. He might be a bit odd-looking, maybe even a tad on the funny-looking side, but all newborns are less than attractive than they should be, with their wrinkly pink skin, missing teeth, and pinched faces. It's perfectly normal. I'm sure he'll look better as he grows. I'll admit he has a few imperfections, but I'm sure we'll get used to them."

"No, I don't think I can, Stephen. I think there is something very wrong with him, with little Stephen's looks. I mean, how in the world could two people as good looking as we are, manage to create such an atrocious looking little child? You have to admit we're both very attractive, Stephen. I don't think it's vain to admit such a thing, do you?"

"No. I suppose not." Stephen replied, not certain if he actually agreed it wasn't vain. He knew what she had said about them was true. They were both quite attractive looking people.

"Maybe there was a mix-up at the hospital. Maybe they gave us some ugly couple's baby, and they got ours by mistake. Do you think that's possible, Stephen?"

"No, I don't. They have all sorts of safeguards in place for that kind of thing. Besides, we both saw him being born. We saw him the second he took his first breath. That's our baby Angela."

"Good Lord," She said.

"Now getting back to your original question Angela, about how we could have a less than attractive child. If you think about it, the only reason we're both so good looking is that we can afford to look so good. Our parents were both wealthy, and we were only children, so fixing our imperfections wasn't a big deal for them. We eat well, we go to the gym, we pamper ourselves at spas, and we generally take good care of ourselves. Also, as you may recall, when we met a few years ago, you told me you had some work done over the years before we knew each other."

"Yes, I did mention I had a few minor alterations. And you admitted to having some cosmetic work done yourself, didn't you?"

"I did. But now that I think about it, I don't believe we ever discussed what sorts of procedures we had done. Perhaps that's something we should have discussed."

"Maybe you're right, Stephen. Perhaps we should have. I mean, it's not really a big deal. When I was a pre-teen, I had a severe overbite, and my parents got me braces to straighten out my teeth. If I remember correctly, you had braces as well, didn't you?"

"Yes, as did most of the boys in my boarding school. My teeth were quite twisted, and a bit gnarly, but the braces and a few orthodontic surgeries took care of that. And we both have poor eyesight and had laser surgery to correct our vision issues, so we don't have to wear glasses. When I was about ten, I also had minor surgery to correct a muscular issue with my left eye that caused it to turn inward sometimes."

"Well, that explains a lot." Angela said with sudden realization, "I think little Stephen might have that same eye thing."

Stephen shot back, "What do you mean? He can't even see yet! His eyes don't have the ability to focus; that's why they seem to roam all over the place. Seriously, are you going to try to blame me for all of this? We made this child together, Angela. He was created from genes from both of us. So, tell me, what else have you have done that I don't know about?"

"As I told you, it was all minor and insignificant things. For example, my nose was a bit wide, and I had it thinned out a bit several years ago. I also just recalled something else I had forgotten about. When I was about four, my ears stuck out, and my mother took me to a doctor who pinned them back for a while until they stayed back on their own."

"Our baby's ears stick way out." Stephen added, "In fact, he looks like a taxi cab driving down the highway with its both doors hanging open. And he has a funny-looking wide nose. So those deformities obviously must have come from you."

"Yeah? Well, what about that weak chin of his? He barely has any chin at all. His mouth hangs open in a hangdog fashion that makes him look half-retarded. I think he got that from you, Stephen. Tell me, was that jutting masculine Hollywood leading man chin of yours with you since birth, or did you have it modified?"

Stephen hesitated for a moment then admitted, "Okay. I might not have had much of a chin when I was younger and may have had minor implant surgery to enhance it, but my chin issues were not as severe as the baby's."

"Ah, ha!" Angela shouted, "Another flaw of yours, which apparently was destined to curse our poor malformed baby." She took off her seat belt and turned around to try to examine the baby closer. But she was unable to see him tucked away as he was in his car seat.

"Angela, for the last time, he's not malformed; he just has a few imperfections. And since we're pointing out those imperfections, what about that unibrow of his? No one in my family ever had any such thing. As I recall from pictures of your Dad when he was alive, he had quite the crop of eyebrow foliage. Tell me, Angela, did you inherit that and maybe have it surgically removed as well?"

"I might have once had a bit more hair between my brows than I would have cared for, and maybe I did have it removed with a bit of laser work."

"So, you're the one responsible for that wooly caterpillar crawling across my baby's eyebrows after all."

"But what about his big bulging eyes? My eyes are normal, and they always have been. You're the one with the protruding mooneyes, Dear!" Angela said sarcastically.

"Mooneyes? You used to call them 'large luminous pools of emotion.' Now you call them mooneyes? Why don't you just call them bug eyes as long as you're being so nasty? And to make matters worse, you think my eyes are ugly on our baby! I really don't get you, Angela."

"Yeah, well, maybe we should have had this discussion before we decided to create that little cave troll in the back seat!"

"Cave troll? Honest to God, Angela! I can't believe you could say such a thing about your own flesh and blood. You're nothing but a self-centered cow!" Steven was now staring daggers at Angela feeling like he was speaking with some horrible creature he had never met before.

"Oh, just wonderful! Make fun of my additional weight after I just gave birth to your little freak."

Stephen was furious. For the first time in his married life, he felt like reaching over and punching his wife right in the face. As a result, he took his eyes off the highway for just a few seconds too long. As he approached a curve in the road, a large buck strolled lazily out of the woods and onto the roadway and right in his path.

"Look out, Stephen!" Angela screamed.

Stephen did the one thing he should never have done, and that was he swerved to avoid hitting the beast. He quickly lost control of his sedan and skidded off the highway, down a steep embankment, and full-bore right into a giant clump of trees.

The front of their sedan slammed into a huge tree, and one of its broken branches crashed through the windshield, piercing Stephen's heart and killing him instantly. His corpse was pinned behind the wheel as the last of his blood spurted from his chest and trickled from his mouth and down his chin. A split second later, Angela, who had not refastened her seat belt, flew through the windshield and became impaled on several other remnants of branches. She unfortunately, took several minutes to die as she hung skewered and screaming in agony. The last sound she heard, as her lifeblood pumped from her body were the cries of her ugly baby, apparently still safe and unharmed, secured in his car seat.

Several hours later, the rescue workers had successfully removed both of the corpses from the scene and had gotten the baby out of the back seat of the sedan. One of the Emergency Medical Technicians was a young woman named Naomi Jacobson. She was holding the baby and rocking it after having determined the boy was uninjured. Naomi was a short, stocky woman who, at first glance, one might consider a bit unattractive if not somewhat homely. However, she was happily married to an equally stout and less than attractive man who owned a plumbing business.

The two had been unable to conceive and had been on a waiting list for possible adoption for many years, yet they had been unsuccessful to date. Naomi wanted a baby more than anything else in the world. She looked down at the wrinkled little boy with his odd-looking nose, uni-brow, slightly twisted mouth, and ears which stuck outward, and she fell instantly in love.

She thought he was the most beautiful baby she had ever seen. Sure, he had a few imperfections, but who didn't? She decided she'd speak with the agent from Child's Services when she arrived and tell her she'd love to be able to adopt this baby if, by some chance, there were no living relatives to claim the child. Unknown to Naomi at that time, her wish would come true.

THE WIND WHISPERS MARY

"And the wind screams Mary."
—JIMI HENDRIX

"Why does it have to be so dark and so incredibly windy?" Mary wondered as she slowly drove along the winding country road. On that particular autumn night, she had found herself experiencing a great deal of trepidation. She had to work late and felt exhausted, not to mention a bit on edge as she drove home in the ever-darkening evening, an imminent rainstorm approaching from the west.

The wind, the dreaded wind, had begun to pick up, and dead leaves and twigs blew across her field of vision, a constant reminder of the wind's growing ferocity. She was driving past high cornfields on the road, which connected the main highway she used to commute to work to the sleepy little town where she lived alone in her apartment with her pet tomcat Wilbur.

Along her route were several large old trees, strategically planted a long time ago by farmers to act as wind barriers. Unfortunately, many of the trees had disappeared throughout the years, and the few remaining appeared ancient and brittle. She was forced to drive slowly along the road to avoid the various twigs and broken tree branches, which fell around her, adding to her anxiety.

She was worried about her car getting hit by a falling branch, or skidding on wet leaves, or perhaps running over a deadfall and damaging its undercarriage. Since she was also late getting home, she knew Wilbur would be giving her the evil eye for not being on time. She had left the cat plenty of food and water as she always did, but that fact seemed to elude the finicky feline. He would not like her arriving home so late and would probably do his best to give her the cold shoulder. Mary often wondered if Wilbur was her pet or if she was his.

Born in the late 1980s, Mary Atkins was a child of the nineties, and now a young adult woman of the twenty-first century. The darkness and the wind shouldn't have bothered her in any way. One would think by now she might have outgrown such childhood fears.

But Mary knew inside she still was capable of being terrified, and often was, not by horror movie images of severed limbs, rolling decapitated heads, torn flesh, gouged eyeballs or gallons of spewing blood. No, these things were so exaggerated as to be unbelievable and had little effect on her whatsoever.

She found that what frightened her most was still the simpler things, both real and imagined. She often thought about what she had heard referred to as the duality of nature; it could, in one moment, produce the most beautiful visions and images, then a moment later could wreak havoc, horror, and devastation.

When she was a young child, her bedroom was located in the southwest corner of her parent's split-level home, and as luck would have it, most of the time, the high winds came from the west, and as such, her bedroom took the brunt of the wind's thunderous tumult.

Mary had a very active imagination and often found it running rampant during her early childhood as she lay in her bed at night with her covers pulled tightly up around her neck; the wind howling against the outside walls of her bedroom, rattling the branches of the large oak tree next to her window, causing them to scratch against her glass like the dead, bony fingers of some unimaginable reanimated lifeless creature.

She often awoke in the middle of the night, thinking she had heard the wind whispering her name. "Maaaaarrrrry. Maaaaarrrrry." she believed it called as if hoping to coerce her to come outside where it could wrap itself around her in an embrace of death and slowly suck her very soul from her body, making her just one more voice in a ghostly chorus of the dead.

Although she had, for the most part, managed to put such childhood fears behind her as she journeyed into adulthood, she often found herself feeling a strange irrational discomfort, like something bad was about to happen to her. This was likely because a few of the fears of her youth still managed to hang on somehow, their claws having dug too deeply into her psyche to relinquish their frightening hold.

One such fear was the fear of the howling wind, and another was her fear of the dark. Combined, they made for the perfect storm of terror. The uncertainty she felt as a child had now suddenly returned to her as she struggled to get back home.

Her fear of the dark was probably tied directly to her fear of the wind, as more often than not during her youth, on a particularly dark and windy night, she could almost guarantee the power would go out, plunging her bedroom into total darkness. The only light she would have available would be the limited moonlight coming in through her window. Still, she could never bring herself to look toward the light because of the skeletal fingers of the oak tree clawing against the outside of the window and the horrible wind whispering her name over and over: "Maaaaarrrrry. Maaaaarrrrry."

She had always been certain if she did muster the courage to look out into the night, she wouldn't see the tree but would see an army of hideous specters brought forth by the wind from their damnation in the depths of Hell, trying to work their way into her room to claim her for their own.

She was becoming agitated not just by the dark and the storm, but the sinister direction her imaginative thoughts were heading. She decided now might be a good time to listen to the radio and maybe find some light up-tempo good-time pop music pumping from the speakers and brightening her mood. She turned on the radio and pressed the "seek" button, and to her pleasure, the first station found was an oldies station playing one of her favorite tunes from her childhood. Actually, it was a tune from her parent's childhood, but her father had played the song many times for her when she was a little girl.

The radio station was playing the 1966 hit by The Association called "Along Comes Mary." This particular tune always made Mary feel great, as she remembered how her Dad often tried to sing it to her with his off-key voice. He could never remember any of the rapid-fire staccato lyrics, which always seemed to shoot from the record player like machine gun fire. The only words he could seem to remember from the song were the lines, "And then along comes Mary" from the chorus and the final lines "sweet as the punch."

Unfortunately, she had tuned in near the end of the song and only got to hear a small piece of the chorus and the final lines. Then the DJ came back on, announcing there would be one more tune in their "Mary" double play coming up right after the commercial break. He didn't mention the song's name but said it was a tune by the late Jimi Hendrix.

At first, she was taken aback by the idea of a Mary double play but then recalled how some stations, especially oldies stations, would look for songs with common titles, themes or names, group them and offer them as "double-plays," "two-fers" or "two for the road" and other such corny names.

Mary knew who Jimi Hendrix had been, she suspected only someone living under a rock might not at least recognize the name, but she wasn't really familiar with his work. Therefore, she didn't know of any song he may have sung with the "Mary" theme in it. She supposed her parents would likely know.

She suddenly lost the little bit of cheer the song had given her as the radio played a commercial for a local technical school in the background. Once again, she brought back to reality, dealing with the high winds, the blowing leaves, the falling branches, and the desolate road. She was mentally kicking herself for taking this shortcut. Sure, it might have taken an extra ten minutes to go her normal route, but at least she wouldn't have been in such a bleak area, and there might be more people around. Out among the cornfields, she felt so isolated, so vulnerable to the forces of nature and whatever the wind and the darkness might have in store for her.

Mary realized the radio announcer had returned and mentioned the song's name, but she hadn't been paying attention and missed it. Then the song began to play, starting a haunting three-chord progression repeated which unknown to Mary had become the song's trademark sound. Mary immediately found the melodic progression to be ominous and unsettling, especially in her current fragile mental state.

Jimi began to sing the first verse's lyrics in his soft, smooth, and mellow voice. Mary couldn't quite understand what the lyrics meant. She wasn't familiar with comprehending such poetic lyrics. She was more for the straight, direct, and to the point style of writing.

The song continued, and the lyrics which followed made no more sense to her than the earlier ones. The words "footprints dressed in red" conjured an image of a set of bare feet, drenched in blood, leaving deep red prints as they stumbled down the street. This image disturbed her greatly. And just when she thought she couldn't possibly feel worse, Jimi softly said the final line of the first verse, "And the wind whispers Maaaarrrrry."

"What!" Mary shouted aloud to herself as an icy chill immediately formed and ran down her spine, and she broke out in a cold sweat. Before she realized it, she had slammed her hand down on the power button, instantly shutting off the radio. She returned her gaze to the roadway in time to see a large tree branch blocking her side of the road. Mary slammed on her breaks, and her car skidded sideways, stopping within inches of the downed branch, where it abruptly stalled.

"Crap!" Mary screamed at the car, at herself, at the fallen tree branch, at the radio DJ, and at the situation in general. She sat for a moment panting, her heart pounding hard in her chest. She could hear the last words of the song echoing in her head, "And the wind whispered Maaaarrrrry." She wanted to forget the words, to put them out of her mind, but she couldn't. The line reminded her so much of the horrible whispering wind she feared as a child, which she always thought had been calling her name specifically.

Tears streamed down her cheeks, and she realized she was crying. She turned the key in the ignition, but the engine wouldn't turn over, and the car wouldn't start. She tried again and again until she was afraid, she might flood the carburetor, and then she pounded her hands against the steering wheel in angry frustration. In her mind, over and over again, she heard the haunting three-chord guitar progression of the song and the final line, "And the wind whispered Maaaarrrrry."

She reached into her purse to retrieve her cell phone, but when she looked at the screen, she saw she had no service. "Damn it!" she swore to no one in particular.

Mary had no idea what she should do next; she was alone on a seldom-used farm road with a dead car and a useless cell phone, with a bad storm on the way. She supposed she could try to walk home, hoping to thumb a ride along the way, but knew not only would she get caught in the rain before she got very far, but doing so would also mean she would have to go out there, where the darkness and the wind waited for her.

As if on cue, she thought she heard someone or something whispering her name outside from the darkness. "Maaarrrryy!" the strange voice called. She decided her best bet might be to stay in her car and wait for someone to come by to offer assistance. Once again, she heard her name called in the wind, "Maaarrrryy!" Icy fingers crept down her spine, and the hairs on the nape of her neck stood on end. Her stomach began to knot, and her hands trembled.

She looked out of her driver's side window and, in the distance, saw something she couldn't at first comprehend. The wind was swirling in a circular motion close to the ground dancing around like a whirling dervish, gathering dirt, leaves, and all sorts of forest debris into its cyclone of air. The circular motion began to rise higher into the air, bringing more and more leaves, broken branches, and other such rubble. Soon the tower of swirling remains was close to twenty or thirty feet tall. Then incredibly, it took what appeared to be a solid form.

The sight Mary saw before herself was beyond anything in her imagination. It was some sort of gargantuan humanoid-shaped beast composed of dirt, leaves, corn stalks, road trash, and similar remnants, including bits of discarded animal fur and feathers. The unnatural golem was massive, and its impossible appearance made Mary quake with fright. For a moment, the creature stood silently across the road glancing side to side, as if becoming acclimated to a strange environment. It looked over in the direction of Mary's car, and as it opened a dark black hole where its mouth should be, she heard the thing's deep voice impossibly whisper her name, "Maaarrrryy!"

Then the creature lifted one leg and dropped it with a crash that vibrated across the roadway, shaking her car. Another step followed this, then another, and then yet another as the incredible beast lurched its way across the road toward Mary's disabled vehicle. Its loping stride was unsure, like those of a newborn animal taking its first steps. However, this hideous abomination of nature was no innocent little creature by any stretch of the imagination.

Before Mary realized it, the hulking creature was standing right outside of her driver's side window, its lower legs pressed up against her glass, which was closed tightly. Up close, she could see the swirling mass of debris still impossibly in constant motion, yet somehow being held together sufficiently to give the beast a semi-solid form. She could see various insects and forest worms squirming among the leaves and other waste products. From above, she heard the creature whisper her name once again. "Maaarrrryy!" the thing spoke in its low, soft, and windy voice.

She saw the creature lift one of its legs, and she was certain it was going to crush her inside of her car, but it didn't. Instead, the leg landed on the other side of her car with a crash, so the beast was straddling the vehicle facing the rear of the car. Looking out through the windshield, she saw the tremendous manifestation squatting down like a small child who might be trying to look into the cab of a toy truck. Likewise, the creature now looked in through the windshield, staring hungrily at Mary.

Its face was beyond description, as it was not quite solid, was inconsistent, and was in constant motion. From deep within the swirling mass of debris, she saw two blazing red embers, which she took to be its eyes. The creature rested a hand on each side of the car, and Mary cried with alarm, fearing the beast might once again try to crush her inside, but again it didn't.

Instead, the creature opened what Mary again took to be its mouth, as a black hole appeared within its indistinct face. Again, she heard the wind created horror murmur her name, "Maaarrrryy!" She shivered from head to toe with fear, and her stomach turned over with disgust.

Then the beast bent its head down and opened its maw wide. Mary feared perhaps it had become angry and was going to shout loud enough to perhaps destroy her eardrums, but instead, it began inhaling air back into its black hole of a mouth. Mary could see leaves and twigs and dirt from all around her being sucked into the creature's unholy maw. As it did so, it appeared to continue to grow in size.

Suddenly she began to feel strange, as if she was light-headed. She worried the beast might be sucking the oxygen out of her car through the air vents; then, she realized she was only partially correct. The horrid thing was not only sucking out all of the life-giving oxygen, but was sucking out her own life force, was inhaling her very soul and making it one with itself, and soon to be one with the wind which had been the creature's creator.

Mary thought back to her childhood fears of the wind coming to get her, coming to take her away and make her part of itself, and as her vision faded to blackness, she realized after all these years the wind had finally gotten what it had always wanted. The wind had whispered Mary one last time and had finally come to claim her.

TOIL AND TROUBLE

The ancient old formerly black cauldron lay on its side across the room where it had sat empty, collecting dust for many years, now appearing more grey than black. Nearby, a withered old crone slumped in her rickety wooden chair, the same chair she once thought of as her throne. Back in those days, it had been magnificent, strong, and unbreakable; then again, so had she been. Now it was like they were competing to see which was the most wretched. And in the chair's occupant's opinion, Selemia believed that, sadly, she was winning that race. Her life as a witch had been one of both toil and trouble, and she instinctively sensed it was coming to an end.

During their time together, the cauldron had served Selemia well, and she likewise had served it in return. That was how such things worked; it was a symbiotic relationship between the witch and her cauldron. It was like a marriage. They were separate, yet they were one, a bond perhaps even stronger than the marriage bond, especially when one considered the divorce rate in the twenty-first century. She had forgotten exactly how long she and that cauldron had been together, but she knew it was a very long time. She had only been about eighteen when they had initially been paired, and that was many typical lifetimes ago.

Although to a casual onlooker, Selemia might appear to have been as old as ninety-five or even one hundred and five, the truth was she was much older than that, perhaps as old as three and a half centuries. Back when she and her cauldron had been at the peak of their power, age was as irrelevant a consideration as most things in life. She could have whatever she wanted in those days; all it took was the right spell and the right concoction from her cauldron. Those days, however, were long gone. Selemia understood death was nearing, and as far as she was concerned, it couldn't come soon enough. She stared at the pitiful looking cauldron, too weak to do anything else but sit, wait to die, and remember better days.

With a dry smile on her creased face, she recalled a time back in the mid-1800s when a local farmer had come to her begging for one of her potions. She had a well-earned reputation throughout the county as a maker of mystic potions and as a healer in general. The man's wife stood by his side.

This was an agreed-upon requirement among the women of the village. Although they were not happy to come anywhere near Selemia, they were more frightened that Selemia might put some spell of seduction upon their husbands, and they might become her slave. The village women knew their husbands didn't have either the brains or the willpower to resist such a temptation. For the sake of their families, they lever let the men go to see Selemia alone.

The farmer's wife had a small bundle she carried close to her breast, a baby wrapped up against the fall chill. As the woman unbundled the blankets, Selemia could see it was a beautiful blond-haired, blue-eyed baby boy. She could also instantly tell by the child's pallor; he was deathly ill, perhaps on death's door.

"Can you please help us?" The farmer asked.

"I can, for a price." She replied, looking at the wife with a cat-like disdain.

The woman spoke up as if challenging Selemia. "And what might that price be? We have very little money."

The witch walked across the room to a dusty cupboard and withdrew a small vile of brown liquid. She turned to the couple, handing the woman the vile, and said, "This will cure your son. After drinking this, he will sleep, perhaps for several days, but he will not die. When he awakes, he will be well."

"The payment," The farmer pleaded, "what is it you require?"

Selemia hesitated then said, "Raise your boy into a strong young man. Treasure what time you have with him. Keep him safe and pure. Then on his sixteenth birthday, send him to me, and he can repay your debt by doing chores for me."

Having no money or little of anything else of value, the couple quickly agreed. If what the woman said was true, their son's life would be saved, and they would have to pay nothing. They never forgot their debt, and neither did the witch. Sixteen years later, a handsome young man knocked on the front door of Selemia's home, eager to repay the debt his parents had incurred. His name was John, and he was a big, muscular, strapping young man.

John had been prepared to encounter a strange older woman at the door but was pleasantly surprised when a beautiful young girl, not more than a year or two older than he was, waited, smiling pleasantly at him. His heart seemed to skip a beat at the sight of her. He learned from the young girl that she was Selemia's niece and her name was Glenalda. He explained how he was there to repay the debt for Selemia. All the while, he watched the beautiful girl; John realized he was falling instantly and uncontrollably in love with her.

The girl seduced John and took him to her bed, where little sleep had occurred that night. By the next morning, he pledged his eternal love to the girl, saying he would return to get her the next day, and they would run off and marry. However, when he returned, the girl was gone, and only Selemia remained. The witch handed him a note from Glenalda, stating that she had gone away and that he should never try to find her.

The boy was heartbroken, and after several months of fruitlessly scouring the countryside trying to find his precious Glenalda, he went to a nearby bridge over a river and jumped to his death, having been unable to imagine living another day without his Glenalda.

But Selemia knew the truth as it had been, she who had posed as Glenalda, with the help of one of her potions. She had saved the boy's life sixteen years earlier for her own eventual purposes, and then as payment, she had chosen to provide the motivation for that life to end. His parents had been so desperate to save their baby they had come to a witch for help, not understanding how high the price for her services would be.

Selemia now sat smiling her withered smile and looking at her ancient cauldron. That one had been a good memory. As she watched, she noticed the small crack which had appeared in the cauldron earlier that morning had grown substantially and seemed to be branching out in every direction. It wouldn't be long now; she could feel it.

Selemia hadn't always been as hard-hearted as she had been with the young farm boy John. Once she had loved and once, she had been hurt so badly as to blacken her heart and change her forever. Charles has been his name. He had been the love of Selemia's life way back when she first took up her chosen vocation. She had given herself fully to Charles and believed he would never betray her, but he had.

Shortly before she had been assigned her cauldron, she discovered that Charles planned on ending their affair to take up with the mayor of the city's daughter. She knew Charles was the ambitious sort, but she never thought he would put his ambition ahead of their love; she had been wrong.

The first spell she had cast with her new cauldron was directed at Charles and his new lover. She transformed Charles into a toad and his lover into a fly. Selemia thoroughly enjoyed watching Charles devour his former lover. She kept Charles the toad in a cage in her cottage for several years until he eventually died. Then she cooked him in her cauldron and ate him. She felt that it was a suitable ending for him. Since that time, she had seduced and used many men, but there had never been another love in her life. It had only been she and her cauldron, and that was just fine with Selemia.

She suddenly felt weak, as if the simple act of slumping in her chair took more energy than she was capable of gathering. Her head sunk down, and her chin rested on her chest as if she might fall asleep again. She heard a rumbling sound and looked across the room to see her cauldron break into hundreds of small pieces and fall in a heap to the ground. Her cauldron was no more.

Selemia looked down at her own aged, withered hands, and saw her skin begin to flake off in layers then blow away like dust. She didn't have a mirror but knew if she did, she would see the same thing happening to her face and the rest of her body.

This joining of Selemia and her cauldron was a relationship where one entity could not survive without the other. As she watched her hands, she could see her bones begin to appear as her flesh, and muscle slowly disintegrated to dust and either fell to the floor or blew away. She was glad there was no pain. She knew what was coming and had been emotionally prepared for it, but she wouldn't have liked pain. Her life as a witch had been one of toil and trouble, and now she was ready to move on to the next adventure, whatever that might be. Several minutes later, her black gown fell to the floor, now nothing more than an empty garment. Over near the fireplace, Selemia's cauldron likewise was just a heap of dust.

93

"We know that in September, we will wander
through the warm winds of summer's wreckage.
We will welcome summer's ghost."
—HENRY ROLLINS

"O Death, rock me asleep, bring me to quiet rest, let pass
my weary guiltless ghost out of my careful breast."
—ANNE BOLEYN

Ellen stood leaning against the edge of the black concrete border, look-ing out at the large stone that marked the former impact crater's site. She had suspected the experience might prove moving, but she had no idea it would have been so emotionally overwhelming. She hadn't known any of those people, nor had they even been distant relatives. They were just forty strangers who had chosen to make the ultimate sacrifice to save thousands. And now being here at the place where they had given all for their country was almost more than she could bear.

She had been all right during the long ride up the winding road-way from the entrance to the memorial park, past the construction site of the future visitor's center and learning center, then to the current visitor area. Ellen had started to feel a bit sad as she walked toward the visitor's shelter, starting to comprehend the significance of the place. It wasn't just some tourist attraction randomly selected from a map for something to do on a boring afternoon; this was a true shrine and tribute to the fallen.

As she approached the visitor's shelter, she heard a man speaking. Out in an open area just beyond the shelter were rows of benches where several dozen people listened to a narrative, given by a man in a park ranger's uniform. She took a seat on a bench under the roof of the shelter and listened to his presentation.

She had known the story of flight ninety-three and what had happened on September 11, 2001, as did almost everyone in the United States who had lived through that horrible day. But more than thirteen years had passed since the terrorist attack, and sadly these memories faded. The park ranger did an amazing job of not only refreshing her memories but also of providing much more detail than she has previously known. For example, she had no idea that when the plane had crashed, it was upside down.

After the presentation, she walked as instructed along the huge black cement walkway with its angular border toward the white wall of names. Along the way, she saw several spots where the black angular border had been cut away to form a shelf where memorial gifts and trinkets could be placed. Ellen saw various gifts, from coins, to flowers, to military patches and even to guitar picks. Each was left by someone in memory of the deceased and each trinket, no matter how seemingly unimportant, meant something significant to the person who left it.

The white wall was long and stood out in contrast to the black walkway. It consisted of individual panels marking the flight path the plane took in its final descent. Each panel bore the name of one of the victims of the Flight 93 crash. During his presentation, the ranger said at the place where the black border ended and the white wall began was a wooden fence where you could look through and see the boulder marking the original crater's location.

Looking through the wooden slats, Ellen saw the huge boulder right where the ranger said it would be. There was a clean patch of mown grass leading up to the bolder following the same flight path. On both sides of the path, the grass and weeds grew wild. Oddly, she saw a black crow sitting directly in the middle of the path. It stopped whatever it had been pecking at to look up directly at her.

Ellen suddenly realized something. The boulder had been visible all the while during her entire walk along the black walkway; she just hadn't realized it. She watched other people coming toward her along the walk she had just taken and saw that they, too, were oblivious to the marker's presence.

She returned to the white wall and studied the names, wishing she had the capacity to remember all of them after she left but knowing she'd likely forget most if not all of them before she got back to her car. She touched each name and whispered, "thank you." This was a genuine and heartfelt thanks because Ellen knew if these people hadn't chosen to fight back against the terrorists and sacrificed their own lives to crash the plane in the rural Pennsylvania field, hundreds if not thousands of innocent people might have perished.

The terrorists planned to fly the plane to Washington DC and crash it into the White House. Ellen figured even if jets could have been scrambled in time to shoot the plane down, it would have likely been over densely populated areas. But because of the sacrifice of these brave few, many lives were spared.

Ellen walked back toward the visitor's shelter along the black concrete walkway and stopped to get a better look at the boulder. That was when she became overwrought with the reality of what had happened that fateful morning in 2001, and she began weeping, openly letting the tears stream down her cheeks with no desire to hide them.

"Are you all right, ma'am?" A male voice said from somewhere off to her right. A handsome man was standing next to her with a concerned expression. Ellen was moved by his desire to help her.

Ellen wiped the tears from her cheeks and, in a voice thick with emotion, replied, "Yes, yes. Thank you, I'm fine. It's just too much, you know, I mean, these people were so brave and so very special. They died so magnanimously, so tragically, to prevent an even bigger tragedy."

The stranger looked out at the boulder as if in deep contemplation and said, "They did what they felt they had to do. I'm sure in a similar situation, you would have done the same."

Ellen said, "But that's the point. I honestly think if I were confronted with such a decision, I wouldn't have the ability to be so brave, so incredibly unselfish."

The man continued to stare out at the boulder and replied, "Look, I don't know you, and I could be completely off base saying this to you, but I'd really like to believe you would do whatever needed to be done. You're shedding tears right now for people you never met. I believe you have within you the same stuff that these folks had."

Ellen looked back at the boulder in the field and began crying once again. The stranger's kind words had touched her deep inside. After a moment or two, she heard another man's voice coming from her left, asking, "Ma'am, is everything okay? Is there anything I can do for you?"

She turned and saw the park ranger who had given the presentation standing next to her.

"Sorry, I'm just a bit emotional."

"This is that sort of place." The ranger agreed.

Ellen turned to the ranger and said, "Thank you for your concern. Both of you."

"Excuse me?" The ranger inquired. "I'm here by myself, Ma'am. I have been for the entire time you've been looking out at the boulder."

"But, but what about—?" Ellen asked, looking for the handsome stranger who had first spoken to her. He was nowhere to be found.

"Anyway, thank you, Sir." She said as she turned and walked slowly back to the visitor's shelter. When she walked around the building, she saw something she hadn't previously noticed. There was an open plaza area with large glass-covered posters depicting various aspects of the Flight 93 tragedy. One of them had a picture of each of the victims from that day.

She looked at each picture, placing her fingertips on each one as she had done with the names on the white wall. Then her eyes focused on one particular photo. It was that of a handsome young man; the same man who had just comforted her at the wall, then vanished.

Ellen smiled at the photograph, then turned and walked back to her car. She was no longer feeling sad but was filled with a sensation of comfort, the likes of which she had never before imagined.

THE BEAST UNSEEN

"Oh, sweet mother of God!" the police officer exclaimed as the ceiling light was switched on, showering the room with an effervescent glow, providing a much too perfect view of the unimaginable carnage neither he nor any of his fellow officers would ever forget. In fact, the horrifying sight would haunt all of their nightmares for many years to come.

"Oh, Good Christ in Heaven," another officer shouted, followed by cries of anguish and revulsion coming from the other officers in the room.

They were standing, mouths agape, staring in disbelief at the butchery surrounding them. The place was a slaughterhouse. Blood, entrails, body parts, and other unrecognizable fleshy fragments were strewn all about the room. The walls were streaked with gore. There was barely a surface anywhere in the room that didn't show signs of the abhorrent violence that had taken place there. It looked as if someone had taken gallons of red paint, added several pounds of boiled noodles then tossed the entire mess into a large industrial fan.

Jim Fredrickson, the youngest member of the police squad, and fortunately the one closest to the front door, turned quickly and staggered outside, his hand covering his mouth as a volcanic eruption of hot vomit forced its way out between his fingers. Once clear of the crime scene, he bent over the porch rail and let the contents of his stomach spew all over a clump of shrubbery. He was certain he would hear about it from Police Chief Matt Sinclair, but at least for the moment, he didn't care.

Bobby O'Neil, another officer, still inside, was far too shocked to even react; he looked around in astonishment as if he had inadvertently found himself immersed in some sort of hellish nightmare landscape, which in fact he had. It was unlike anything he had ever seen in his life, and he hoped to God he would never have to see anything like it again.

"What the hell could have possibly done this?" Police Chief Sinclair said in a stunned raspy voice. He was standing at the front of the group and was equally as shocked as they were. Matthew Sinclair had seen many horrors in his twenty-seven years on the force, including victims of automobile fatalities and even small passenger plane crashes. Still, he had never seen anything like the sight he was now witnessing. "This place is a charnel house! What kind of savage would even think to do such a thing?"

It looked like a thousand spinning blades had flown into the room and puréed the victims like a giant blender chewing them into tiny crimson pieces. Sinclair wasn't even sure at this point how many victims he had. Worse, he had no idea where to begin the identification process. He suspected this would be one for the lab boys to sort through, and he was very grateful for that fact. Because right now, all he wanted to do was be as far away from this horror as possible.

Taking a deep swallow, trying to keep his own upset stomach from turning over, he asked, "What do we know about this place? Who's supposed to live here?"

O'Neill stepped up with a note pad, which trembled in his quivering hand, and said in an equally shaky voice, "The 911 dispatcher said a John and Maria Stinson own the house. They live, I mean, lived here with . . . Oh, Christ!"

"Come on, man." Sinclair demanded, "Spit it out."

"They lived here with their five children, all under twelve," O'Neil said, then looked around the gut-wrenching spectacle in the room, realizing that somewhere among the tatters of what was once human beings were likely bits and pieces of this precious family. He swallowed hard and continued, "Two boys and three, three little girls."

"Sweet Jesus!" Sinclair said, "What sort of maniac are we dealing with here?"

O'Neil hesitated for a moment then said, "Chief, I don't think any man did this; any human."

Sinclair looked at him curiously and said, "What are you saying, Bob? Do you think an animal of some kind did this?"

"Well." O'Neil said, "Look at this place Chief. I doubt anything but some sort of animal, or maybe a bunch of animals could have done this."

The Chief looked around the room reluctantly, knowing he had to study every aspect of the crime scene but wanting desperately not to have these images burned into his memory, yet knowing they would be. Maybe O'Neill had something there. In all of his years on the job, Sinclair had never seen any human inflict this sort of atrocity, even the craziest of the crazy.

He noticed a large framed blood-splattered family portrait hanging askew on the wall to his right. It was of the Stinson family; father, mother, and the five young children. Each of the kids was fair-haired with blue eyes, as were the parents. Large ruby-stained clumps of that same hair, attached to shredded sections of scalp, were scattered all about the horrifying scene.

It was becoming more difficult by the minute for the Chief to keep his focus. Suddenly, all he could think about were his own beautiful grandkids. He couldn't imagine such a fate befalling them. His emotions were heading in a variety of directions simultaneously. He wanted to run to his daughter's house and hug his grandkids, while at the same time, he wanted to find whoever had wiped out this family and put a bullet between their accursed eyes.

Then he noticed something he had missed during his initial glance around the room. On the far wall amid the stipples of crimson was a series of small blood-smeared handprints, looking as if a young child had walked along the wall using it for support. Sinclair carefully walked among the carnage, doing his best not to disturb anything, and when he got closer to the wall, he noticed small bloody footprints on the tile floor, not shoeprints, but bare footprints. The prints led down a hall and stopped outside of a hall closet.

"O'Neil!" Sinclair called, trying not to sound too excited. As Bobby O'Neil approached, Sinclair said nothing but pointed first to the handprints on the wall, then to the tiny footprints, then to the hall closet door. He signaled for O'Neil to walk with him down the hall. Once outside of the closet, O'Neil drew his service revolver and pointed it along with his flashlight at the closet as Sinclair, using a handkerchief, grabbed the handle, twisted, and threw open the door.

At first, the closet appeared empty. Then O'Neil shouted. "Chief. There's a little girl in there! She's huddled near the back of the closet."

Sinclair looked around the door and peered inside. O'Neil was right. On the floor near the back of the closet, a little girl of about six years old was sitting tightly against the wall with her bloody hands wrapped around her knees, which she used to hide her face; as if in doing so she could protect herself from who or whatever had murdered the family outside. She was also barefoot, and Sinclair could see dried blood covering the bottoms of her feet as well.

O'Neil looked expectantly at Sinclair as if waiting for him to provide guidance on what he should do next. Sinclair looked at him sternly and jerked his head in the direction of the child, suggesting that O'Neil take the lead. O'Neil had young kids of his own and didn't project as large or intimidating a figure as Sinclair did. He placed his gun back into his holster, put away his flashlight, and got down on his hands and knees, crawling into the closet to speak to the girl.

After a few minutes, O'Neil backed out of the closet with the small girl in tow. Sinclair immediately noticed the girl was dark-haired and likely not one of the Stinson kids. Perhaps she was a cousin or a friend visiting or sleeping over for the night. Sinclair called out to officer Mary Mortenson, the only female officer on the squad.

When Mortenson approached, Sinclair whispered, "This kid was hiding in the closet; she's likely traumatized. From what I can tell, she isn't one of the Stinson kids. They were all towheads. Maybe she's a friend or relative. We need to get her to talk. Take her outside away from all of this mess and see if you can get her to tell you anything. The ambulance should be here soon. Have them check her out as well. Mary, she may be the closest thing we have to a witness."

Mary nodded, then bent down and looked at the child's downcast face saying, "Honey? Don't be afraid. My name is Mary, and I'm here to take care of you. What's your name?" The young girl looked up with eyes that were devoid of all emotion, saying nothing. Mary sensed this girl would need a lot more help than she or any paramedics would be capable of providing. It would likely take years of psychological therapy to get over an ordeal as horrible as the one she must have witnessed. Mary could only hope the child had made it safely to the closet before the worst of the bloody carnage had taken place.

To Mary's surprise, the little girl let go of O'Neil's hand and raised both of her arms to go with Mary, who bent down and lifted the girl up, burying the child's head in the crook of her neck before heading down the hall. There was no reason for the poor darling to have to see the horror waiting in the main living room again. Once had most certainly been too much.

As Mary carefully made her way toward the front door, across what seemed like the vast expanse of the gruesome living room turned slaughterhouse, Mary could see young Jim Fredrickson staggering back into the house, looking pale and worse for wear. She hated to leave her fellow officers in here, but the Chief had asked her to take care of the girl, so that was what she knew she had to do.

Sinclair and O'Neil reentered the living room, seeing two officers, Jones and Farley, still standing in stunned silence. Sinclair also noticed that young Jim Frederickson had made it back inside. He didn't blame Jim for not being able to keep from puking his guts out. Sinclair was barely able to keep his own lunch in his stomach.

"Farley!" Sinclair called, "If you haven't already done so, call the forensic team and tell them we need them pronto!"

Sinclair was fairly certain that neither of the two officers had thought to call anyone and had probably been standing there like two slack-jawed morons since entering the terrible room of death.

"Uh, Um," Farley stammered. "Will do, Chief." Then he got on his radio and passed the necessary information on to the dispatcher.

Sinclair said, "Jonesie and Fredrickson. Watch the front door and make sure no one but the forensic crew comes in here without clearing it with me." They both looked relieved to have a chance to turn their backs on this horror.

"Affirmative, Chief!" Jones said as the two officers turned to head toward the door. But after only a few steps, they stopped dead in their tracks.

Mary Mortenson, who had been carrying the little girl to safety, stood at the front door and seemed to be shaking almost uncontrollably. She still held the little girl in her arms. But the two officers could see something was very, very wrong, not just with Mary, but with the little girl as well.

The child was impossibly changing somehow. When they had last seen her, the girl's face had still been hidden, buried in the crook of Mary's neck, where she was apparently shielding her eyes from the horrors of the room, but now . . .

"What the hell!" Jones shouted as Mary began to spasm even more violently. The little girl raised her head slightly, her eyes now peering out at the police officers. But they were no longer the eyes of a child, the eyes they had expected to see. It was as if the girl's head had tripled in size and two huge segmented insect eyes the size of softballs bugged out from under a bulbous wrinkled, leathery forehead. Her mouth, its mouth—they could no longer think of this creature as a little girl—had also become inhumanly large with massive lips and what seemed like hundreds of blood-stained long needle-like teeth, most of which were sunk several inches into Mary's neck.

As Mary's body twitched horribly, the stunned officers saw five long sharp claws exploding from inside her and out through her back, rapidly tearing upward until they reached her neck. At that point, the body split in half, and the now-dead woman's head flew across the room, striking an unsuspecting officer Jones directly between the eyes, killing him instantly. In a few seconds, the remaining officers would wish that they had been as lucky as Jones had just been.

The creature now standing over Mary Mortenson's shattered corpse looked unlike anything Officer Farley, or young Officer Frederickson had ever seen in their soon to be terminated lives. Farley reached to grab for his gun, but at a speed he had never anticipated, the creature shot across the room, simultaneously slicing off his right arm and raking its razor-sharp talons across Jim Frederickson's throat; severing his head from his shoulders. It buried its talons deep into Farley's stomach, ripping out his entrails and flinging them haphazardly across the room where they splattered against a wall, clinging momentarily until they slid down and oozed onto the floor.

Bob O'Neil rushed across the room toward the beast, his gun drawn and firing blindly, unfortunately not even hitting the creature once. Then just before the thing attacked him, O'Neil had a brief second of clarity before his life was ended, where he saw the creature in its entirety.

The thing stood about four feet tall in its current hunkered position; it's head was a huge light bulb shaped thing with a high, bald forehead leading back to a horse's mane of long black hair. Between its two widely spaced segmented insectile eyes was a pig-like snout with two flaring nostrils, glistening with snot. The mouth from top to bottom had to be eight or ten inches containing its hideously long, sharp fangs. O'Neill could see pieces of Mary's flesh still clinging to the bloody needle-like teeth.

Its arms seemed to start near the top of its head and hung down ape-like, dragging on the floor. The hands were huge, at least a foot or more long, and were tipped with long talon-like claws. Its torso was small compared to its head and long arms but was still very muscular and covered with long matted hair or fur. Its legs were equally long and currently bent in the squatted position. O'Neil could tell in his momentary glance that if it were standing up to its full height, the beast would be well over nine feet tall. Its feet were huge and had similar claws to those on its hands.

Before this brief moment of observation even had a chance to register, the creature sprang forward from its squatted location and, in the matter of a millisecond, was using those claws to slash and shred O'Neil to pieces. Although he was killed nearly instantly, those few seconds were the most agonizing he had ever experienced.

Then the thing turned and looked across the room at Chief of Police Matt Sinclair. He was the only remaining human still alive in the slaughterhouse. He already had his gun drawn and pointed directly at the hideous creature. Before the thing even had a chance to think about attacking, it heard the thunderous boom of Sinclair's weapon at the same instant the back of its skull exploded in a shower of blood, bone, and grey matter. It collapsed on its back, dead on the floor.

By the time Sinclair walked over to examine the corpse, he was horrified to see it had returned to its human form; that of an innocent looking six-year-old girl. She lay sprawled on the floor with a large caliber bullet hole in her forehead and the back of her skull blown out.

"What in the name of God have you done?" A frightened voice called out from the front door. Sinclair turned to see several people looking at him with horrified expressions of both disbelief and revulsion on their shocked faces.

Seeing their confusion, Sinclair stammered, "No, no, you don't, you don't understand. It, it wasn't. . . ."

///

The official report of the incident from the local district attorney, which came out a few weeks after the incident, called the event "a tragedy" and Chief Sinclair's actions "unintentional and accidental." The official take on the event was that a collection of unknown wild animals had somehow found their way into the Stinson home, killing and partially devouring the unfortunate family. When the police came onto the scene, the home had been cleared, and the threat was no longer deemed present.

Unfortunately, at some point during the investigation, the wild animals must have returned and caught the police by surprise and slaughtering most of them. It was assumed that in the chaos, Chief Sinclair must have tried to shoot one of the creatures, which apparently had been attacking a young girl, but he had inadvertently shot and killed the girl by mistake. Attempts to identify the girl or her next of kin were futile, and the girl remains a Jane Doe.

The report stated that Chief Sinclair had been relieved of duty and voluntarily agreed to retire from the police force. At the time the report was written, there were no plans to file criminal charges against Sinclair since the girl remains unidentified, no civil suit would likely follow either.

What the official report failed to mention was that former Police Chief Matthew Sinclair was committed to a psychiatric facility where he remains to this day sedated, lying in a hospital bed in an eight by ten padded room on twenty-four-hour suicide watch. He is completely non-communicative and spends his days staring into space, drooling, and repeating, "The beast unseen. The beast unseen."

THE GHOST OF GARMONDA MONDURA LAKE

Authors Note: In early 2017, my friend, fellow author, and publisher Mark Slade asked if I would be interested in writing a short ghost story of fewer than 1500 words for a special publication coming out in the fall. I was intrigued by the idea because he wanted it to occur in a fantasy-type world of my own creation. How could I pass up such an interesting challenge? —Thomas M. Malafarina

The twin moons Ojoita and Dalusa cast their eerie magenta glows upon the barely moving surface of Garmonda Mondura Lake. Kar-Ron Del Majosotic sat on a small stone-covered beach surrounded by a forest of hundreds of wild Jungbung trees, their gnarled and twisted silhouettes wraith-like in the moons' afterglow. He was more than a trifle anxious. He'd heard all the stories, and although he'd never believed any of them, that knowledge did little to comfort him as he waited alone.

Although the Land of Narg was full of fantastic and amazing creatures and was a place where the impossible was made possible daily, the concept of the dead returning in spiritual form was something Kar-Ron felt should be reserved for old wives' tales and campfire legends. Yet as the evening darkened, his anxiety grew.

"What in the name of Orlion's beard I am doing here?" He asked himself. He had left Mubb-Faan City an hour earlier to make the more than two-sector journey on his Hovatrans to this fabled body of water. But now that he was here, he was second-guessing that decision.

Kar-Ron was a creative scribing student at the Charr-Drogg University, named for its founders, industrial giants Montagero Charr and Festerious Drogg. Of late, he had found himself in a bit of a funk, creatively speaking. This was something his fellow students like to refer to as "scriber's block." He needed something to jump-start his creative juices, to get him back in the game. He felt spending an evening in a place where more horrifying legends and stories abounded than anywhere else in the sector might be just what the medic-man ordered.

The strange tales of terror revolved around a woman, that is to say, the supposed ghost of a woman named Karamon Lee. The legend said Karamon Lee had been beheaded along the banks of Garmonda Mondura Lake more than one hundred revs previous after having run afoul of a gang of murderous criminals who had been terrorizing the sector at that time.

The legend said the headless spirit of Karamon Lee roamed the shores of Garmonda Mondura, looking not only for her missing head, but seeking vengeance on her attackers. The ghost was said to kill anyone who crossed its path indiscriminately.

Over the previous dekatury, many residents' bodies had been found along Garamonda Mondura's rocky beaches, apparently dead of natural causes. Yet each of them bore a look of unbridled terror frozen on their faces as if they had seen the demon Yargon himself. No one had a medical explanation for the deaths, so the blame naturally fell upon the legendary ghost of Karamon Lee.

Despite his lack of belief in spirits or the occult, Kar-Ron had hoped that by coming to Garmonda alone on such a dark and moonslit night, he might at the very least succeed in stirring a myriad of primitive emotions sufficient to put his imagination back in high gear. A parchment scroll lay unfurled at his feet, completely blank save for the finely etched title, "Karamon Lee: The Ghost of Garmonda Mondura Lake." Kar-Ron hoped that before the evening was over, he would be inspired to fill the empty scroll. That single act would put him on the road to what he hoped would be many more creative endeavors.

He heard the rattling of leaves, and then out of the corner of his eye, he saw a slight movement along the shoreline. His heart leaped into his throat as his head snapped in that direction. At first, it was hard to discern what was lurking in the shadows. Then to his relief, he realized it was nothing more than a pair of squiddles, busy gathering fallen nuts from the Jungbung trees. He breathed a sigh of relief, seeing his breath in the rapidly chilling air for the first time. That was when he felt the hairs on the back of his neck begin to rise as he sensed the presence behind him.

Slowly and with mounting trepidation, Kar-Ron began to turn as his heart practically stopped beating in his chest at the sight floating before him. It was a translucent image of a creature, a woman dressed in nightclothes, arms dangling loosely by her side. Her head was missing.

As the apparition hovered before the terrified man, a night bird, perhaps an Erlgrew or maybe an Owergrat flew over Kar-Ron's head and straight toward the specter. Faster than Kar-Ron's eye could perceive, the creature raised its hand, and the bird flew right through it. Then it instantly fell from the air and lay dead on the rocky beach.

The spirit turned its headless body back in Kar-Ron's direction and began to advance toward him, floating above the ground. He knew now what had happened to all the dead bodies found along the shore. He also understood he would likely be the next corpse to be discovered.

The floating specter leaned down, coming ever closer to Kar-Ron. He could see clearly into the stump of the hideous thing's neck, where its head had been viciously hacked off so many revs earlier. It was teeming with translucent larvae of some sort, all of which were squirming among each other in the withered ethereal flesh. A few of the ghastly things fell from the stump and puffed out of existence when they hit the ground. The ghost reached out its hand and came within a minamuter of Kar-Ron's face when it stopped unexpectedly.

The thing turned in the direction of the unfurled scroll as Kar-Ron sat on the cold ground, frozen in terror. It seemed to be reading the title

Kar-Ron had written earlier. He couldn't comprehend how something without a head could possibly be capable of reading anything. Then again, a few secilants earlier, he hadn't even believed such a ghost could actually exist. Apparently, the Land of Narg had more amazing things than even he had realized.

The ghost stood up straight and pointed down first at the document then at Kar-Ron. Still almost paralyzed with mortal terror, he slowly nodded his head, acknowledging that at some point in the future, he had hoped to fill the page. The specter then pointed at itself, nodded its headless neck, then slowly turned away. Within a few moments, the thing was gone, having vanished into the gathering fog billowing off Garamonda Mondura Lake.

Kar-Ron let out a sigh of relief, realizing how close he had just come to dying. Then he looked down at the parchment and smiled, knowing his scribers block was gone, and he was ready to write what would likely be the greatest story of his young life. And now the ghost of Karamon Lee was no mere legend.

TALK TO ME

"We live in a world of transgressions and selfishness, and no
pictures that represent us otherwise can be true, though, happily,
for human nature, gleamings of that pure spirit in whose likeness
man has been fashioned are to be seen, relieving its deformities,
and mitigating if not excusing its crimes."
—JAMES FENIMORE COOPER

Although food prepared and served in a diner wasn't his first choice
for fine cuisine, Jason nonetheless sat at the counter of the Mountain
Street Diner, surprised to find himself enjoying his meal much more
than he ever thought he could have. The open-face hot roast turkey
sandwich with a side order of French fries and the entire works smothered in gravy was surprisingly tasty. He wasn't the pretentious sort by
any means, but he did enjoy the finer things in life and was therefore
pleasantly surprised to find this meal so enjoyable. That was a good
thing, since unknown to the man, it would be the last meal he would
ever eat.

The door to the diner opened, and the warning buzzer above the
door droned loudly to make the staff aware another customer had
entered. A tall man walked into the diner dressed in black pants, a long
black leather trench coat closed tightly around him, a wide-brimmed

floppy black leather hat under which long black hair flowed, and wearing black leather gloves. He kept his head cast downward, avoiding eye contact with any of the patrons. Several of them noticed the peculiar dress of the man and must have thought him an oddity, as they seemed to chat among themselves, commenting in whispers about his appearance.

As Jason quietly enjoyed his meal, the man approached from the right and took the stool at the counter next to him. Jason gave the man a cursory nod, not really paying much attention to him. He didn't know or, for that matter, particularly care if the patron returned his gesture. It had been simply a reflexive friendly greeting, and he was too engrossed in his delicious meal to care one way or the other. Through his peripheral vision, Jason could see the man's black pants and the tail of his long black coat. He had considered trying to get a better look at the stranger, but with his close proximity to the man, he wouldn't be able to do so without being outwardly obvious. He suspected the stranger to be a very large man.

The sleeve of the man's coat had ridden up somewhat, and Jason could see the skin of his exposed wrist between the glove and the sleeve. It appeared as if the man's flesh was strangely wrinkled; no, perhaps rippled or bunched up might be better words for what Jason saw. He immediately had an image of the alien character from the 1997 sci-fi movie "Men in Black." He believed the character's name was Edgar and had been played by actor Vincent D'Onofrio. He always found it odd how he could recall such meaningless trivia at the strangest of times. Jason remembered how in the movie, the alien had taken over the character's body, wearing his flesh like a suit, which apparently didn't fit him properly and was bunched and rippled in places. Suddenly he began to develop a strange sensation in the pit of his stomach as if there might be something very wrong with the man sitting next to him and that something bad was about to happen.

Before the feeling had time to take shape and become an actual conscious thought, Jason felt someone grab his hair and pull his head backward. Then he felt a sharp pain across his neck and instantly knew the stranger next to him had just slit his throat. He felt the warmth of his lifeblood flow down the front of his chest as he tried to cry out but couldn't. Then the room swam away to blackness before he ever had time to react.

Suddenly the restaurant erupted in chaos, with patrons screaming and running for the front door. Jason's dead and practically decapitated body fell to the floor with a sickening thud. The waitress behind the counter screamed and ran into the diner's kitchen area, presumably to call 911, or perhaps simply to escape and save herself. The man slowly stood, turned, stepped over the top of the still twitching corpse, and walked casually out of the diner, his collar turned up, and his hat pulled down, his face obscured.

///

A young couple sat quietly on a park bench, enjoying the sunny fall afternoon. The woman, Cindy, was feeding peanuts to the numerous squirrels, which were prevalent in the park while her husband, Barry, sat reading a mystery novel. They often came to this park to relax, read, and feed the birds. It was also a great place to meet friends and was one of the city's favorite public gathering places. Nearby two policemen on park duty stood talking and watching the many people come and go.

Suddenly the air was filled with blood-curdling screams as the two police officers grabbed for their guns and ran in the direction of the shriek. They saw Cindy screaming and crying in terror, her white flowered dress and light pink sweater both splattered red with Barry's spurting blood. She had apparently fallen to the ground and was looking up at the park bench in horror. Her husband sat on the bench, grabbing helplessly at his throat, which was spraying blood like a fountain. Behind him, a tall man dressed in dark clothing, under a long black trench coat and floppy hat, stood calmly with a bloody butcher's knife in one hand while his other held tightly onto the dying man's hair.

The two officers approached the man with their guns drawn and ordered him to drop his weapon. The man calmly complied and offered no resistance whatsoever as the officers pulled his hands roughly behind his back and cuffed him. One of the officers noticed how the cuffs seemed to snag and catch in the rippled loose flesh of the large man's wrist. He didn't particularly care if the perpetrator was suffering pain from the pinching cuffs; he was too shocked by what he had just seen. The man's body on the bench fell to the ground with a thud, his throat slit so extremely, his head was practically severed from the exposed bloody neck stump. More blood pooled in a crimson puddle under his fallen body.

Once the big man was properly secured, the other officer called for backup and then went over to comfort the shocked woman sitting on the ground next to her husband's fallen body, too terrified to touch him, knowing he was dead.

///

Sometime later, the large man was booked and placed in an interrogation room at police headquarters. He appeared to be even larger in the confines of the small eight by ten room. The walls were painted a drab shade of tan, and a large two-way mirror occupied the wall opposite from where the man sat silently. The room's only furniture was a four-foot-long gray metal table and two mismatched metal chairs; both painted the same shade of gray as the table. A single bare light bulb hung from the ceiling casting shadows around the small confining space.

The man sat with his arms cuffed behind his back. He still wore the long black leather trench coat, but his black gloves had been removed as well as his wide-brimmed black leather hat. They both sat on the table next to the man. His hair was long and greasy and hung down over his face. His head was cast down as if he was in deep concentration, uninterested in his surroundings.

Suddenly the door to the room burst open, and two plain-clothes detectives walked in. One of the two stood like a sentry at the door while the other walked directly over to the table, grabbed the top of the metal interviewer's chair, spun it around, slammed it down on the concrete floor with a bang, and straddled it while staring intently at the sullen man who didn't pay him the slightest bit of attention.

"Okay, asshole." The detective shouted at the killer. "What's your story? You obviously have some kind of sob story. All you douchebags have some sort of sob story; my daddy abused me, my mommy was a junkie, the devil made me do it. Come on, moron, what's your story?"

The large man sat silently, never raising his head to make eye contact with the officer, never moving a muscle, completely ignoring the detective as if he wasn't even there.

The detective, Jack McArthur, looked up at his partner Matthew Shannon, who stood quietly by the door and said, "Can you believe this friggin' moron. He offs two innocent people in public by slittin' their throats, one of 'em right in front of two beat cops, and the other in front of a diner full of people. Then he offers no resistance on the takedown, and now here he is with nothin' to say for himself. What the hell am I supposed to do with an idiot like that?"

Then suddenly, without warning or provocation, the detective slapped the large man across the top of his head, causing it to shift slightly to the right from the impact as his long greasy hair flopped loosely from side to side. Yet the man offered no resistance or even acknowledgment of the attack.

Detective Shannon cleared his throat as if to indicate to his partner he may have gone too far, which was part of the illusion they were attempting to create and which they needed to make their ruse work.

"Oh, excuse me." McArthur said theatrically, "It appears my partner feels I may have crossed some sort of line here. He is a bit of a bleeding heart, don't you know, and he don't like it much when I lose my temper and maybe rough a few scumbags like you up a bit. See, he is more of a touchy-feely kind of cop. Ain't that right, Shannon?"

Shannon didn't reply. He simply stood quietly and observed his partner, pretending to be offended by the remark and hoped he appeared somewhat angry. Like most teams, they often did the good cop/bad cop routine when interrogating suspects. But in their case, it wasn't really much of an act. The fact was, Shannon really was a nice guy and did believe in the subtler, more affable approach to getting suspects to talk, while McArthur was a bit of a loose cannon and enjoyed screaming and intimidating the suspects. He was also not opposed to slapping them around a bit, as he had just demonstrated.

The result was a made-to-order good/bad cop team, which more often than not managed to result in better closure rates on their cases than most of the plain-clothes teams on the squad. The other cops often called the pair Jekyll and Hyde. McArthur never minded the ribbing, even though he knew they were all referring to him as the evil Mr. Hyde part of the team. Instead, he loved the attention and the obvious jealousy the other cops blatantly exhibited.

Shannon decided to let McArthur continue his interrogation a bit longer before they did their patented "old switch-eroo" as they called it when McArthur would fake being frustrated with the suspect and storm out angrily of the room, leaving Shannon to step in and work his mellow magic on the unsuspecting criminal.

"So tell me, numbnuts," McArthur insulted, "What is it that makes a big lug like you suddenly go postal and start offing innocent civilians for no apparent reason? Come on and tell me, tall, dark, and ugly. Inquiring minds want to know."

Then McArthur turned on the heat. "Hey, scum sucker. I'm talking to you." Once again, he slapped the man across his downcast head. "Look at me, monkey boy. I'm talking to you." The man silently sat with his head looking downward, refusing to acknowledge the detective.

"Screw you, scumbag," McArthur shouted on cue, spittle flying angrily from his mouth. "I've had it up to here with slime like you. You don't want to talk? Fine. No problemo. We got you dead to rights. We don't need you to talk. I'm outta here."

With that, McArthur headed for the door and gave Shannon a sly wink. Then trying to sound disgusted with his partner, he said, "Fine, mister touchy-feely, he is all yours. You go right ahead with your stupid psychobabble and see if you can get the creep to talk to you. Waste your time if you want to. I'm leaving before I'm tempted to put a bullet in his idiot brain."

The truth was McArthur would only be a few feet away, watching from behind the two-way mirror. If Shannon had any problems with the psycho, McArthur would be back in the room within a few seconds, ready to play full-contact hockey, using the perp's head as a puck.

Shannon walked cautiously over to the chair, which McArthur had previously occupied, quietly turned it around so it faced the mysterious suspect, and slowly sat down with his hands calmly folded on his lap. He looked carefully at the huge man sitting across the table from him but couldn't tell much about his facial appearance as his long greasy black hair hung down, obscuring his features.

He did, however, notice a strange foul odor coming from the man, not just sweat or the stench of the unclean, but something deeper, something rank. Shannon had been on the scene of many murders in his career and had smelled plenty of decomposing bodies. That was very much like what he was now sensing; decomposition. The man didn't look up when he sat on the chair or show any sign of noticing Shannon's arrival.

"Sir, my name is detective Matt Shannon. I am going to sit here with you for a while, and if you feel like talking, I'll be here to listen. I'd truly appreciate it if you'd talk to me. You won't only be helping me, but you'll be helping yourself as well."

The hulking giant remained silent, staring downward. Shannon tried to look under the man's chin inside his coat, but the area was cast in shadows and hard to distinguish. He thought he noticed that the skin of the man's neck was somewhat bunched up, as if the man had once been very overweight and had lost the equivalent of a person or two, leaving a collection of loose fleshy folds. It strangely reminded Shannon of a shirt, which had come loose from its pants and had wrinkled, needing to be pulled down, tucked in, and straightened out once again.

"Sir?" Shannon asked as politely as he could manage. "I don't know if you realize it or not, but you're in a lot of trouble here. I really wish you'd just talk to me." This excessive politeness was also part of their good cop/bad cop routine. Shannon would go out of his way to project the caring police officer image, hoping the suspect would fall for it and let his guard down.

Although he was naturally more easy-going than his partner, Shannon secretly would have liked nothing better than to have the murdering creep try to escape, so he'd have an excuse to put him down with one shot through the center of his forehead. No lawyer, no trial, no muss, no fuss. This man was definitely guilty, and Shannon had no problem being his judge, jury, and executioner if the need arose. But he struggled to maintain his false air of calm, caring concern, hoping to get the murderer to open up. A confession would save a good deal of potentially wasted time.

Shannon decided to try another approach. "You see, there isn't a lot I can do for you unless you open up and talk to me. In fact, there still might not be very much I can do for you since we both know you did kill two men in front of many witnesses. But either way, I wish you could help me to understand why you did what you did. It might benefit you at your trial. I assume you had a reason for wanting to kill those two men. Am I right? Please, please talk to me."

Then Shannon suddenly experienced a strange sensation in his skull, feeling like thousands of multi-legged insects were scrambling about inside his brain. It felt as though his brain was being scanned or probed in some way, which he knew was impossible. And more than that, Shannon seemed to think somehow the strange man across the table from him might be responsible for the strange feeling he was experiencing. He didn't know how it might be possible, but he couldn't seem to shake the impression.

"Taaaaak toooo meeeee." The large man said from below his downcast head with a strange voice of a tonal quality unlike any Shannon had ever heard before. It sounded as if there were two or three voices, each in a different octave, simultaneously speaking, but Shannon didn't know how such a thing might be possible. The strange multi-toned voice caused Shannon to shiver as a chill ran through his body involuntarily.

He forced himself to get over the creepy tickling sensation he felt inside of his mind and tried to focus on the fact he was genuinely pleased the man had actually responded to him. It meant he was making at least some progress. "Yes, yes, that's good." Shannon encouraged, "Talk to me. Yes. You need to talk to me and to answer my questions. I might be able to help you." Then he again felt the strange multi-legged insect tickle inside of his head.

"Taaalk toooo meeee." The large man repeated, sounding a bit more understandable. Shannon believed the man was about to open up to him unless, of course, he was simply repeating the phrase Shannon had spoken and not really understanding what he was saying. He had to try something else to assure himself the large man actually understood. He had to find a way to get through to this suspect. The prisoner had still not lifted his head to acknowledge Shannon.

"What is your name, sir?" Shannon asked again, returning to his calm and careful demeanor. "Who are you?"

The man hesitated for a moment, and Shannon half expected the man to repeat what he had just said in his strange style of speech sounding like "whoooo aaaarrrrr yooooo." Again, he suddenly felt the strange tickling inside his skull resume and was surprised when a few seconds later, the man clumsily answered his question. "I . . . nottt of . . . dis . . . contree . . . I haaave . . . no naaaame." The man still kept his head cast downward as if wishing to prevent Shannon from seeing his face.

"Are you saying you come from somewhere else?" Shannon asked, feeling excited at his progress yet still desiring to appear calm. Again, he felt the squirming sensation in his mind. He noticed the strange feelings in his brain always seemed to occur just before the man spoke as if somehow, this man was probing his mind to find the proper words to use to communicate. He thought the idea ridiculous, yet some part of Shannon seemed to believe it might be true.

Before Shannon had a chance to pursue the idea further, the man spoke again, saying, "It's . . . jusst . . . dat . . . I comm . . . frumm an . . . old country . . . old ways." Shannon had no idea what that statement might have meant. Did the man really mean he came from an old country? He didn't believe so, as "old country" didn't feel right to him.

And what did he mean by "old ways"? Shannon had dealt with many mobsters from foreign countries attempting to set up their criminal enterprises in the United States. They all talked about the old country and the old ways when they explained why they might have murdered someone who had crossed them. It was their way of saying, "In the old country, this is how we dealt with such things, and this is how we will deal with them here."

However, he didn't believe this was what the strange man before him was trying to explain. He thought the man's reference to "country" meant something else, something much more sinister. The way the murderer had said "old country" and "old ways" and the man's strange demeanor seemed somehow to suggest Shannon was in the presence of something not just old, but ancient, and not just foreign but perhaps alien.

Shannon decided to get right to the point. "Can you tell me what these men did to make you want to kill them as you did?"

The ragged man slowly lifted his head and looked Shannon directly in the eyes. Shannon's breath caught in his throat at the sight before him. This man was definitely not right; something was very horribly wrong with him. His eyes were large and round and covered over with a translucent gray film like eyes stricken with cataracts. Although they seemed to look at him, they didn't seem to focus properly, as if they were the eyes of a dead man.

At the place where the skin of the man's ruddy cheeks should have met his eyes, there were dark openings, suggesting the fleshy face he wore wasn't his face at all, but some sort of mask. And not a mask constructed of plastic or latex or other such synthetic material, but one unbelievably appearing to be constructed of actual human skin. Through the slight openings, Shannon could see what looked like some gray and brown dusky dried flesh just beneath the outside loose layer of skin. Again, he smelled the sickening odor of decomposition. Shannon had the image of a man's head and torso with all of the bones, organs, and musculature removed, leaving essentially an empty costume of flesh, which somehow this person or thing or whatever it might be across the table from him had apparently crawled into.

The flesh below the man's neck at the place where it entered his coat was bunched up in ripples. He sat staring, fighting back the feeling of gut-wrenching nausea and cold chills that appeared to spread throughout his body. He wondered what sort of sick bastard this character was, and although he considered signaling his partner to return, he chose not to for the moment. Once again, Shannon felt the strange sensation inside his skull.

Then the killer spoke again, "I . . . keelt . . . dem for fun . . . for sportt . . . like da . . . huuumonzzz doz."

Shannon was shocked at the revelation the bizarre man had just made to him. The murderer had just confessed to killing the two men, but he also said he did so because he thought it would be fun as if it was simply something all humans do.

Shannon wasn't at all surprised to hear the murderer speak of himself as some sort of being apparently separate from humanity. Maniacs such as this often did. In his experience, Shannon felt for some reason, psychos tended to think of themselves as something other than human, as if their ability to take lives made them some sort of new non-human species. Perhaps they were correct; perhaps they were no longer just human. Maybe they lost their humanity. Perhaps they never actually had it to lose. Shannon was starting to wonder if the man before him was really a human at all, or if he might, in fact, be something else, but what that might be he didn't know.

He realized with embarrassment it was beyond ridiculous for him to be entertaining such bizarre thoughts, but he couldn't keep himself from having them nonetheless. Shannon was a sensible man, a thoughtful man who believed only in things he could see or touch and never had any time for nonsense such as ghosts, demons, space aliens, or anything of the sort. Yet here he was, starting to believe the man he had in custody might somehow be something other than a human being.

He asked the man in a shaky voice, "You mean to say, you killed these two men in cold blood just for the fun of it, for sport? Is that what you are trying to tell me?" Once more, he felt as if his mind was being probed as if long thin invisible tendrils were reaching through his skull into his brain and extracting words.

"Yass." The deranged man replied, trying to form the words through the mask's lips; the face didn't seem to move properly. "To . . . keeel . . . foor funn . . . for spurt . . . to . . . muuurrrr . . . derrr . . . like da huuumonzzz."

"I don't understand," Shannon asked, confused. "Did you mean to say you wanted to commit murder like you think humans do? That makes no sense to me. Not all humans kill and commit murder; you should know that." Then he decided to try to determine just what this strange man thought about himself; despite his misgivings, he asked, "After all, you are a human, aren't you?" There it was, the question he had been criticizing himself for thinking was out there on the table.

The strange man looked intently at Shannon as the detective felt the creeping, tickling sensation in his brain intensify and the start of a headache beginning. Then the man replied, "No . . . not . . . huuu- mon . . . I . . . arrr . . . else . . . not . . . huuumon."

Shannon understood he had a genuine loony on his hands. The man either believed he wasn't a human and ran around killing people in cold blood for sport. Otherwise, he was clever enough to be already acting crazy in an attempt to set himself up to go for an insanity plea eventually. Shannon looked again at the strange way the man's skin hung wrinkly on his face and was now certain the man had somehow acquired the flesh of some other man and was unbelievably wearing that flesh as a mask. If the killer was going for an insanity plea, he certainly had taken all the right steps. He definitely had Shannon con- vinced he was madder than a hatter.

Suddenly, Shannon wished his partner were sitting in the driver's seat instead of him. McArthur seemed always to handle the weirdest situations effortlessly and could take the most unbelievable circum- stances with a grain of salt. Shannon knew McArthur was watching from behind the glass, and with one subtle sign, Shannon could indi- cate it was time for him to return to the room. But he was determined to see this through on his own. Sure, the guy was some sort of whack-job, and he may have killed two men, maybe more, but he was now subdued and handcuffed and completely harmless to anyone.

He decided to play this out a bit longer and asked again. "So, you are trying to tell me you're not a human?"

"Not . . . huuumon." The man replied through the hideous fleshy mask. "I . . . else . . . sum . . . ting . . . else."

"You're not human? You're something else other than human?" Shannon asked, "And you come from an old country where they practice old ways, not like those of humans?" Shannon realized he was getting used to the weird crawling feelings inside of his skull.

"Yass" The man replied. "Manny of uss . . . wit da old ways."

Shannon understood this madman truly believed what he was saying. The man thought he was some form of life other than human. Shannon could imagine McArthur laughing his ass off behind the mirror at the mess he had gotten himself into.

But despite his high level of patience, Shannon had just about reached the end of his rope with the psycho. He had just essentially gotten the guy to confess. They didn't need to hear any more. There was no point in dragging it out any longer. He would leave the room and have this nut-job dumped into a holding cell, pending a mandatory psych exam, after which the man would probably be locked up for the rest of his unnatural life. He just wanted to make sure he was nowhere around when they finally removed the guy's atrocious flesh suit. He knew seeing such a sight would likely cause him to puke his guts out, and he just didn't need that.

As Shannon stood to leave, he suddenly stopped in his tracks when he heard a clanking sound coming from behind the murderer, who sat with his hands still positioned behind his back. Shannon's stomach tightened with alarm as he reached his hand up into his jacket to grab for his pistol from his shoulder holster. At the same time, the door to the interrogation room burst open, and McArthur rushed in with his own pistol at the ready, pointing it straight at the huge man. The prisoner slowly rose to a standing position as he brought his hands around to the front of his body, now free of the handcuffs.

"Hold it right there, ass-wipe!" McArthur shouted. "I've just been lookin' for an excuse to blow your worthless brains all over that back wall, and you look like you are about to give me all the encouragement I need." The big man looked up, and Shannon heard McArthur's breath hitch with alarm at his first close-up view of the flesh-mask the maniac wore.

McArthur quickly regained his composure and screamed, "What kind of twisted crap is this?" He tried to pull the trigger but found he was paralyzed and unable to complete the act. Shannon discovered he, too, was unable to move. He had managed to take his own gun out of his holster and positioned it in front of his body but couldn't bring it up to aim it at the killer. He was completely helpless to do anything but stand and stare. Shannon felt the tickling and squirming sensation once again inside of his head, but now it was much more intense than he had experienced before, as was the ever-increasing ache in his skull.

The enormous man now stood to his full six feet seven inches, and after looking back and forth between Shannon and McArthur for a few seconds, he unfastened the front of his leather trench coat, pulled it open, and allowed it to flop to the floor with a slapping sound.

Neither Shannon nor McArthur could believe their eyes as what they were seeing defied all logic or reason. The man was most definitely not human; Shannon didn't know what sort of being it might be, but human was nowhere among the choices. The room was filled with the raw stench of decomposition. Although the creature wore black pants held up with a worn and tattered rope, fashioned into a makeshift belt, it was otherwise completely unclothed from the waist up. However, no human flesh was present on its torso and upper arms, but instead, they saw a dark gray, black and brown, dried translucent mass, appearing to be in constant motion, somehow making up the approximate shape of a man.

Behind the semi-transparent outer layer, thousands, if not hundreds of thousands of coal-black, worm-like creatures with glowing red eyes squirmed and writhed, swirling amongst each other in a macabre frantic dance of horror. From the outside, the thing resembled the ancient long-dead remains of some mummified corpse of what once might have been a human at one time. But whatever the unimaginable worm-things were which made up the creature's insides, the sight was unlike anything Shannon had ever seen or could have ever possibly imagined. He sensed a single consciousness coming from the mass of crawling worms like they all moved and thought as a single entity.

Shannon suspected the man, although now he realized he could no longer think of the revolting thing before him as a man but a horrid unearthly creature, was using some strange form of telepathic will power to keep the filthy putrid remains in the shape it needed to simulate a human form. He also assumed this was the same force that kept McArthur and himself in their paralyzed state.

He didn't believe the thing before him was extraterrestrial, although it very well could have been. He had a sense that it had come from somewhere on earth, perhaps below the earth, deep down inside the earth. Shannon couldn't know for certain, but he had a primal intuition, which told him it might be a more reasonable explanation, although what he saw before him defied all reason.

He allowed his gaze to follow the simulated body upward, knowing full well what he would find, and not wanting to see it; yet for some reason compelled by perhaps a morbid human curiosity which wouldn't allow him to stop. Near the top of what would be the creature's chest area, he saw a large flap of human flesh hanging loosely, indicating the neckline and start of the mask, which the creature wore. He also saw the creature's flesh-covered hands traveled up to its arms, ending just below where its elbows would be if it had elbows and where the skin bunched like that of a sagging leather sleeve.

Unfortunately, he realized his original assessment had been correct; the beast, the disgusting creature of unknown origin, made up of millions of squirming maggot-like things, was wearing the hollowed-out head and hands of some poor soul to disguise itself and travel freely among people. Unable to move or speak, Shannon didn't know what terrible fate he was destined to suffer under the will of the murderous being. Shannon felt the tingling inside of his brain increasing and realized the thing across the room was once again scanning his mind for the words it needed.

"I . . . haav . . . good . . . vaacaashun. Muchhh . . . funnn. Gooood hunnnting." The creature said through the wrinkled fleshy face it wore as a mask.

Whatever the creature was, or more accurately, whatever these creatures were and wherever they came from, Shannon finally understood their purpose for being there. They, or it, as he found the thing easier to refer to, had come for sport, to hunt, to gain pleasure from killing humans. For a moment, he thought of all of his friends who were hunters, who took days off from work and went into the woods to hunt various game for sport. In essence, this is what the being standing before him was doing. It didn't think of humans as anything more than animals to be hunted for sport.

Shannon realized the only reason the creature had been taken into custody is that it had chosen to be taken. It wanted to be captured and to be brought to the police station, specifically to that place. It must have realized that killing unarmed humans in the street didn't pose a sufficient enough test of its hunting skills and wanted to come to a place where it might find more challenging game. What better place than a police station brimming with trained, armed officers?

Shannon could see with his peripheral vision that McArthur was, like himself, still unable to move, positioned with his gun pointed directly at the creature but unable to squeeze off a shot. Standing tall in front of them, the horrible beast began to slowly peel its skin gloves from its withered, dark and filthy body, dropping the shriveled flesh bags to the concrete floor with a sickening sound which made Shannon's own skin crawl and his stomach turn over with disgust. Then, as if that hadn't been enough to cause him nightmares for the rest of his life, however long that might be, the thing reached up and pulled off the mask of flesh, which also flopped to the floor with a wet slopping thud.

He couldn't comprehend the details of the face of the creature. Like the rest of its constantly moving body, its face was a similar mass of pulsating dark black worm-like things squirming in constant motion, sloshing just under a translucent layer of brownish-gray membrane. At the place where the creature's eyes should have been, Shannon saw two spherical globes in deep black sockets, and to his horror and disgust, he realized they were the eyes of the original owner of the flesh. They were suspended in a dark brown syrupy liquid substance, bobbing erratically like two hard-boiled eggs in a bowl of runny chocolate pudding. He suspected if he somehow survived this, he might never be able to consider eating either of the foods again.

The creature turned what passed for its head in the direction of McArthur as Shannon saw the man's gun barrel slowly begin to rise, just out beyond his field of vision, yet he somehow knew exactly what the creature had planned. He tried to scream "no" but could scarcely get a sound to pass through his paralyzed lips. He shouted the word in his mind hoping to distract the creature or perhaps make him stop his murderous act.

A few seconds later, Shannon's ears were ringing with the deafening sound of the blast of McArthur's gun, and he heard the distant thud of the man's now practically headless body hit the floor. The smell of the gun blast hung in the air as well as the coppery aroma of McArthur's pooling blood. Shannon waited, unmoving, certain at any moment the creature would use its strange mind control to command his body to raise his own pistol and blow his own head off.

Instead, the creature reached down, picked up the revolting fleshy gloves and headpiece, allowing its unimaginable worm-infested form to ooze into the appliances, filling them to the point where they once again resembled their formerly living counterparts. The creature slipped his trench coat over his thin hideous body and buttoned it, hiding his alien form.

The strange non-human creature looked at Shannon with the roaming dead eyes of one of its victims and said, "Gooood . . . copppp . . . I . . . lak . . . yoooo." Then Shannon felt his own gun hand begin to rise toward his head, and he knew it was all over.

/ / /

Matt Shannon awoke to the sounds of alarms, sirens, and many people shouting. He slowly opened his eyes and realized he was lying on the floor of the interrogation room. The first sight, which came into focus, was the knee of someone who was hunched down next to him. Behind the person's leg, he saw the practically headless body of Jack McArthur blocking the doorway with several other people examining him.

"Detective Shannon." The voice said from above him. "Can you hear me, Shannon?"

"Yes, I . . . I can hear you." Shannon replied with a raspy croak, trying to sit up. "Oh, crap! My head!" he complained, grasping the sides of his head as he was suddenly hit with a massive skull-splitting headache. "What the hell happened to me?"

"Well," The voice replied, it appears you took a major blow to your head with the barrel of your own gun. It appears you were pistol-whipped into unconsciousness. The EMTs suspect you might have a concussion. We'll be sending you to the hospital shortly as a precaution. Right now, we are quite surprised to have found you alive."

"What's going on? Who are you? What happened?" Shannon asked, confused.

The voice replied, "My name is Detective Mark Ralston from the East Side division. And it appears the perp you and your partner McArthur were interrogating managed to get somehow free of his bonds, grab hold of your gun, and clubbed you on the head. Then he must have shot your partner when he came in to assist."

"On no. Not Jack." Shannon said, momentarily forgetting that McArthur had been forced to shoot himself before he had been forced to knock himself unconscious.

"Afraid so," Ralston replied. "But that ain't the half of it. The perp apparently took both weapons and went on a shooting spree, killing everyone in the stationhouse before disappearing. You're lucky to be alive."

"Video?" Shannon asked. "Someone must have video."

Ralston said, "Yeah, we have plenty of video of him shooting up the stationhouse but no video of your interrogation. Do you know anything about that, Detective Shannon?" His voice had a suspicious tone, which Shannon recognized as the natural distrust all cops seemed to have.

"No.," Shannon said, confused and concerned. "I'm certain the video was running when we started the interrogation. I never shut it off, and I doubt McArthur would have done so either. I can't explain what happened." But in the back of his mind, he realized the creature had mentally shut down the recording equipment, choosing not to have any video of the interview and, therefore, no evidence of its true form.

Then Shannon had another realization, one he knew he might never be able to come to terms with. He couldn't understand why every single cop in the stationhouse had been killed, yet he had been left alive as the lone survivor. He wanted to tell someone about the strange creature, which inhabited the flesh mask. Still, he knew if he did, everyone would either assume the blow to the head had caused him to hallucinate or else he was faking confusion because he was covering for some screw-up he and McArthur had made. He had no proof of the creature's existence and no idea where the creature came from or where it may have gone. He couldn't even comprehend why he was still alive.

Then he recalled the hideous creature's final words, "Gooood . . . copppp . . . I . . . lak . . . yoooo." Apparently, he had played his role of good cop very well, perhaps too well. For whatever reason, the bizarre murderous creature had chosen to let him live, although he knew its repulsive countenance would haunt his nightmares for the rest of his life.

AFTER MIDNIGHT

The security guard stared at the bank of idle displays, all in bright, vivid colors. Each one showed a separate area of the huge department store. Since there were only eight video screens and dozens of cameras strategically placed around the store, the images on the monitors updated every few seconds when in cycle mode to show whichever area was next to be screened. The higher ticket areas were repeated more often, and were displayed on more screens than the lower-priced sections.

Chet had only started his shift less than an hour earlier at 11:00 P.M., and already the boredom was beginning to set in. He was hoping at least something a bit interesting might happen that evening, as the previous three nights had been strangely uneventful. This is not to suggest Chet was looking for any sort of major altercation, either. God knew he had experienced enough of that for several lifetimes.

Many years earlier, Chester Dalton had graduated from high school, and instead of heading off to college like many of his friends, he had decided to see what the world had to offer him. He had enlisted in the army right before 9-11 and quickly found himself part of Desert Storm. As soon as his hitch was up, Chet left the service, and using his army experience, he was accepted by the local police department in the town where he lived. But after several years of that, he became bored and left the force. This was followed by several gigs for everything from a private security agent to a bounty hunter to a night club bouncer. Now, at forty-five, Chet had just about had his fill of such violent jobs.

Although not a big man, Chet was solid, well-built, and could handle himself in a fight if it became necessary. He had done so more times in the past than he cared to think about. Now he was content to sit alone at night in the quiet of his security booth watching video screens and chilling.

He glanced up at the wall clock next to the bank of monitors and saw it was 11:55. Five minutes until midnight. Then things would start to get interesting. Chet liked interesting as long as it stayed calm and secure. After midnight was when the freaks made their nightly appearance. They were seldom the same freaks each night, but they were all very similar in their peculiarities. He realized P. T. Barnum would have had difficulty putting together a sideshow with more oddities than Chet encountered on any given night on his job.

There were the fat lady and the thin man, usually found together for whatever bizarre reason. The woman trucked her way around the store on one of the electric scooters, which Chet referred to as "Lard Carts." The scooters, meant for legitimately handicapped shoppers, were more often than not used by these lard butts and fatties. Several times he had seen some disabled shoppers looking for a cart to ride only to discover them all either being used by one of the gravity butts or else recharging because their batteries had drained hauling these bulbous sacks of undulating flesh around the store.

He also wondered why it seemed these huge freakish women often had such skinny husbands dutifully following them and their carts around the store. Were these guys simply chubby chasers? Did they stay slim from constantly enabling their partners by running around getting them whatever they wanted and following their lard carts around stores? Or did the women eat everything in sight, leaving nothing for their mates?

There were also the illustrated men and women, all adorned with more tattoos than he would ever have imagined possible. Chet wasn't anti-tattoo by any means. He even had two of his own. But some of the freaks he saw in his store defied all logic and common sense. Arms, legs, and even necks, heads, and faces were covered with ink. And the body piercings were even more bizarre. He often wondered where these freaks worked. Who in their right mind would even hire such a walking mutant?

Then there were the midgets, the giants, the hermaphrodites, the transvestites, the hookers, the pimps, the potheads, the crack heads, and the meth-mouths. Not to forget about the goths, the punks, and God only knew what else some of these freakish creatures could be called. Chet often wondered to himself, at what point does a human stop being a human and becomes something new and not necessarily better.

To the best of his knowledge, Chet believed there were few if any freak shows and sideshows remaining. He knew why. All someone had to do was stop by his big box store after midnight, and you could see all the freaks your twisted heart desired. Most of them were harmless, just folks coming out in the privacy of night to do their shopping away from the staring, judgmental eyes of the so-called normal people who were now at home fast asleep. Every so often, Chet might have to subdue someone for shoplifting and turn them over to the local police. But that had also become a rare occurrence.

At 12:10 A.M., as he studied the bank of video screens, he noticed something suspicious that caught his attention. It was an extremely tall man entering the store wearing a long black leather coat hanging down below his knees. He also wore a dark leather wide-brimmed hat, black leather pants, motorcycle boots, and leather gloves with the fingers cut out. It wasn't just the style of the man's dress that caught Chet's attention, but the fact that the man was wearing such an outfit on a hot ninety-plus degree July night. Of course, the store was air-conditioned but even so, to wear such a getup on such a muggy night was bound to attract suspicion. Chet knew that often professional shoplifters used long coats to hide all sorts of stolen merchandise.

Chet's security office was located near the front entrance of the store. Its mirrored window allowed him to see out, but no one could see in. He watched the odd stranger walk by his window, heading into the store. It was then he saw the man had long, greasy black hair that hung down from his hat, hiding much of his face. He also wore dark sunglasses and sported a thick black beard. His face and exposed fingers appeared to be coated with filth and glistening with sweat.

As the man passed the window, he stopped for a moment, then slowly turned his head in Chet's direction. Chet knew the man couldn't see in through the mirror, but he nonetheless felt as if the stranger was looking right at him and could see everything. A cold chill raced down Chet's spine, and he felt a bead of sweat begin to form on his upper lip. After what seemed like an eternity but was actually only a second or two, the stranger turned back and continued walking into the store. Chet found himself suddenly taking a deep breath, realizing that he had been unconsciously holding his breath during the time the stranger was staring at him.

"Wow. That was creepy." Chet thought, "Now that is one freaky dude."

However, that wisecrack was only his way of trying to deflect his concentration from the real issue. That being the fact that he knew there was something bad about that character, and Chet instinctively knew the stranger would be trouble for him that night. He had developed that awareness from a lifetime of dealing with trouble in all the various forms it took. His problem was he didn't know what sort of trouble the odd man was bringing with him.

Chet went back to his desk and began following the man with his overhead cameras as he moved about the store. The big man moved quickly through the store, bypassing all the high-ticket areas normally targeted by shoplifters. He completely ignored the jewelry department, hurried by electronics, and past the sporting goods area before eventually slowing down at the food and produce section.

"What's this guy up to?" Chet wondered aloud in the quiet of his office.

He saw the man approach the open cold display case, which held various packaged cheeses and lunch meats. Unfortunately, his back was to the camera, and although Chet suspected the man might be stealing food, he couldn't see from the view he had available. The man's back seemed to be moving as if he were picking things up and pulling them into his coat, yet his arms were still visible hanging at his side. A moment later, Chet saw the wrapper from one of the meat packages fall to the floor, and he suddenly realized what the man was doing.

It was obvious that the arms hanging by his side weren't real but were props. The man's actual arms were hidden inside his long coat, which probably was lined with dozens of deep pockets. With his back to the camera and his "arms" visible, anyone watching might not realize his scam and that he was filling his pockets with fresh meats and cheeses. Then the man moved over to the area, which held a variety of freshly cut high-priced steaks.

After a moment, the man turned and began making his way back toward the store entrance. Chet could see his coat was closed, and because of the thickness of the garment, not a single sign of anything inappropriate could be discerned. Chet got up from his desk and opened the door to the office, getting ready to head this character off before leaving the store. He didn't have to wait long. After just a few minutes, the man was walking right toward Chet, who was blocking his exit from the store.

"Excuse me, sir." Chet said using more cordiality than he would have liked to, but which was expected of him, "I need to speak to you about something important."

The strange man just stood silently, looking down at Chet. The security guard hadn't realized just how large the stranger was. He was certain the man was well over six-seven, and his shoulders were much broader than Chet had originally noticed. If this character decided to get violent, Chet might have a real struggle on his hands. He decided to handle this by the book and not risk any unwarranted danger to himself.

"Sir. I need you to step into my office over there and answer a few questions for me."

The stranger still said nothing but slowly turned his head and looked toward the security office. Chet had the feeling that not only did this character know exactly what was coming next, but he had no fear of Chet, the police, or anyone. Without a word, the huge man turned and walked toward the open door of the security office.

Chet followed, and as he did, he pressed a special auto-dial icon on his smartphone, which sent an automated message to the local police requesting a unit be dispatched to the store. The store was part of a multi-billion-dollar chain that spared no expense when it came to security and paid a significant annual stipend to the local police department for this level of service. He knew that a squad car would arrive and head directly to his office in less than a half-hour. All he had to do is keep this guy calm until then, and the locals could deal with him.

As they entered the office, the man stood in front of Chet's desk and stared at the bank of video screens illuminating the darkroom. Chet knew if the guy was going to bolt for the parking lot, it would likely be in the next second or two. But the man either didn't realize he was in trouble or didn't care. Chet looked at his watch as he saw that only two minutes had passed since he sent the automated request for backup. He decided to try to talk with the man until help arrived.

"Sir, do you know why I asked you to come in here?"

The man didn't reply. He just stood staring down at the security guard. Chet thought he noticed a slight movement just beneath the front of the man's coat. He suddenly became concerned, realizing the stranger might have a knife, gun, or other weapon hidden under that coat. The man opened and closed his gloved hands a few times as if bored. It was then Chet realized the arms weren't props but where his real arms. But then, whose arms were busy stealing food?

"Sir, I have reason to suspect you were shoplifting food from our meat and cheese section. Would you like to explain your actions?"

The man looked down at Chet and, after releasing a sigh of frustration, mumbled, "I dint wanna, but my brother, he hungry."

Chet suddenly felt a bit of sympathy for the man. Looking at his worn and dirty clothing, he could see the man was obviously poor. And if he had a brother at home who was depending on him for food, perhaps Chet could understand his plight. Maybe he could give the man a break this one time, and then he might never return to the store. Then he'd become someone else's problem.

"Look. I understand where you're coming from. I've been poor from time to time in my life as well. I get that you want to get food for your brother, but I can't permit shoplifting. I'll tell you what I'll do, this one time only. If you just open your coat and leave the food you stole on my desk, I'll let you leave. I've already called the police, but I'll tell them you ran away when they get here. I don't want to see you go to jail, especially if your brother depends upon you to supply him with food."

The man lowered his head as if in contrition, then slowly began to pull down the zipper on his long leather coat. As the coat opened, Chet expected to see packages of food fall out onto his desk but was in no way prepared for what he saw instead. The man was naked from the waist up, but that wasn't what made Chet's breath catch in his throat. Hidden under the coat was some sort of freakish deformity, the likes of which Chet had never seen in even the worst horror movie.

Just above the top of the man's pants was a face, or at least it might be called a face of some type. It was a mouth, a huge mouth perhaps a foot wide and two feet high with large red lips and rows of long shark-like teeth. At the center was a long lapping tongue that rolled out of the maw like a snake and danced serpent-like in the air in front of Chet's face. He was paralyzed with fear. At the top of the mouth was a deformed, twisted nose and on each side of the nose were large wandering eyes.

"My brother still hungry." The man said in a deep, monotone voice.

Before Chet had been able to even comprehend what, he was looking at, four long flapping tentacles seemed to fly out from the man's sides under the coat. On the ends of the rope-like appendages were small human hands. The hands grabbed tightly onto various points around Chet's body and, with a strength he never would have imagined, began to pull him toward that gaping, waiting maw.

Chet opened his mouth to scream, and the large man punched him hard in the face, smashing his nose to a bloody pulp and shattering several of his teeth.

"I sorry, mister, but my brother still hungry."

As Chet was slowly pulled into the fang-filled chomping wood chipper of a mouth, and as the agony coursed through his dying body, he realized that all of the people who entered his store after midnight, the ones he thought of as freaks, were just regular people with a few odd peculiarities. This thing, this horrible creature that was ending his life and feasting on his flesh was the real freak.

THIS RUBS ME THE WRONG WAY

"You know Jimmy, this isn't exactly what I'd call my idea of a great date," Annie said as the pair drove through the front gates of the Heavenly View Cemetery while the sun was just beginning to set over the western horizon. The car pulled over to the side of the narrow gravel road, and her boyfriend turned off the engine.

"Come on, Annie. Lighten up a bit." Jim Dobson said casually. "I told you my hobby was grave rubbing. You saw the hundreds of rubbings I have in my apartment. You agree to come with me sometime I was going to collect new images. That's why we're here." Jim reached into the back seat, where he grabbed a backpack of supplies. The couple got out of the car and stood near the front bumper.

Annie hesitated, "I know I said I'd come along, and I really want to try to embrace your hobby, but to be perfectly honest with you, this rubs me the wrong way; no pun intended."

Jim gave a sly smile. "I'd like to rub you the right way." He said, nudging his crotch toward her and giving her a Groucho Marx eyebrow twitch.

"Forget it, Jimmy." Annie insisted. "Your chances of getting anywhere with me in this horrible place are less than zero."

Jim said, "Ah, come on, Annie. Where's your sense of adventure?"

"My sense of adventure is at home, where I should be. I'm sorry, Jimmy. It's just that it's all so creepy for me."

Jim looked as if he had been offended, "Annie. I've told you it's not creepy, and it's not ghoulish. Grave rubbing is a legitimate hobby based on the desires of people like myself to collect historical documentation. It has nothing to do with hanging out in graveyards just for some sort of sick fun or something."

"Then why didn't we come out here during the day? You know, like when the sun was shining, and there was no chance of running into ghosts or zombies?" She asked.

"Seriously? Ghosts? Zombies?" Jimmy said with an air of condescension. "You honestly don't believe in such things, do you, Annie?"

She replied, "No, of course I don't. But that doesn't make this place any less creepy. And it still doesn't explain why we came out here at night. Are you planning on doing something illegal here, Jimmy?"

Jim said, "No, not at all. It's just . . ."

"Just what?" Annie shot back. "I knew it! James Charles Dobson! You're trying to get me involved in doing something that's going to get me in trouble, aren't you?" Whenever Annie wanted to make a point, she used his full name. He figured it must be a woman thing because his mother always did the same thing when he was a kid.

"No, I swear," Jim said, raising his right hand in the air like a boy scout. "I assure you we're not doing anything illegal. The reason we're here now is that I know the evening groundskeeper. There's like this ancient section of the cemetery over that way with graves from back in the seventeen and eighteen hundreds. The only way a grave rubber like me can get in there is with special permission. The truth is, the managers of the cemetery don't want any of us in there. As a result, there's a sort of deal we have to make with the groundskeepers. If you agree to give them something special, sometimes they'll agree to let you sneak in. It's not illegal."

"Really? Trespassing isn't illegal? Bribery isn't illegal?" Annie insisted. "I may be wrong, but the last time I checked, they were both illegal."

"Not really." Jim insisted weakly. "It's not trespassing because we'll have the permission of the night caretaker. And it's not bribery. It a simple trade. I'm going to do a few rubbings in exchange for a small gift." He reached into his backpack.

"What gift?" Annie asked.

Jim retrieved a whiskey bottle from the backpack and said. "Crown Royal baby. Nothing but the best for Art the caretaker."

"God! You're impossible, Jimmy!"

"Yeah. But that's what you love about me."

As the two walked toward the cemetery's back end, Annie was reluctantly trailing behind studying the various tombstones in the more modern section and noticed something, which made her stop in her tracks. "What's that?" She asked.

"What's what?"

"That tombstone over there. It has a birthdate but no death date. What's up with that?" She asked.

"Oh, that's no big deal," Jim said. "You see that a lot nowadays. People pre-plan their funerals and stuff. You know, to get it all paid for ahead of time? Well, now a lot of people are including their headstones in the process and filling out everything except for the expiration date."

"Blecch!" She cried. "You mean like a hotel reservation for the dead?"

Jim thought for a moment then said, "Yeah. I guess you could think of it like that. They have their spot reserved, and when they pass on, the tombstone engraver comes back and etches on the death date."

"Jeezus! That's really creepy!" Annie exclaimed. "Like this whole cemetery and twisted hobby wasn't weird enough. Remind me again, what is it I see in you, Jimmy? Because right now, I'm starting to wonder."

Jim bent down and kissed her passionately on the lips, flicking his tongue gently against hers. At the same time, he reached up and softly cupped her breast. She gasped audibly.

"Oh yeah." She said dreamily. "There's that."

Then she suddenly snapped back to reality and said, "No. No. No. There's no way that's happening here. No way at all."

"Annie, Baby! What? No likie a little kinky-kinky?" Jim persisted.

"For-get-it." She said emphatically.

"Fine," Jim said. "Besides, I'm starting to get a nasty headache, probably a migraine. I recognize the signs."

"Want a pill or something?" She was starting to sift through her purse.

"No need. I'll be fine till we get home."

Then Annie suddenly let out a small shriek of fright.

Jim said, "Now what's wrong?"

"There's someone over there behind that tree. I swear I saw something move over there."

"Hey," Jim shouted toward the tree. "Art? Is that you over there lurking in the shadows like a freakin' vampire or something?" He laughed.

A figure slowly moved out of the darkness as a grizzled old disheveled man in faded jeans and a well-worn work shirt lurched forward.

"Zat you, Jimmy?" The figure asked, shielding his eyes from the setting sun.

"Yeah. It's me, Art, and this is my girl Annie." Jim replied.

"Nice, real nice." Art said, casting a lecherous smile complete with several missing teeth while leering at Annie as if she were a juicy pork chop.

Jim interrupted the man's gawking and said, "Easy old-timer. That one's taken."

"So, ya got what ya promised me?" Art said, abruptly taking his attention away from Annie.

"You bet. Crown Royal. A whole bottle of it."

"Yar, that's what I'm talkin' about, Jimmy, me boy. Bring it on over here."

Jim handed the bottle to the wizened old-timer, and the man turned to lead the pair to the older section of the cemetery.

"Now you to be careful over here wit all dem old stones. If any ting happens to dem, da boss will have me balls nailed to his office wall. Get me drift?" The man instructed.

"Yes, I understand," Jim replied.

"Ya better." Art insisted, pulling something from his dirty pants pocket. He raised his arm with a clicking sound, revealing a switchblade, rusted, yet glimmering in the setting sunlight. "Cause if he comes after my balls, I'll be comin' after yers."

Once again, Annie let out a gasp as she grabbed tightly to Jim's arm and the two of them slinked past the groundskeeper who already had lost interest in them. He had put away his blade and was unscrewing the top to the whiskey bottle.

As they entered the now open gates of the old part of the cemetery, Annie asked, "Is he serious, Jimmy? Would he really come after you?"

"Not to worry, Babe. He's nothin' but a burnt-out old drunk who every so often has to make himself feel like he still has something he lost a long time ago. Besides, knife or no knife, I could take him stone-cold sober, and he hasn't been sober in more than a decade from what I hear."

They began to look around at the ancient tombstones as the sun continued descending in the west. With excitement, Jim dropped to the ground near a particularly old-looking headstone and shouted. "Look at this one Annie. It's from the early seventeen hundreds. And look at the quality of the carving. I mean, think about it, these were all done by hand! Those stone masons were true artisans."

Still recovering from the encounter with Art and the general morbid feeling of the entire evening, Annie said, "Oooo wow, how amazing." The dripping sarcasm in her voice was apparent.

"Okay," Jim said. "I get it. You don't like being here. No problem. Let me get a rubbing of this one and a few more, and we'll be on our way before it gets too dark. Besides, this headache of mine is getting worse by the minute."

"As far as I'm concerned, the sooner we leave here, the better." She replied as she began to look around at the other ancient stones with disinterest. Then she shouted, "Holy crap, Jimmy! Look at this one."

Happy to see her showing at least some interest in his chosen hobby, Jim said, "Almost done here, Babe. I'll be there in a minute."

Annie bent down to study the tombstone more closely. She still couldn't believe her eyes. She read the name repeatedly as her lips moved silently along. The name inscribed on the stone was James Charles Dobson, Jimmy's name! She heard leaves crackle behind her as Jim approached.

"Holy crap is right. Just look at that." Jim said.

What's your name doing on here, Jimmy?"

"It's not my name," Jim said. "I mean it is, but it's not. It's the same name, but some other James Dobson."

Annie asked, "You said you just moved here a few years ago from the Midwest. Any chance you had some relatives living here in the East a few centuries ago?"

"No. I don't think. At least, not that I know of." Jim said. "But you know, Dobson's not an uncommon name. Could be just a coincidence, I suppose."

Then Jim took out his flashlight to get a closer look at the stone's worn face and practically dropped it when he saw the birthdate. The stone read, "Born, April 9, 1793."

"Annie. Look at that." Jim said. "This dude was born on the exact same date I was born but two hundred years earlier than me. How freakin' bizarro is that?"

"That's really, really weird, Jimmy. Way too weird." Annie replied. "I think maybe I've had enough of this creepy place. Let's get out of here, now!"

"Not just yet," Jim said. "I can't let this go without getting a rubbing of it. It's just too cool. Man, I'll take this home, frame it, and put it in my living room."

"Honestly, Jimmy?" Annie chastised. "I really don't like this. It's starting to make my skin crawl just being here."

Without answering, Jim bent down, grabbed a stick of charcoal, and a fresh piece of paper, which he fastened to the top of the stone with masking tape and began furiously rubbing the face of the paper, transferring the inscription from the tombstone to the paper. He was intently working on his rubbing and not paying much attention to Annie, who was staring all around the graveyard with terror in her eyes. As she moved in a slow circular motion scanning the area, she heard

Jimmy let out a sharp cry of pain, followed by the sound of his body falling to the soft earth in front of the tombstone.

"Jimmy!" She screamed as she raced to his side. His body was still, and he wasn't breathing. There was a thin trickle of blood seeping from his ear and one of his nostrils as he lay stone-cold dead on top of the grave, the one bearing the name identical to his own. The rubbing paper was still fastened to the grave marker. He had just completed it before collapsing. As Annie looked at the paper, she noticed the paper's death date for the first time. It was the same date as that very day, only two hundred years earlier.

BETTER OFF BURIED

*Author's Note: This is a twisted homage to a story, which has had many dif-
ferent incarnations since the late 1980s, both as a joke as well as an urban
legend. As is typical of such tales, the originator is unknown. I decided to
take the story's basic premise and create my own special version of it as an
ironic horror tale.* —*Thomas M. Malafarina*

"Oh no, Bo, what have you done? For the love of God! Why would you
ever do such a thing?"

Elmer Huggins was staring angrily down at his black Labrador
retriever, Bo, whose head now hung in supplication at the sudden
realization he had angered his master. Elmer had seen Bo approach,
seemingly happy to show off his most recent prize. But all of that had
changed very quickly.

Bo was standing on Elmer's second floor back porch with the mud-
covered remains of something in his mouth. The dog must have chased
the thing through God-knows-where because similar grime covered the
dog's face and paws. Despite the accumulation of filth, Elmer distin-
guished what it was that his dog held between his jaws. The body hung
limply from his jowls, the head and front paws hanging to the left, and
its back legs and tail dangling to the right. Bo had his massive maw
tightly gripped around the thing's middle, and Elmer could see the
poor creature was obviously dead.

The sight of the dead kitten made Elmer's heart skip a beat because he knew what this would mean to him, and it wouldn't be good. Elmer had searched for months trying desperately to find a rental unit that would accept him and his huge dog but had failed miserably. Then one lucky day, he had answered an ad for an apartment for rent, which indicated pets were welcome. It was a small one-bedroom efficiency located above a garage behind the property of an elderly woman named Mrs. Thelma Balthasar. She was a widow with no children but had several cats. Although she often seemed to be a bit quirky in Elmer's opinion, Mrs. Balthasar wasn't what you would call a typical "crazy cat lady". However, she did have six of the things. Well, at least she did until Bo made his recent revelation.

Elmer had been beyond thankful the woman was willing to rent him the unit along with his dog after having so many doors slammed in his face. Mrs. Balthasar had told Elmer she loved all animals, often more than she liked people, but she favored her cats most of all.

She had also made it clear from the start that her only requirement was that he keep Bo locked up, so the dog didn't get out and do anything to harm her cats. She called them her babies and said they weren't strictly house cats. She told him they often spent time lounging in the back yard, a small parcel of land separating her house from the garage above which he and Bo were to reside. As a result, she instructed Elmer to keep Bo under lock and key for her little ones' welfare.

Yet now, after only a month and a half in the place, he saw his future as a resident of this apartment as dead as the filthy kitten dangling from his dog's mouth.

"What the hell am I gonna do now, Bo?" Elmer asked his dog, who still stood with the cat in his mouth. Elmer said sternly, "Drop that damned thing, Bo. Drop it now."

The dog obeyed and let the corpse fall to the porch with a dull thud. He stared down at the tiny body, wondering how he was going to make this all right again. It was then he noticed that there were no obvious signs of damage or anything that might tie Bo to the death. He had expected to see the cat's stomach torn open, and its innards spilled all over his porch, but Bo's teeth hadn't pierced the cat's flesh, and there was no blood or gore whatsoever. Likewise, the cat's neck hadn't been broken and stretched, as often happens when a dog grabs a kitten and shakes it to death. The cat just looked like it had been sleeping.

This gave Elmer an idea. He let the corpse lying on his porch while he took the dog inside. He put Bo in the bathtub and cleaned all the grime from his body until not a trace remained. Then he took a basin of soapy water and went out onto the porch to clean the mud and grime off the remains. He noticed it wore a pink silk ribbon that likely had been tied into a bow until it had become untied. He cleaned that up as well. When he was finished, he took the body inside and did his best to blow it dry with his hairdryer. Then he tied the bow carefully back around the kitten's neck.

When night arrived, and it was completely dark, Elmer carefully sneaked down the stairs with the kitten tucked under his arm and made his way through the yard to Mrs. Balthasar's back porch. Once there, he double-checked to assure no one was watching and gently placed the kitten's body on the decking by the back door. Then he skulked back to his apartment, confident that neither he nor Bo would ever be tied to the crime. As far as anyone could tell, the cat was simply sick from some unknown cause and had managed to make it onto the porch before succumbing.

Early the next morning, Elmer was awakened by the sound of an ear-piercing scream that was like the cry of a banshee. Seconds later, he heard a hard, thumping sound. He raced to his porch and looked over at Mrs. Balthasar's house to see her sprawled on the back porch, apparently unconscious. Neighbors were racing from their homes after hearing the woman's scream to see what was wrong. One woman was dialing her cell phone, obviously calling for help, while another was on her knees next to Mrs. Balthasar, taking her pulse. That woman was one who Elmer knew was a nurse who lived next door to the old woman. A second later, the nurse began administering CPR.

Elmer could hear ambulance sirens in the background getting louder by the second. After a time, the nurse stopped, looked up at the woman with the cell phone, and shook her head. Elmer could read her lips as she mouthed the words, "She's gone."

Elmer felt horrible. His stomach clenched with revulsion. He had absolutely no idea that finding her kitten dead would be so devastating to the woman. He also was unaware of the woman having any history of heart problems. He suspected she would be sad but never guessed she would drop dead. Had he known this, he certainly wouldn't have taken the coward's way out but would have owned up to what his dog had done and accepted the consequences. Now he realized he would have to live for the rest of his life with the knowledge that his actions had caused the old woman's death. He was sickened with grief. He turned and hurried back into his apartment bathroom, where he vomited uncontrollably into the toilet, while Bo watched from the living room.

The problem was, Elmer didn't know the truth. But, how could he? He had no way of knowing why the woman had been stricken so fatally at the sight of her dead kitten. This was because he was unaware the kitten had actually died two days earlier, and Mrs. Balthasar had tied the pink bow around the kitten's neck herself when she buried it in her flowerbed.

FULL MOON, DEAD MEN WALKING

The troubled young man peeked cautiously through the cracks between the boards he had used to block the hole left by the shattered window. It was the only way to keep them out; the undead, the zombies, the dead men walking. It didn't matter what anyone chose to call them; they were the new reality. Even with the boards nailed firmly in place, there was no guarantee they wouldn't find some way to break in, especially if they sensed him and came in great numbers.

Lonnie Talbert looked across the calendar on the wall above a candle, which was almost burned away to nothing and cast little illumination as a result. He didn't want to do anything to attract their attention. In the dancing shadow light, he saw the date and the round icon indicating the coming full moon. He turned to look at the battery-powered clock on the wall and saw moonrise was less than an hour away.

He always paid close attention to such things since Lonnie knew what would happen when the sun set and the full moon climbed high in the sky. He would change and become the hunter and creature he had been cursed to be, the creature which that woman Casandra had turned him into years earlier when she had bitten him. It mattered little that he had eventually killed the strange Goth chick; the curse remained. As a result, he'd become a werewolf as he had every month for the past several years. But this was the first time he would experience that change in a world overrun with zombies.

He remembered a time when he couldn't imagine anything worse than bearing the burden of the werewolf's curse. That was, until a month ago. He recalled again how he had awoken naked in an alley covered with gore and surrounded by the tattered remains of his latest victims. It was difficult to tell how many because of the severe degree of savage mutilation. He could recall nothing of the victims or the evening's attack, but now after more than two years of being what he had become, Lonnie tended to give such things little thought. He recalled a day when he would have felt guilty waking up to such carnage. Now it was just another night at the office.

That morning Lonnie had managed to slink through the maze of alleys and side streets, doing his best to wipe himself clean on discarded rags, all the while digging in dumpsters for half-finished water bottles to assist with the cleanup. He was sorry he hadn't ended up down by the docks as he had on several previous occasions because it always made the job much easier if he was near the river.

He dug through another dumpster, searching for a last remnant of clothing to make himself appear at least somewhat presentable. This was always the easy part since his typical crowd of peers was the throng of human refuse known as the homeless. He lived among them and dressed in the same sorts of rags they used for clothing. It was what he had to do to go unnoticed. He tended to ignore the other indigents, and for the most part, they left him alone as well. He did his best to be invisible, just another sad, pathetic soul wandering the alleys, struggling to survive another day.

That morning, Lonnie heard shouting from the end of the alley nearest to the cross street and saw one man attacking another. This wasn't unusual in New York City, especially in the sorts of downtrodden areas where he chose to live. But he immediately noticed something was very wrong with the situation unfolding not more than thirty feet away.

It appeared as if one of the men was actually biting into and tearing out the other's throat. For a werewolf, such a sight shouldn't seem all that disturbing, but the idea that one human being might be doing such a thing to another was beyond his understanding. Then a moment later, another strange looking human lurched up to join the first and began tearing open the victim's stomach and fishing out long coils of intestines which steamed in the cool morning air. The man bit down on the glistening sausage-like morsels and sucked heartily, withdrawing their contents. The links of innards seemed to flow like playthings through the creature's clumsy fingers, landing on the ground amid a gleaming pool of blood. All the while, the victim screamed helplessly until the screams turned to a death rattle.

Lonnie suddenly realized he had been correct in referring to the attackers as creatures because it was obvious, they were no longer human. At one time, he might have found the concept hard to comprehend, but being a werewolf, he was prone to accepting things that might previously have been construed as impossible. However, he decided he had seen enough and chose to leave through the opposite end of the alley doing all he could to avoid contact with anyone else.

He had to find a place to get away from whatever madness seemed to be gripping the people of the city. As he searched, he noticed more sirens were going off than was normal as police cars, ambulances, and rescue units flew past at breakneck speeds heading to destinations unknown. Running from street to street, he was shocked to see more of the same, people attacking and devouring other people. It was as if the entire city had gone insane.

The streets were clogged with vehicles slamming mindlessly into each other, and Lonnie saw dozens of fights breaking out all around him. He saw humans beating, shooting, stabbing, and killing each other in the streets. Then he saw the dead men rise and begin feasting on their attackers. There were hundreds of alarms ringing as crowds of looters shattered storefront glass. Lonnie was astonished at how quickly what he thought of as civilization breaking down all around him. He had no idea what was happening or why, but he knew that he would have to find shelter and do so quickly if he were to survive.

He located an abandoned apartment building and was surprised to find the door open on a first-floor one-room unit. It was perfect for his needs as it only had one window, and everything could be seen from this single living space. He checked out the attached bathroom and was pleased to see it only had a tiny ventilation window, much too small for anyone to climb through. Lonnie opened a few cabinets and was surprised to find not only some utensils but also more than two dozen unopened cans of soup and several unopened boxes of cereal and crackers.

In another cabinet, he found a case of bottled water and several two-liter bottles of cola. Obviously, someone else had been squatting in this place before his discovering it. He wondered if the squatter would return and if he might have to fight him for the space. Lonnie walked to the front door and secured the deadbolt. As it turned out, the former resident never returned. At least Lonnie didn't think he ever returned, although he might have been among the undead creatures who eventually tried repeatedly to gain access.

One night toward the middle of the month, Lonnie awoke to hear pounding on the window. He looked out and saw five or six of the zombies outside slapping spastically against the glass pane. Some of them were scratching the surface as if doing so would allow them to get inside. He looked around the apartment and found an old toolbox, which contained an assortment of tools, including a hammer and some eight penny nails. He smashed up an old wardrobe, which was practically falling apart anyway, and secured the boards to the window frame. It was a good thing too, because only moments after he had finished, the creatures managed to break the window and would have come in had it not been for the wooden barrier.

Lonnie found a steak knife in the utensil drawer of the kitchen, and using the cracks between the boards, he managed to kill a few of the zombies by shoving the blade through their eye sockets and into their brains. Each time he pulled the knife back through the wood, he could smell the rank, revolting stench of their decomposing flesh. He knew he eventually would have to leave the place since his food supply was running low, and his un-flushable toilet was running over.

He also understood the days were slipping by, and the next full moon was rapidly approaching.

Now he was once again looking out through the cracks between those same boards, knowing that shortly Lonnie Talbert would be gone and the wolf would return. He wondered once the "change" came over him, what the wolf-beast would think of the walking corpses and how it might react to its new environment.

Lonnie had already come to terms with the possibility his wolf manifestation might not survive in a world occupied by thousands of the rotting undead. There was nothing he could do about that any more than he could do anything about preventing the forthcoming transformation from occurring. What would be would be. In a few minutes, it would all be out of his control anyway.

Lonnie felt a familiar twinge start to occur deep in his stomach. He looked again through the cracks between the boards and saw the full moon had ascended in all its brilliant glory. He placed his palms against the boarded opening and, staring down at the floor, braced himself for what was to come. He called it "the change," but it was much more than that, even more than a shape-shifting as ancient Indian tribes referred to it. It was a transformation, a complete rearranging of bone and musculature. As a result, it always brought with it the type of agonizing pain one would expect such a dramatic conversion to bring.

Once again, as he had experienced every month for several years, Lonnie Talbert was suffering from that agony as his bones cracked, his muscles twisted, and his flesh stretched into its new wolf form. The transformation wasn't just physical, either. When he became the beast, he remembered nothing of being Lonnie Talbert. He became instead a savage, flesh-craving creature bent on bringing death and feeding his insatiable hunger. Lonnie suddenly thought it ironic how he was not much different from the undead creatures roaming the city streets in that respect. When he eventually reverted to his human form, Lonnie likewise recalled nothing of the time when he was the beast.

Then again, he didn't believe this was entirely true. During the time between full moons, he often had reoccurring nightmares of people being torn limb from limb, their entrails eviscerated, and their flesh consumed raw. He was never sure if these were nothing more than nocturnal imaginings or if they were actual flashbacks to events that had occurred in his alternate wolf reality.

As the agonizing transformation reached its completion, the wolf persona awoke and was shocked to find itself trapped inside a room. The space smelled of the stink of humanity. It reeked of human scat as if the creature living here had not left the place in weeks. The scent was strongest near a closed door at the far side of the room. There appeared to be the only window in the room, which was boarded over for some reason. The wolf looked frantically around the space for any signs of the filthy man. If it found the human, it would feast upon the pathetic creature's flesh. But the wolf found no one.

Frustrated and hungry, the beast became enraged and threw the space's meager furnishings about the room. One of the chairs struck the boarded window, and it moved slightly. The beast smelled the air coming in from the outside. It wasn't the familiar scent of the city the creature had expected but was an odd, rank stench. The beast could smell the acrid odor of smoke and the stink of rotting meat. The sensation caused the creature's hackles to rise as it sensed the unseen presence of some as of yet unidentified danger lurking outside.

Instinctively the wolf knew it needed to feed, and it would also have to be aware of whatever form that potential danger it sensed might take. It could tell by the foul scent this unknown threat had something to do with the incredible rotting pong, which was assaulting its senses.

In a fit of savage rage, the wolf tore into the wooden slats, shredding the lumber into splinters, raining a storm of shards and slivers down upon the floor below. In a matter of seconds, the opening was large enough for the beast to jump through. It landed hunched, alert, and always ready to either attack or to defend.

It suddenly heard a growl, not unlike its own coming from its right. The beast turned and saw a human shambling toward it. How strange that the stupid human hadn't run in terror; they always ran for their lives at the sight of the beast, but for some reason, this human didn't.

This one kept coming as if it intended to attack. Something else wasn't right about this human. Its scent was all wrong, not the scent of fresh, delicious blood coursing through healthy veins, but a smack of stagnant blood pooling in pockets throughout the creature's body. And the disgusting odor of putrefaction was overpowering. The beast couldn't comprehend how this human-like creature could appear alive, walking and moving about when every sense the wolf possessed told him the thing was dead. It intuitively understood that whatever this creature was, it wasn't food. The lumbering human thing kept coming toward the wolf as if it had no comprehension of the danger awaiting it.

When the stinking human was within its reach, the wolf swiped at the creature's head with its massive claws and, in a single slash, separated the thing's head from its body. A second later, the human collapsed in a headless heap on the ground. The wolf knew it had stumbled onto something important. If it came upon any more of these creatures, and it suspected it would, separating the head from the body would kill them quickly. This was good to know because the beast was sickened by the thought of having to bite down on any of the decomposing flesh. It, of course, would do so if required, but it wasn't a creature who feasted on rotting carrion; it craved warm blood-filled living flesh. But where would it find what it so urgently needed? All around it was the stench of death and decay. It was as if all of the living creatures had vanished.

The wolf heard a sound, a small female voice calling from the alley ahead. "Please. Please don't hurt us."

Then another voice, a rough masculine voice, replied, "Oh, don't worry, you sweet little thing. I'm not gonna hurt you. In fact, I'm gonna make you feel real good."

The wolf entered the alley stealthily and saw a young girl pressed tightly against a brick building with her arms encircling a little boy, who she was holding tightly in front of her. They were dirty and unwashed, as was evident by their foul scent. They were coated in grime, dressed in rags, emaciated, and obviously starving. The beast felt there was scarcely enough meat on both of them to satisfy its hunger.

However, the man standing in front of them, blocking any chance of escape, was a different story. Although he too was dressed in rags and covered in filth, he was a well-fed bulky muscular man who was currently brandishing a large knife at the two youngsters. The wolf was repulsed by the caked-on stench of unwashed human filth, which surrounded the three of them, but at least it was not as repugnant as the stink of decay. The beast could also smell the two children's fear and the angry sweat of aggression emanating from the large man. More importantly, the wolf could sense the warm blood coursing through their veins. It cared nothing for the scene playing out in the alley. All it wanted was to feed and feed it would.

The wolf fell upon the large man, sinking its teeth deep into the attacker's throat while simultaneously burying its claws into the man's abdomen and tearing out his guts. It could hear the children's' screams as the big man's entrails spilled to the ground with a sickening plop. As the beast tore out the man's throat, it sensed the pair fleeing the alley. It didn't care, as they were too small, too thin. They were also sickly and frail, while the wolf was fast and strong. It would catch them easily once it was finished with this delicious human.

After a time, the wolf dropped the remains to the ground and turned to pursue the fleeing children. It suddenly heard a low moaning and guttural growling coming from behind. The beast turned to see the once dead remains of its victim had somehow returned to life. It couldn't understand how this could occur since there was so little left of the corpse except for a torso with only a head and half of one arm remaining. The body was separated from the waist down, and its head was barely attached to its neck. As a result, the head hung askew at an impossible angle. However, that didn't keep the thing's mouth from rapidly opening and closing as if desperate to feed as it twitched and jerked on the ground.

The wolf's animal mind seemed to comprehend that somehow the dead were not remaining dead. They were somehow walking as they decomposed and had some need to feed constantly. The wolf recalled that strange decayed human it had decapitated earlier, remembering that separating the head from the body seemed to kill the creatures. The beast raised its muscular leg and brought its massive foot down on the dead thing's skull, crushing it to a bloody pulp. The creature stopped moving.

The wolf turned again to go after the little humans but noticed their scent was faint, almost completely gone. A moment later, at the end of the alley, there was a crowd of shadowed creatures. The beast knew by the reek of decomposition that these were more of the dead humans, the stinking walking meat sacks.

Instinctively, it understood what the creatures wanted; they wanted to feed, and the wolf was to be their meal. This caused an animal rage to build inside the beast. Flexing its massive muscles, extending its razor-sharp claws, the wolf opened its fanged mouth and released a mighty roar that rattled the broken windows of the abandoned buildings. But the undead creatures didn't back off and continued to slowly lurch toward the beast. The wolf ran like a mindless savage down the alley toward the mass of stinking walking corpses and dove directly into the crowd, arms flailing and jaws snapping.

///

Lonnie awoke as if from a dream, or perhaps a nightmare would be more accurate. He was lying on his back, staring up at the sky. He felt something cold, wet, soft, and sticky below him as if he were lying on a thick mattress soaked with rainwater. There was an ungodly familiar smell surrounding him as he struggled to sit up, finding it difficult to do. He looked at his naked arms and saw he was covered with blood and fragments of flesh. Although this was common, after returning from his wolf manifestation, something was different. The blood was black, and the flesh was grey and rotten.

He quickly struggled to stand up and saw he had been lying on a pile of dismembered zombies. Limbs, heads, torsos, and innards were scattered all about the alley and piled on top of each other. Looking down, Lonnie saw his entire body was covered with the foul remains of the undead, obviously from the wolf's latest carnage.

Then he heard a growling noise coming from directly behind him. He turned and saw dozens of the wretched undead creatures walking aimlessly along the street, seeming to pay no attention to him whatsoever. He looked down again at the decomposition, which coated his body and realized the creatures couldn't tell he wasn't one of them.

Lonnie walked from the alley into the main street, strolling among the dead men walking, eager to rid himself of the foul stink which coated him but knowing that would be impossible until he found a safe place to hide out until once again the next full moon brought back the wolf.

SHADY REST

"Climate change is happening, humans are causing it, and I think
this is perhaps the most serious environmental issue facing us."
—BILL NYE

"I find it very sad that by the time corporate science realizes
the value of nature, that it may be too late"
—STEVEN MAGEE, SOLAR RADIATION, GLOBAL WARMING,
AND HUMAN DISEASE

"Do you remember back in the early part of the century everyone was
going crazy about 'global warming,' 'climate change' and all that other
tree-hugging crap, Frank?" Jonathan said, making air quotes with his
arthritic fingers as he enunciated global warming and climate change.

"Yeah, yeah, John, I remember for sure," Franklin replied. He was
Jonathan's best friend and had been since childhood back during the
nineteen sixties. Now it was 2040, and they had both lived past the
eighty-year-old milestone.

Jonathan said, "What a bunch of nonsense that was. Here we are
some thirty years later, and everything is exactly the same as it was back
then. It was a lot of worry over nothing."

The two were sitting in wheelchairs in their private room of the Shady Rest Senior facility looking out the massive window at what was one of the most beautiful spring mornings either of them could recall. Both of their spouses had passed away years earlier, and the friends had checked into Shady Rest at the same time. Because of their status in the world and their financial resources, their request to be roommates had, of course, been promptly granted.

Franklin said, "Remember how they had dozens of different scenarios consisting of various end-of-the-world disasters? Polar ice caps melting, oceans rising, skin cancer running rampant, world-wide famine, plagues, disease, mutation of the human genome; you name it, and one of those wacko groups would come up with it."

"You're telling me." Jonathan agreed, "And people like you and me took so much of the heat it was ridiculous; just because we happened to be rich and successful industrialists. What the Hell did we ever do wrong except maybe to put tens of thousands of people to work, help them earn a good income, and boost the economy?"

"And not just the US economy either, my friend. We had factories all over the world. We brought prosperity to those foreign Godless heathens the likes of which they'd never seen before. And if we happened to make ourselves rich in the process, well, that was just icing on the cake as they say."

"Lucky for us too, Frank, or instead of living in this fancy-schmancy retirement home, we might be struggling like so many others who were less fortunate."

Franklin thought for a moment, "We certainly did pay our share of taxes and contributed to charities as well. Remember, John?"

"Yeah, how could I forget? Now here we are sitting in the lap of luxury and enjoying this lovely spring day. I can't think of a better way to spend our twilight years. It doesn't get much better than this."

The two released simultaneous sighs of contentment as they stared out the window at the lush, green lawn, the many blooming trees, and the gorgeous late morning sky. Every so often, a bluebird or robin would fly by and twitter. Far out among a grove of trees was a bird feeder, which the staff at Shady Rest always kept overflowing with seed. Besides the occasional finch or wren, a chubby squirrel or chipmunk would scurry up the pole and help himself to a mouthful of seed.

Jonathan suddenly said, "Watch this. In a minute or two, that fat squirrel is going to jump down off the feeder, tumble one time, then get up and scamper away through the grass."

"What do you mean?" Franklin asked.

"Just watch."

Sure enough, about a minute later, the fat squirrel jumped down to the ground, tumbled once, then regained its balance and ran away.

"How the Hell did you know that?" Franklin asked.

"It was easy." Jonathan said, "He does the same thing every single day right around this same time. I suppose squirrels are as much creatures of habit as we are." Not taking his eye off the squirrel, he asked, "So what time is it now? About two minutes to ten?"

Franklin looked over at the clock on the wall and saw it was exactly two minutes to ten. He gave his friend a strange look and asked again, "How the Hell are you doing this, John? It's getting a bit creepy. Is it some sort of trick?"

"No trick Frank. I'm just being observant. Here's another one for you. In exactly two minutes, Nurse Maggie will be arriving with our morning pills."

"Nurse Maggie." Franklin said dreamily, "What I wouldn't do for five minutes alone with the lovely Nurse Maggie."

Margaret Esselman was a short, stocky nurse in her late-fifties who, although one of the oldest nurses on staff, the two octogenarians still considered her to be a "hot number."

Jonathan asked, "And what in the Hell would you do with good Nurse Maggie if you had such an opportunity, not that you ever would."

"I'd give her a taste something special that would have her following me around all day like a lost puppy; that's what I'd do."

"And how, pray tell would you manage such a chore with that shriveled old useless thing you have between your legs. It'd be like trying to push a rope up an alley." Jonathan said, laughing hysterically. It didn't matter that the pair had this similar discussion at least twice a day; it always seemed fresh to them at medicine time and usually brought about raucous laughter.

"Well, you know John; they've got meds nowadays for such afflictions. One magic blue pill, and I'd be like a twenty-year-old all over again."

"And what about your high blood pressure, or your bad ticker, not to mention your enlarged prostate?"

"They probably have some kind of pill for that. And if they do, God knows we can afford to buy whatever they have out there."

"Maybe you should just take it easy for a bit and take that dirty old man mind of yours off Nurse Maggie for a while."

As if on command, the pair heard the familiar sound of shoes on the vinyl floor as the nurse was arriving to give them their daily medicines. Just as Franklin was about to give a hardy "Good Morning Maggie," they heard an unfamiliar young voice call, "Mr. Bleaker, Mr. Stone, it's time for your meds."

This was most unusual and equally unappreciated. For as long as the pair had been staying at Shady Rest, they had never had any nurse care for them but Maggie. Jonathan decided he'd have to get to the bottom of this outrage immediately.

Before he even looked at the nurse, he harrumphed, "Now see here. Where's Nurse Maggie? She always comes to give us our medicines." But before he could finish his thoughts, he stared in awe at one of the most gorgeous creatures he had ever seen in his life. He had no idea who this nurse was, but she had to be only about twenty-five, and she was built like the proverbial brick outhouse, with long flowing blonde hair, a cute button nose, and more curves than any road he had ever ridden on.

His friend Franklin hadn't missed the beauty of this new arrival, either. He was staring at the young woman dumbfounded, apparently unable to speak. Johnathan believed, if Franklin had had fantasies about Nurse Maggie, they had all evaporated by now. This sweetheart was the real deal.

"So, which of you handsome gentlemen is Mr. Bleaker, and which one is Mr. Stone?" She said, and for the first time, Jonathan got a look at her strange hypnotic eyes, one of which was bright green while the other was piercing blue. He had heard of this sort of genetic anomaly in the past. He had never seen it up close before, and instead of his being disturbed by the feature, he found it to be surprisingly tantalizing.

"I'm Jonathan Bleaker." He said, "But please, call me Jonathan or John, or even Johnny if you prefer."

"I'd be happy to, Johnny." She said, and he noticed a slight southern accent to her voice, which only made her even more alluring. "So then this here good-looking big guy must be Mr. Stone."

"B . . . b . . . b . . ." Franklin said, apparently unable to form even a single coherent word.

"Yes," Jonathan said on his behalf. "That's Franklin Stone."

The young nurse bent down toward Franklin, giving him an eye-full of her more than ample cleavage. "Is Franklin okay, Johnny, or did the poor man have a stroke?"

"No, he's okay." Jonathan said, "He just sometimes gets a bit tongue-tied around, well, around beautiful women."

"Why, aren't you just the most adorable charmer?" She said, standing upright then turning and wiggling over to her medicine cart, speaking as she went. "Your regular nurse, Maggie, called in sick today. There's apparently some new virus or flu going around. Since Shady Rest is a bit understaffed, they requested I stop by and take over Maggie's duties for the day. I hope that's okay with you, boys. I can tell you're very fond of Nurse Maggie. My name is Joslyn, but y'all can call me Josie if you like." She made a show of bending over to look into her medicine cart, allowing her already short skirt to ride enticingly high. Jonathan heard an involuntary gasp escape Franklin's throat.

"Some stud-muffin he is." Jonathan thought to himself.

"Well, here you go, boys," Joslyn said, handing both men their pills and a glass of water.

As she did, Jonathan noticed something strange about her hands. Both of them had what looked like a partial finger, a sixth finger jutting off the side slightly behind the pinky finger. At first, the sight gave him a bit of a start, but then he caught himself and looked away before the lovely young woman noticed his surprise. If he was anything, it was a gentleman, especially when it came to the female gender. As such, the last thing he wanted to do was to cause her any embarrassment. He lifted the pills to his mouth, closed his eyes, and took a gulp of water to wash them down. He noticed Franklin had taken his pills as well.

He was in no hurry to see this sweet young girl leave, so he searched his mind for something to ask to keep her talking, even though it appeared as if she wasn't in any real hurry to go either.

"Do you work at one of the other Shady Rest facilities?" He asked, "Both Franklin and were always major contributors to the Shady Rest organization, and for a time, we both served on the board of directors."

"You did?" She said, surprised, but not answering his question, "Why that's so very special! You both must be very important men."

"Well." Jonathan said, feigning humility, "We were both fortunate to have owned successful businesses during our early lives, which netted us both substantial incomes. Isn't that right, Frank?"

Franklin was sitting silently, apparently still gawking at the beautiful nurse. Then Jonathan noticed there was also something else about Franklin that seemed a bit off. There was a thin string of drool starting to trickle down from the corner of his mouth. Jonathan wondered what was wrong with his friend. He decided to ask Nurse Josie if she could check Franklin to make sure he was okay.

But when he tried to speak, he realized he was no longer able to do so. It was as if his mouth and throat were frozen, and he couldn't force out a single syllable. Then he noticed that he couldn't move his head or any part of his body for that matter. What was wrong with him? He felt fine, yet he couldn't move.

"Well, now," Nurse Josie said with a knowing air, "I believe the pill I gave both of you has done its job just splendidly. Wouldn't you agree?"

Jonathan suddenly realized he was in trouble. This stranger, this woman, had drugged both he and Franklin with some paralytic substance, and he didn't even want to imagine what her motivation might be. He was certain he'd never met her before. But it was possible that maybe he had wronged her father or grandfather in some business deal sometime in the past, and perhaps she was here for revenge. He had driven many companies out of business during his career, and as such, was no stranger to having enemies. He didn't feel this was the case with this woman, but he couldn't develop any other ideas for why she would do such a thing. Then the woman lifted a sheet of printer paper from her cart and began to read from it.

"Jonathan Marvin Bleaker and Franklin William Stone, two of the country's greatest and most successful industrialists. Net worth in the neighborhood of several billion dollars." Then she interjected, "Sadly, I don't get to hang out in that neighborhood very often, boys. It says here over the years, you both were repeatedly sued by environmental organizations trying to force you to stop your polluting and contributing to greenhouse emissions. However, because of your wealth, you were able to afford an unbeatable team of lawyers who never lost a single judgment. This report says you both are considered criminals against the world and have been responsible for much of the climate change we've been experiencing for years."

Jonathan and Franklin looked on silently. They had no choice since they were unable to move.

"By the way, I made sure you were unable to speak." Joslyn said, "I've read the trial transcripts and watched all of your press conferences and have heard your rhetoric about how global warming and climate change was nothing more than a lot of liberal fantasizing. Well, gentlemen, I'm here to tell you that you were both very wrong."

Jonathan had no idea what this raving psychopath was talking about. There was nothing wrong with the world. There was no climate change. All she had to do was look out the window, and she could see how lush and beautiful the landscape was here at Shady Rest. Of course, the grounds here got special treatment by a staff of gardeners, but the rest of the world was just as fine. What was wrong with her, anyway? Then as if reading his mind, she turned and walked toward the large bank of windows looking out over the lawn.

"And you know what really makes us sick?" She said, and Jonathan suddenly noted her use of the word "us." She was obviously part of some sort of radical tree-hugging organization. "What makes us sick is how the people here at Shady Rest have kept the truth from both of you for so many years. They're just as greedy as the both of you are. They needed your steady influx of funds to keep the place going, so they created this special room just for you two. Think about this for a minute Johnny. When was the last time either of you has actually been outside?"

Jonathan realized he couldn't recall when he had last actually gone outside. He was no longer steady on his feet, and to go outside, he'd have had to have someone wheel him around in his wheelchair. Besides, neither he nor Franklin had ever really wanted or needed to go outside. Why should they? They had a beautiful view from this room and a great cool breeze of fresh air blowing in from the side windows. They could watch nature at work, hear the birds chirping and watch the squirrels playing. It was just like being outside, but without the mosquitoes and other annoying insects. Then he thought for a moment about the fat squirrel he saw jumping and rolling at the same time every day and got a sudden disquieting feeling in the pit of his stomach.

Nurse Josie, if she really was a nurse, walked over to the screen in one of the side windows, grabbed it with both hands, and pulled it out, throwing it to the floor. In the place where the screen had been, Jonathan saw a large industrial fan encased in a steel frame, spinning steadily.

"There's your fresh air Johnny. It's completely manufactured in the room behind this one and treated to make you believe it's actually fresh air coming in from outside. Now, what about this amazing view of the Shady Rest gardens, Johnny?"

Jonathan noticed that her alluring southern accent had suddenly disappeared completely. She walked over to a panel set in the wall, typed a code into a keypad, which popped the panel open. Then she pressed a series of switches inside the panel. Suddenly the glass wall looking out onto the manicured lawn vanished, replaced by a series of blank video displays, each one framed to look like a window panel.

"Before I came in to see you both, I was eavesdropping and over-heard you telling Frank about how you thought you saw the same squirrel do the same thing every day at the same time. Well, you were absolutely correct, Johnny boy. You see, this too has all been an illusion, a video holographic projection of what the good folks here at Shady Rest thought you both wanted to see. None of it was real. And just so you know, the world no longer looks anything like what you've been seeing in here."

"I also saw you noticing my two different colored eyes as well as my extra fingers Johnny. You probably thought you were being discrete, but I'm used to such looks like most of us born over two decades ago are. We all have one sort of genetic mutation or another, so much so that we no longer consider it rude to stare, just inquisitive."

She began to undo the buttons on her blouse, and Jonathan's heart skipped a beat. She turned and grabbed an antiseptic wipe from a box on the medicine cart and began wiping what appeared to be tan makeup from her partially exposed chest. The flesh underneath was mottled and riddled with boils and other such sores.

"In case you're wondering, Johnny boy, these are all cancerous lesions caused by the lack of ozone, which permits harmful UV radiation to flood the earth, scorching it and killing virtually everything that lives. The average life expectancy for anyone in my generation is about thirty years if we're lucky. Also, that number is declining every year. I'm twenty-six and terminal. I'll likely be dead before the end of this year. Thanks to you gentlemen and others like you."

"You see, we have a list. It contains the names and history of all of you people still living who we consider directly responsible for destroying our blessed planet. And our goal is to see that as many of you pay for your crimes against nature before we die."

"Now's the time when I'm supposed to read this to you." She studied the document in her hands then said, "Jonathan Marvin Bleaker and Franklin William Stone. Having been found guilty of crimes against nature and humanity, we, the people of the United Environmental Salvation Core, have sentenced you to death by exposure to the world you are responsible for destroying. May Satan welcome your accursed souls."

Jonathan and Franklin watched helplessly as the young nurse reached into her shoulder bag and withdrew what appeared to be a gas mask of some sort. She placed the mask over her face then nodded to some individuals who walked around behind the two old men. They, too, wore similar protective masks. Soon their wheelchairs began to move backward out of the room before turning and being pushed down a long corridor.

Although his paralysis made his vision limited, Jonathan could see the bodies of several of the nursing home staff lying dead in the hallway; each of them apparently shot to death. He hadn't heard any gunfire, so he had to assume the killers had used silenced weapons. These same killers were now pushing him and Franklin down the hall. But why hadn't they just shot them? Where were they taking them?

Then he recalled what Josie had said, that he and Franklin would be killed by exposure to the world they had destroyed. Then she had put on that gas mask. Jonathan saw the glass front doors up ahead with the outside world waiting beyond. What he saw through the filthy glass made his heart sink with foreboding. There was no sunshine, no blue sky, no green grass, and no little animals scurrying about.

What he saw was a dark grey, bleak and dismal world of smoke and smog. What little lawn remained was nothing more than brown, wilted grass. Lying dead on the former grass was Nurse Maggie and several more of the Shady Rest staff. They had apparently not been shot; they had been marched outside without the benefit of protective gear.

The front of his wheelchair pushed against the glass doors, and in a matter of seconds, he and Franklin were outside. He heard the voice of Josie, muffled by the gas mask in his left ear.

"This won't take long, Johnny. You'll probably try your best not to breathe, but eventually, you'll have to. And a few seconds after that, it'll be all over."

Jonathan held his breath but heard a gasp from his right and realized Franklin had just inhaled some of the toxic atmosphere. A few seconds later, he saw his friend collapse from his wheelchair and sprawl dead at his feet. Jonathan's lungs burned for oxygen as he held his breath for as long as possible. He could smell something foul, trying to work its way up into his nostrils. Finally, when he couldn't hold his breath any longer, he had no choice but to inhale. He felt it first in his mouth, then his throat and finally his lungs. It was a white-hot burning as he sensed the very lining of his lungs eaten away. As Josie promised, within a few seconds, it was all over.

THE CABINET

David heard the van pull up out in front of his house, knowing his wife Lindsey had returned from the estate sale she'd been attending. For the past several months, she had been searching, hoping to find a cabinet of the specific size and style that she had in mind. Although frustrated by her numerous failed attempts to fulfill her quest, she had decided to try the sale occurring that morning to see if her luck would change.

Lindsey had called David moments earlier, excitedly explaining that she had found the perfect cabinet and that she'd be arriving home in a few minutes. He had let her use his van for the trip since it was capable of hauling larger items.

Earlier that morning, she had asked, "David? Why don't you come along with me to the sale today?"

"Ah Babe, you know I hate those sorts of things."

"Yeah, I know you do, but what if I get lucky and find a cabinet today?"

David said, "No problem. If you do, then I'm sure someone there will load it into the van for you. I'll unload it when you get home."

After receiving the call, David slipped on his shoes and went outside through the garage, opening the double bay door to bring the cabinet inside. Neither of them ever parked their cars in their garage. Actually, they couldn't if they wanted to as there was no room. The garage was full of David's many partially-completed projects. Someday he knew he would have to finish them, but today was apparently not going to be that day.

After wrestling the large cabinet into the garage, David stepped back to take a good look at it. It was in surprisingly decent condition and was perhaps three feet wide by seven feet tall and about a foot and a half deep. He didn't know what Lindsey paid for it, but knowing his wife, she got a bargain. There was one thing he couldn't help but notice and something which he hadn't expected to find. That was the cabinet's hideous, weathered coat of flat-black paint. He found that feature as surprising as it was perplexing.

Lindsey told him that, during the sale, the auctioneer informed her the cabinet had been a favorite of the property owner, a stodgy old woman of wealth who'd only recently passed away. David could tell by the cabinet's feel and weight that it was a very well-built piece of furniture. He also understood that sometimes the rich could be a bit eccentric, but he wondered what sort of woman would paint such a lovely piece of furniture such a horrible color. Then he was caught completely by surprise when for some unknown reason, as he stood staring at the cabinet, an icy chill suddenly raced down the center of his back. He felt gooseflesh rise on his arms. Then he gave an involuntary shiver.

David couldn't wait to get this thing painted. In its current state, it gave him the creeps. He was quite certain it would likely take two coats of primer and three coats of paint to adequately cover the ebony cabinet. But then he learned that Lindsey had a different plan in mind. On the way home, she purchased a quart of paint, which she said was mauve, but David thought it looked pink. She said she wanted him to give the cabinet just one thin coat of paint, allowing some of the black undercoat to show through in places, feeling it would give the cabinet a more "rustic" look.

"Whatever she wants." David thought to himself. He figured applying a single coat of paint was a lot less work and took a lot less time than trying to apply five, and that was just fine with him. Even if he didn't completely cover the strange black finish, he could at least drastically change its appearance. He decided not to wait any longer and immediately set to work painting the old cabinet.

The task went quickly, and when he was finished, the cabinet looked surprisingly good. He never would've believed it possible that such a hideously colored piece of furniture could turn out so well. He decided it would be best to let the paint dry until the next day when he'd come out and check on it.

David slept restlessly that night, having a variety of disturbing nightmares, none of which he could recall the next morning. But he knew he had slept fitfully because instead of awakening refreshed, he felt every bit as exhausted as when he went to bed the previous night. He decided to go out and examine his project.

He was pleased with how the flat mauve outer coating allowed just traces of the original black paint to show through, and the effect was both interesting and pleasing to the eye. He could see many different shades of black and various shapes and patterns lying just beneath the new outer mauve covering.

David opened the cabinet to check out the inside of the doors and was pleased to see they likewise had turned out just as good as the outside. Then he noticed an odd pattern on the flat panel on the inside of the door. He stood back and stared as the shape seemed to form into something David could scarcely believe. The shape appeared to be the image of an old woman with her eyes closed right there lurking just under the new outer layer of paint.

He couldn't believe he hadn't noticed it the previous day while painting the inside of the door. Maybe it had always been there, but it had taken the new coat of paint to bring the image out completely.

David thought this discovery was incredible, and he couldn't wait to show it to Lindsey. But then, just as he was about to call out her name, the eyes opened.

BEAL

"Why do we have to go to this ridiculous dinner, Blake? You know I can't stand that man?"

"Yeah, I know, Sheryl. But if it's any consolation, you're in good company. No one can stand him."

"So what the hell are we doing going to a dinner with someone nobody likes?"

"Do you love our house?" Blake asked. "And do you love this Mercedes we're driving?"

"Of course, I do. You know that."

"Well, Seymour Mason, and more importantly Mason's Meats, our biggest client, is the reason we're driving in this car and living in our fine house rather than living in that one-bedroom apartment and driving that domestic subcompact."

"Hey. I liked that little car." Sheryl argued.

"Maybe so, but you love this car."

Sheryl hesitated for a second then conceded, "Yeah. I suppose you've got me there. But you'd think with all of his money and prestige, Seymour would be less of a crude and obnoxious a-hole than he is."

"You know the old saying, 'You can't polish a turd.' Money doesn't always equate to class, I'm afraid, my dear. Seymour Mason is a self-made millionaire who built his business from the ground up.

Unfortunately, during those long years of hard work, he never found the time to properly educate himself or acquire an appreciation for culture."

"That's certainly true." Sheryl said, "He's about as crass and uncouth as they come."

"Look, Sheryl. If it helps any, I'm fairly certain Seymour won't be entertaining us with any of his typical dinner conversation."

"Oh, God! I certainly hope not. I can't think of any worse dinner conversation while trying to eat a fine steak dinner than hearing all the details of his slaughterhouse operation. Last time it took everything I had not to puke all over his dinner table."

"Yeah, I know. And the fact that you were in the early stages of pregnancy didn't help matters either."

"That's for sure. But you know? Even though I'm almost due and way past the morning sickness days, I still don't think I could handle his disgusting descriptions of how his cattle are slaughtered. How much common sense does it take to know that's not acceptable dinner conversation, for God's sake?"

"I agree. So I spoke with Seymour about it the other day. After that last dinner disaster six months ago, I delicately requested that when we all got together this time, he might want to keep his dinner topics away from the slaughterhouse."

"And what did he say to that?"

"Surprisingly, he agreed. He actually apologized. I think Seymour knows he's an odd duck and socially awkward. I think he really wants to fit in with normal people, but he doesn't quite know how. He's obviously a genius of sorts to have built such an empire from nothing, but it might be that same genius that makes him so unacceptable in social situations."

"So, I shouldn't expect any details about how his cows are slaughtered, butchered, and prepared for sale?"

"Nope. Not if he's true to his word, which I believe he is. He knows you're just days from having our baby, and I think he's really eager to make up for the last time."

"Well, I certainly hope so."

The couple entered the two massive black iron gates at the front of the Mason estate and headed up the long, well-lit asphalt driveway, which wound through beautifully manicured landscaping. In front of the mansion was a large, brightly illuminated portico where Blake pulled his Mercedes. A moment later, a man dressed in a porter style uniform walked up and requested Blake's keys.

"Valet parking?" Sheryl asked, "Pretty impressive."

"Only the best for Seymour Mason, my dear. Only the best."

A moment later, they were entering the mansion's front hall, where another servant met them and escorted them both to the dining room. The room was enormous and brightly illuminated with various lights and the massive crystal chandelier, which Sheryl had all but forgotten about. The place was the epitome of elegance with a large rectangular table lavishly adorned with obviously expensive place settings. The place reeked of money. The servant directed them both to their seats and poured them each a glass of wine while they awaited their host's arrival.

"Are we early?" Sheryl asked, feeling awkward.

"No. In fact, we're actually a few minutes late."

"But, where is everyone?"

Blake looked around for a moment noticing there were only three place settings at the table. "Look at the table." He told Sheryl, "There are only three settings. Maybe it's just Seymour and us. I just realized he hadn't specified that others would be coming. I just suppose I assumed."

"Wonderful!" Sheryl said in a sarcastic whisper out of the side of her mouth, "Just the three of us? You are going to owe me big time for this one, Blake."

Blake gulped, knowing he was suddenly in big trouble with the little woman. He wondered what he might have to buy her to get back in her good graces.

"Blake. Sheryl. I'm so glad you could make it." A loud voice boomed from the hall. The couple turned to see their host Seymour Mason standing in the doorway. He was staring at Sheryl with a very strange look, which made her skin crawl for some unknown reason.

"I've been looking forward to this dinner for such a long time. And don't worry Sheryl; no talk about the business tonight, I promise."

Sheryl felt her face redden slightly as she became embarrassed at the man knowing about how he had upset her. Perhaps it was the idea of actually having to deal with the issue face to face, or maybe it was that odd way Seymour seemed to be looking at her. She truly did feel flustered nonetheless, which was unusual for her.

"Um, look Seymour. I'm sorry about that whole thing; you know it was the early part of my pregnancy. I wasn't feeling quite myself."

"No need to apologize, my dear. I understand completely. I realize that I often tend to be a bit, shall we say unrefined, a diamond in the rough, so to speak. It's I who owe you an apology. So now that all of the formalities are out of the way, let's all sit down and enjoy an evening of friendship, good food, and pleasant conversation."

Sheryl couldn't get over the change in Seymour. He might not be perfect, but he had obviously been paying attention, and in her opinion, he had come a long way from the crude man he had been several months earlier. Perhaps Blake was right. Maybe Seymour just needed someone to point out his flaws in order for him to rectify them. Whatever the reason, it was a welcome change.

The couple and their host chatted for a few minutes while enjoying some of Seymour's vintage wine. Sheryl drank water because of her pregnancy, while Blake seemed to be guzzling his wine. She usually didn't keep track of such things, but Blake was already on his second glass if she wasn't mistaken. She'd have to tell him about that later when they got home.

After a few minutes, the man who had answered the door brought in plates of food. Sheryl supposed he must be Seymour's butler. Each platter was lavishly garnished with a variety of vegetables surrounding what looked like a perfectly cooked, luscious petite veal steak smothered in a dark au jus sauce.

"Please taste it and tell me what you think," Seymour said proudly.

Sheryl cut a thin slice noting how easily her knife slid through the meat as if it was slicing butter. She glided the morsel into her mouth and was astonished by how tender, juicy, and flavorful the meat was. It had such an exotic and so deliciously distinctive flavor. At first, she tasted pork, and then she thought she tasted a hint of chicken, then finally beef. Perhaps it was the result of the dressing or perhaps the various spices used in its preparation. Whatever the reason, this was the most incredible flavor she had ever experienced.

She let go with an involuntary moan and said breathily, "Excuse me, Seymour. I'm so sorry, but oh my God, this is the best veal I have ever tasted. Blake, try your veal; it's beyond incredible."

Blake seemed to be not paying attention staring off into space, his wine glass empty once again. Had that only been his second, or perhaps it had been his third?

"Blake?" Sheryl tried once again, "I asked you to try your veal. What's wrong? Can't you hear me? Oh my God, are you drunk, Blake? You had better not be drunk. Now stop fooling around and try your veal."

"It's not veal, Sheryl," Seymour said from across the table. "It's my own special product, which I call 'Beal.' It's very rare and costly to produce. Beal is my personal brand name for baby veal."

Sheryl looked a bit confused. "Baby veal? Isn't that a bit redundant? I always thought veal came from calves, which are baby cows. So why bother to call it Beal?" She recalled seeing pictures online of veal farms where hundreds of calves were kept in tiny huts, denied exercise, and fed special feed to make them fat and tender. Although she had to admit the practice disgusted her, she, like most people, chose to put it out of her mind. What else could she do? She loved meat but didn't need to know the gruesome details about its preparation.

Suddenly she heard a thudding sound and turned to see Blake passed out, headfirst into his veal or Beal or whatever Seymour chose to call it. Blake's eyes were still open, staring down at the meat as his cheeks rested in a mound of mash potatoes and gravy.

"Blake? Blake? Dammit, Blake!" Sheryl shouted angrily as she tried to shake him awake. A thin stream of drool ran from the corner of his mouth down over a pile of caramelized carrots.

She turned to their host and said apologetically, "Seymour. I'm so terribly sorry about this. Blake never usually drinks very much, and I don't think I've ever seen him so drunk on a few glasses of wine. I don't know what's wrong with him this evening."

"Oh, not to worry, my dear. You see, Blake's not drunk. He's dead."

Suddenly Sheryl's world seemed to spin out of control around her. "Dead? Dead? No Seymour. You're mistaken. He's just a bit tipsy."

"No. He's dead all right. I should know because I was the one who poisoned him." Seymour admitted.

"What are you saying? You, you poisoned him? But, but why Seymour? Why would you ever do such a thing?" She cried, her voice breaking.

Seymour smiled and said, "For two reasons, my dear. First of all, I did it for my personal amusement. After all, your husband had the nerve to try to lecture me on the proper dinner conversation. I played along with him, pretending to be genuinely concerned about how I conducted myself when I couldn't care less in reality. The second reason I did it is simply that I can. I have tons of money, and because of that, I can get away with things that common men cannot, such as murder. Oh, and now that I think about it, I suppose there's a third reason. I did it for the Beal."

Sheryl's heart was thudding manically in her chest as tears spilled down her cheeks. She shook her head disbelievingly while crying, "For the Beal? I don't understand. What the hell are you talking about?"

"For the Beal." Seymour repeated with a strange knowing look in his eyes, For the baby veal."

Suddenly Sheryl felt a pinching sensation in the back of her neck and turned angrily to see the butler standing behind her with a syringe half full of some clear liquid.

"You see, Sheryl, I had to get Blake out of the way so my assistant George could administer your anesthetic."

The room started to fade in and out of focus as Seymour's voice had become like an echo in a large cavern.

"Please allow me to explain, Sheryl. I know you can hear me. The anesthetic George gave you will not render you completely unconscious. It will just paralyze you from the neck down, making it easier for us to perform the C-section."

"C-section? Caesarian? What is he talking about?" Sheryl thought through her haze. She couldn't move or speak. She could barely hear or even comprehend.

Seymour continued, "You see. The term Beal is not redundant, as you had suggested, Sheryl. Beal is a completely new, never-before coined name. Also, I said earlier, Beal means baby veal. It's not made from calves, but from real human babies."

Then she sensed herself behind lifted out of her chair. George was joined by the valet who helped him carry her out of the room to God only knew where. The last thing she heard was Seymour's knife and fork scraping on his plate as he enjoyed his plate of Beal.

PUNKIN HEAD PARKER

Joel Parker sat staring into the fire burning in the hearth of his stone fireplace, enjoying the way the heat took the chill off the cold cabin this Halloween night. The place was completely isolated deep in the woods of northern Schuylkill County, accessible only by a single-lane dirt road that usually washed out during bad weather. The cabin was one his parents had left him in their will. He was surprised they had done it since he had been such a disappointment to them in life. Then again, he was their only child.

He noted that this was the fifth annual event and could very well be his last because his work was almost done. He was sorry to see the end of such an enjoyable tradition, but it made little sense to keep going. Although Joel had to admit a tiny voice inside him was suggesting that continuing, regardless of his original plan, might be a good idea after all.

He looked across the room to the large pumpkin sitting on the oak plank table. It was almost time for him to get busy and carve the face, as he had done faithfully for the past four years. It was all part of the tradition.

Sadly, Joel realized that whether he continued or not, his nickname, Punk, would likely remain; there was little he could do about that other than to pick up and move across country where no one knew him. That wouldn't work because his home was here. Besides, if he were honest with himself, he had actually gotten used to the name over the years, and most people who still called him Punk either had no idea of its origin or had long since forgotten.

He was thinking back, as he often did at this special time of year, to the start of everything, back to the day when he was simply Joel Parker before he had gotten saddled with that horrible nickname "Punkin Head Parker." Then his life had been much simpler. He was just a seven-year-old second-grade student in Schuylkill County, doing all he could to fit in with the other students. He had managed to survive kindergarten and first grade at his previous school with no problems, but that had been before his parents moved. This meant he was introduced to a whole new crop of kids he had never met before.

Joel had quite a large, round head even as an adult. But as a young boy, it was much more noticeable on his small frame. He started at his new school just a week or so before Halloween, which was unfortunate timing. On his first day of school, his teacher brought him to the front of the classroom and introduced him.

"Class. This is a new student transferred here from First Street School. His name is Joel Parker."

"You mean Punkin Head Parker," a voice said from somewhere out among the myriad of strange faces.

"Who said that?" the teacher demanded, but no one accepted credit for the slight. "Well, whoever said that you should be ashamed of yourself. That's no way to welcome a new student to our class. And besides, you broadcast your ignorance as well by the mispronunciation of the word. It is pronounced Pumpkin, not Punkin, so you are doubly wrong."

But his teacher's admonishment did little good. What was said could not be unsaid, and like many terrible nicknames, this one stuck. From that day forward, Joel Parker was known as Punkin Head Parker. At first, Joel spent many nights crying alone in his bedroom, unable to deal with the unfortunate moniker. He often looked in the mirror at his large round Charlie Brown head and cursed his hideousness. To make matters worse, the school bully Ronald Walker and his toadies did everything they could not only to enforce the nickname but intimidate and ridicule Joel, their new unfortunate favorite target.

Ronald's four henchmen were Jimmy Yoder, Charlie Smith, Wally Benson, and Joey Ruddell. Each of them made Joel's life miserable every chance they got throughout the second, third, fourth, and fifth grades, although each year, the taunts became less until eventually the gag lost its appeal and began to fade away.

But the nickname stuck. Then after a time, the name Punkin Head Parker was abbreviated to Punkin Parker, and by the time Joel was entering junior high, he had been known simply as Punk. This actually proved to be an improvement because, with a nickname like Punk, many of the students who hadn't known Joel assumed he had gotten the name from being a tough kid, one of those sorts you didn't mess with. Soon Joel allowed the nickname to define him, and as such, he became involved with a group of students who had embraced the new emerging "Punk Rock" music scene.

Eventually, as Punk, Joel got involved with drugs and alcohol, and his grades began to suffer because of his new less than desirable lifestyle. By the time he was sixteen, he felt he had no choice be to drop out of school. Because of this, he could not get a good job and had to go from one menial source of employment to another. Then one day, in frustration, he sat down to re-evaluate his situation and try to determine who or what had been responsible for his downfall. He knew it wasn't his own fault, but surely someone had to be responsible.

Then it hit him; the name. That stupid, ridiculous nickname, which still haunted him, was the reason he had never been able to fit in anywhere except among the punkers. And where did that name come from? It had come from Ronald Walker and his four toadies. It was then that he decided he would make them all pay for what they had done to him.

Now Joel stood up and approached the large pumpkin sitting on his table. Laid out in front of the pumpkin was a series of different carving knives, some long and thin, others short and wider. Each served a purpose and was necessary to transform the subject into the perfect Jack-O-Lantern. He had become quite skilled at carving over the years and was looking forward to this year's project as he hoped it would be the best one yet.

He reached down with both hands and lifted the large, pre-hollowed pumpkin from the table. Its bottom had been removed as a necessary aspect of his carving. As the pumpkin rose higher, it revealed what was hidden underneath. A man's head protruded from a hole cut in the center of the table. His body, bound with tightly tied bull rope, was below the surface of the tabletop.

The eyes blinked as they tried to focus in the meager light of the room after being in complete darkness for so long. Besides, the effects of the drugs Joel had injected in the man hadn't yet completely worn off.

"Good evening, Ronald," Joel said in a jovial manner. "Welcome to my cabin in the woods on the fine Halloween night."

"Who the hell are you, and what the hell have you done to me?" Ronald had grown into a large, muscular man and had never lost his bullying ways. He had most recently been employed as a supervisor at a local cement factory and was hated by all of his subordinates.

"Ronald, really. Don't you recognize me?"

He likely didn't because Joel no longer looked anything like the young boy Ronald had bullied. He was extremely tall and gaunt with dyed black hair, eye makeup, black fingernails, and was covered with body piercings and tattoos.

"Recognize you? No, I don't recognize you! All I see is some skinny half-a-fag who's going to get his ass kicked as soon as I get out of here."

"Look closer, Ronald. Isn't there anything familiar about me? Like maybe my head. Don't you think it might be a little on the large side?"

"Head? What are you talking abo . . ." Then, like a light going on in a dark room, a look of recognition suddenly appeared on Ronald's face. "You? Punkin Head Parker? Is it you?"

"Yeah, Ronald, it's me. And now I suppose you want to know why I brought you here."

"I don't give a rat's rosy red ass why you brought me here, Parker. You just better untie me pronto. Maybe then I'll let you off easy with just a few broken bones. But if you don't, I'm gonna have to kill you."

"No need for threats, Ronald. There's no way you can get free unless I set you free, and that's not going to happen until after my annual Halloween Pumpkin carving."

"What the hell are you talking about, you freak? Let me out of here, now!"

"Before I begin carving, I have to show you something special. Do you remember Jimmy Yoder, Charlie Smith, Wally Benson, and Joey Ruddell?"

"Yeah. I remember them, but we've lost touch over the years, not that it's any of your damned business."

"Do you ever wonder what became of them?"

"No, of course not. I have a job and bills to pay, sleazeball. I ain't got time to worry about such things."

"Well, Ronald. I know exactly what happened to each one of them. Aren't you even a little curious?"

"No. Now get me the hell out of here and do it now."

Without responding further, Joel turned and pulled the curtain's string behind him, raising the cloth to reveal a glass display shelf, which held four separate square glass aquarium-style containers full of a light-yellow liquid. Inside each container was a severed head. He looked over at Ronald's shocked face as he stared at the horrific tableau in unrestrained terror. Each of the heads had the eyes removed, leaving behind two black triangular holes similar to those of a Jack-O-Lantern. Likewise, where the noses had been was now gaping holes, carved into similar triangular shapes. Large, jagged, irregular semicircles like those carved to form a pumpkin's mouth replaced the victims' mouths in the ravaged heads.

Joel was proud of the way the heads floated preserved in formalde-hyde displayed in all their wretched glory. A series of lights under the glass shelve shone upward, illuminating them in a gruesome manner, making something already horrible to behold even more heinous. Below the heads were four individual nametags at the bottom of each tank reading, James Yoder, Toady; Charles Smith, Toady; Walter Benson, Toady, and Joseph Ruddell, Toady.

The disgusting decapitated heads were all that remained of the four individuals who had once been Ronald's cronies. The fifth tank was empty but displayed a label reading, "Ronald Walker, Bully in Charge."

"You bastard!" Ronald shouted.

Joel reveled in the satisfaction of knowing that nothing Ronald could do or say would change the fate that awaited him and that he, Punkin Head Parker, was going to be the one to bring that final judgment.

Joel picked up one of the thin sharp implements, placed his left hand firmly on the top of Ronald's head, and began carving this year's project. It took many hours for the screaming to stop and the Jack-O-Lantern to be complete. It was then that Joel looked down at his work with admiration.

"You know what I've been thinking, Ronald?" But of course, the corpse didn't reply, "I been thinking you five guys weren't the only ones who were responsible for all of my problems. Sure, you may have started things, but there were others."

He stood staring out into the gloom of his cabin and said, "Yes, I'm sure there were others; many others."

THE TELL-TALE TRACKS

Author's Note: This is a twenty-first-century homage to the great Edgar Allen Poe and his incredible work, The Tell-Tale Heart. It was one of the first horror stories I ever read as a kid, and it scared the crap out of me. If the writing style seems different from my own, it's because I took Poe's story a paragraph at a time and tried to follow his storyline using a modern setting and current style language. —Thomas M. Malafarina

Look, I recognize it's true that sometimes I tend to come across as a bit nervous and maybe a little highly-strung, but hey, I'm a musician, I've got A.D.D. all right? So that's to be expected. That doesn't necessarily mean I'm nuts. Right? I mean, it may not be easy being this way, but I'm telling you it's done wonders in helping me become better at what I do. When I'm off my meds, my senses feel sharper, and, despite the high level of volume we use when we play, I swear my hearing, if anything, has gotten better. It's like not only can I hear everything on Earth, but now don't laugh, but it's like I can hear everything in Heaven and Hell as well. Does that sound crazy to you? Maybe it does, but you should listen carefully and pay attention to how calmly I tell you my whole story.

I don't know when or why the idea suddenly popped into my brain, but as is often the case with extremely intense creative ideas, this one haunted me night and day. I don't know why the thought came to me because, in truth, I really did love the old guy. He'd never dissed me or done me wrong in any way. He was rich, and he owned the music studio where my band was currently recording tracks for our new CD.

He also served as the recording engineer and producer. But I'm telling you I didn't want or envy his money either. To be honest, I think it was his eye. Yeah, I'm sure it was. I know this sounds crazy even to my own ears, but one of his eyes looked just like a buzzard's protruding eyeball. It was pale blue with a disgusting gray film covering it. I tried to avoid it, but I swear my blood ran cold whenever it looked at me. It was a slow and gradual thing but grew worse with each encounter. I simply couldn't take looking at that eye any longer, so I decided to murder him.

Now here's the point I'm trying to make. You probably think I'm completely nuts but trust me; crazy men are ignorant and have no sense for planning such a thing. But you should have seen me in action. I couldn't have been nicer to the old studio engineer than during the week before I killed him. I spent the entire time recording a series of special solo tracks, which meant only the two of us alone in the studio. The old guy lived in an apartment above the studio, and he liked to work into the late hours, mixing and refining the tracks. It was more common than not for him to fall asleep in the recording booth.

My work usually finished up at around eleven, and I'd leave. But then every night about midnight I'd sneak back to the studio, to the door of the sound room, gently open the door and silently peek inside to see him there sleeping with his head resting on the mixing board. When the opening of the door was just wide enough, I'd quietly thrust my head in, along with an unlit flashlight. I always moved very slowly so as not to disrupt the old man's sleep.

It often took me as long as an hour to get my entire head into the sound room far enough to get a good look at his sleeping form. See? Would a crazy man do that? Then when I was sufficiently inside the room, I'd very cautiously turn on the flashlight while covering it with my hand so that only a single ray of light fell on the buzzard's eye. I did this every night for seven long nights, after midnight. Each time I found the eye closed.

This made it impossible for me to do what I had to do because it wasn't the old man who was driving me to murder, but that evil eye of his. Then every following day, I would return to the recording studio and speak to him in friendly terms as if nothing was wrong. He would've needed to be as sharp as a tack to realize that I was watching him each night after midnight or what my intentions were.

On the eighth night, I was more cautious than I had been previously. In fact, if you were to watch the minute hand on my watch, it moved much more quickly than my own hands did. I was astonished how never before that night had I experienced such an awakening of my senses. I could barely contain my feelings of success at how I was opening the door little by little, and, as he slept, the old man had no idea of what I was planning. I actually chuckled, thinking about that. He may have heard me because his head moved slightly as it rested on the control panel. Most people would have pulled back out of the room at that time, and you might suspect I did, but I didn't. The control room was still black as coal, and so I knew he couldn't see me as I kept sliding it open ever so slowly.

I had my head in the room and was about to turn on the flashlight when my thumb slipped on the knob, and the old man jumped back from the mixing board and cried out, "Who the hell's that?"

I was silent, completely still, and said nothing. I didn't speak or move for over an hour, and while I waited, I listened but didn't hear him return to sleep. He was sitting on the rotating chair near the mixing board panel doing exactly what I was doing, listening just as I had done every night for the previous week.

Suddenly I heard a strange groaning sound, which I knew well. It wasn't the sound of someone in pain but of a soul overcome with sheer terror. I had experienced similar sensations waking up in the dead of night, so I knew what the old man was feeling. Although part of me pitied him, another part had to laugh inside because I knew he'd been sitting there for over an hour since hearing that first sound. Ever since then, his fears had been steadily growing. He'd been likely trying to convince himself he'd only heard the wind rustling along the roof or perhaps some insect flying around the room. His self-comfort was useless. Useless because death was awaiting him in the form of me, an unseen shadow, which he couldn't see or hear but somehow sensed the presence of my head poking into the room.

After I had waited patiently, still not hearing him fall back asleep, I decided to very slowly and stealthily cover the face of the flashlight and carefully turn it on. A ray of light no bigger than a thread shot from the flashlight and landed right on that horrible buzzard eye.

It was wide open and staring right at me. The more I looked at it, the angrier and more out of control I became. I saw it with perfect clarity; its dead blue gaze covered by its heinous film of gray. The sight of it chilled me to the bone so much that I didn't even notice the old man's face. It was like the ray of light had instinctively found its way to the damnable eye.

With my senses on high alert—please don't mistake this for insanity because it wasn't—I began to hear a low, dull thudding sound which I knew well yet could scarcely believe I was hearing. It was the beating of the old man's thumping heart. Like a death metal band driven to frenzy by the steady beating of bass and drums, my rage began to increase, growing stronger by the second.

I somehow managed to remain still, scarcely breathing and still holding the covered flashlight with the thin beam focused on that buzzard's eye. All the while, that hellish beating of the old man's heart continued to increase, growing louder with every second. The old man must have been terrified for his heart to be beating so loudly. I thought for a moment; it must be ready to burst. Then suddenly, I became very anxious, certain that a neighbor might be awakened by the terrible sound of that rhythmic heartbeat.

I couldn't wait any longer; his time had come. With a shout, I removed my hand from the face of the flashlight and raced into the room. The old man let out a cry for help, but only one time, because

I had grabbed one of the solid-body guitars from its wall hanger and brought it down hard on his head. At first, I smiled, knowing the eye was finally dead, even though the sound of that beating heart continued inside my head. After a few seconds, it stopped, and the old man was truly dead. I checked for signs of life, and there were none; that horrible eye would never plague me again.

If you still think me crazy, you won't when I tell you about all the precise precautions, I took to get rid of the corpse. I took care of it that night, working quickly and silently.

The old man had once shown me a secret place under a trap door below a carpet where he kept his special stash of marijuana and other recreational drugs. I checked and found it empty. I shoved the body into the space and put everything back the way it had been so that no one could have noticed anything out of place. I had been clever and lucky as there hadn't even been a single drop of blood splatter.

By the time I was finished, it was four o'clock and still as dark as midnight. Oddly I heard a knock at the main door to the studio. I went down and opened it as if I had every right to be there at four in the morning. To my surprise, when I opened the door, my three bandmates were standing there on the pavement with strange smiles on their faces. They said they were heading home from a party and had seen my car parked outside. They figured I was working late and wanted to hear the latest tracks I'd recorded.

I gave them my best "no sweat" smile and invited them in. When they asked about the old recording engineer, I told them he'd gone up to his apartment and left me alone in the studio. I told them to bring in a few chairs to the sound booth, to relax, and to listen to some of the latest tracks we'd recorded. I sat down in the very same chair where the old man had sat when I bashed in his skull a few hours earlier.

My mates seemed to be relaxed, and as such, I assumed by how I, too, was relaxed and spoke of the recording that I had been convincing in my deception. I began to play the latest tracks the old man had finished. The bass began to thud in syncopation to the drums as the guitar, and vocal tracks joined in. Suddenly, I felt a bit off, my head ached, and I felt as if I was getting a strange ringing, then humming in my ears. I tried to ignore it and cover it with casual conversation, but then I realized the sound was coming from the recorded tracks, and the strange thing was that no one seemed to notice it by me. That was when I realized the sound was coming from inside my own head.

I felt as if all the color was draining from my face. No matter how loud I spoke, that sound seemed to grow stronger and then change to more of a thumping sound, the sound of a heartbeat. Why didn't they notice it? Why couldn't they hear it? Why were they smiling and talking as if nothing was wrong? I had no idea what to do. The sound was driving me mad. I stood up, cursed, and shouted, grabbing the studio chair and slamming it down against the floor while my bandmates watched, unimpressed. They were used to my tantrums, but I'd never acted quite like this before. The thumping beats grew louder and louder while they looked on at me as if disinterested. Then I realized they knew; somehow, they knew. They weren't just looking at me, they were mocking me, ridiculing me in my moment of anguish, and the thumping heartbeat grew louder in my brain.

"Bastards!" I shouted, "I admit it. I killed the old man. I did it! Look under that carpet and lift the floorboards. You'll find him and the beating of his hideous heart!"

FUNERAL FOR A FRIEND

Sam could think of little he dreaded more than attending funerals. It was something that had plagued him for as long as he could remember. The phobia was severe enough to be crippling for him. The simple act of attempting to walk into a funeral home always made Sam's blood run cold. As soon as he felt the unearthly solemn stillness and smelled the pungent overpowering fragrance of flowers, his legs would begin to tremble, and he wanted nothing more than to bolt for the door. Just attempting to pass through the doorway felt as if he were breaking through some membrane-like barrier separating life and death itself. His phobia had been so bad that he avoided funerals at all costs. Even when his beloved wife had passed away ten years earlier, he hadn't had a formal funeral service for her. He simply was unable to deal with the idea.

He recalled a time from his childhood. Sam was about nine or ten years old at the time. One of his friends, whose uncle was a mortician, had called Sam and asked him to meet at his uncle's funeral home. The plan was for them to meet there then head to a local park to hang out.

Sam stood at the funeral home's front door with his hand gripped tightly on the handle, frightened beyond reason and unable to pull it open. It was like some genetic primitive survival mechanism built into his brain wouldn't permit him to pull the door open. After a few tense moments, when he finally gathered the courage to pull, the large wooden and leaded glass door slowly opened a few inches; his senses were accosted with the overpowering smell of funeral flowers.

One would normally think such an aroma might be pleasant and calming, but not for young Sam. The odor, which was actually a combination of many different types of flowers that had spent the day filling the funeral home with their various blended scents, seemed to Sam to be a vile and revolting stench, which when he opened the door hit him like a baseball bat to the face.

This repulsive stink caused his young stomach to turn over with revulsion. Instead of the aroma of pleasing flowers, Sam's senses had been bombarded with the smells of rotting, decaying vegetation. His mind was filled with the image of an unrecognizable pile of putrid sludge, infested with worms and other crawling insects. To Sam, the rotting mass was representative of the same type of decomposition, which would eventually overtake the current resident of the funeral parlor once he or she was put deep into the ground.

At first, the young boy felt he might pass out from the offensive wall of reek, and then he thought he might vomit. Instead, he stood staring into the darkness of the interior of the funeral parlor while the invisible barrier of fumes surrounded his face and blocked his entry, terrifying him to the very core of his young soul.

Sam had been certain if he tried to pass through that transparent wall of noxious vapors, the air might have felt thick and perhaps liquid or gelatinous. The boy just knew if he tried to enter the funeral parlor, the festering floral putrefaction would surround him like an invisible nest of living, deadly vines as its suffocating tendrils wrapped tightly about him in a final grip of death.

He imagined long, thin, serpentine fingers of unseen stench, crawling up into his nostrils, their slimy essence stealing slowly into his skull and penetrating his brain, while still others crept down into his throat, eventually cutting off his air supply before slithering further down into his stomach, where they'd begin to devour him from the inside out.

Overcome with terror, the young boy immediately turned and fled from the horrifying house of the dead, forgetting completely about his friend and not even caring if he ever saw him or the dreaded funeral parlor again. Sam recalled how, when he had been running madly from the building, he could have sworn he heard a voice inside his head, calling him to come back and face his fate. But he refused to even turn around as he fled in terror.

Yet here he was, so many years later, standing in the rear of what was obviously a funeral parlor, and he had absolutely no idea why he was here or how had he even gotten here. If he had walked in through the main door and made his way to his present location, he couldn't remember doing so. His head felt thick and foggy. He seemed unable to concentrate or focus. The sensations he was feeling were surrealistic and dreamlike. He thought he was dreaming at first, but as he looked around the place, he could tell he wasn't.

Whose funeral was this anyway? He assumed the deceased must have been someone special, perhaps a very close friend. Otherwise, he would never have agreed to come. Had he actually agreed to come? He couldn't remember anything. Sam knew he was getting old but not so old that he wouldn't be able to remember walking into a funeral parlor. That sort of thing would have been so traumatic for him that surely, he would have remembered. Had he been drugged by someone and brought here against his will? Was the drug beginning to wear off, and that was why he felt so strange? And why wasn't he feeling the familiar sensations of discomfort and stress he always felt upon entering a funeral parlor?

Looking around the room, Sam saw about a dozen people, all of whom appeared to be strangers to him. No, that wasn't quite right. When he looked more closely at the people, it seemed like perhaps he should recognize them, yet for some unexplainable reason, he couldn't quite make the connections.

His curiosity was beginning to get the better of him. He had to figure out what was going on, who all of these people were, and why he had been brought here against his will. Sam was now certain someone had drugged and forced him to come to this place. He walked slowly along the side of the room, keeping his back pressed tight against the wall, avoiding eye contact with any of the people in the room. They seemed not to notice him, which was just fine as far as he was concerned.

He began working his way steadily up toward the front of the place where the coffin stood with its lid open. Sam hoped that once he saw which of his friends it was in the box, his memory might return, and this all might make more sense. He was feeling surprisingly comfortable, and his legs weren't wobbling in the least. Perhaps after all these years, he had finally gotten over his phobia. Maybe he should be grateful to whoever it was that managed to bring him here.

Sam walked past the front row of people. His head was still feeling muddled and cloudy. None of the people seemed to pay any attention to him as they were all engaged in their own private conversations. To his discomfort, his old apprehensions began to return as he cautiously approached the open coffin. He knew he had to find out what this was all about despite his resignations. He took a deep breath and looked down inside.

This friend he recognized. Suddenly it all made sense to him, and his apprehensions were all gone. Sam wondered why he had spent so many years dealing with his irrational fears. Now that he was here, he realized it wasn't all that bad at all. Perhaps facing our innermost fears was all it took to beat them.

He turned and looked out at the other mourners and suddenly realized he recognized all of them now as well. Sam smiled with relief. These people were all friends of the man in the coffin, and that meant they were friends of his as well since it was his body in the box.

STATUS QUO

"He who rejects change is the architect of decay. The only human institution which rejects progress is the cemetery."
—HAROLD WILSON

"God, grant me the serenity to accept the things I cannot change, the courage to change the things I can, and the wisdom to know the difference."
—REINHOLD NIEBUHR, ALSO KNOWN AS THE "SERENITY PRAYER"

"The man who looks for security, even in the mind, is like a man who would chop off his limbs in order to have artificial ones which will give him no pain or trouble."
—HENRY MILLER

For some, change is a natural part of life, something to be expected and embraced with the anticipation of whatever new and potentially exciting events might follow. For others, change is something to be hated, feared, distrusted, and looked upon as something to be avoided whenever possible.

Frank Delveccio was one of the latter types of people. In all of his forty-nine years of life, Frank had despised change in any of the many forms it might take, from the simplest alteration of his daily routine to the major life-changing events everyone must face from time to time. Frank did everything within his power to keep his life running as smoothly as possible, with little variation to his daily routine.

Five days a week, he woke at precisely 5:45 A.M. and went into the bathroom to complete his daily ritual of emptying his bladder, brushing his teeth, and showering, always in that order. After dressing in blue work pants and a grey work shirt (he had a sufficient supply of each), he would walk downstairs to the kitchen and put a pot of water on the stove to boil for his morning tea. After eating a bowl of corn flakes, never oatmeal, or any other type of cereal, he would drink the last of his tea. By 6:25 A.M., he would be in the first-floor powder room sitting comfortably and reading the morning newspaper while enjoying his regular-as-clockwork morning constitutional.

By 6:35 A.M., he was out the door and was in his car heading for his job as a machinist for a local manufacturing firm about five to ten minutes outside of the coal region town of Ashton, Pennsylvania. Although he didn't clock in until 7:00, he liked to be on-site between 6:45 and 6:50 to prepare his various activities for the day. Frank hated to be rushed and arriving an extra ten minutes early allowed him to maintain that comfortable rhythm of life he required so intently.

If someone familiar with Frank's actual job function were to describe it as boring, they would be quite correct, both descriptively as well as literally. Frank worked for Technofacture International Corporation as a setup-operator of a semi-automatic machine called a Bore-O-Matic double end boring machine; hence the literal reason why his job was boring.

The descriptive reason why his job was boring was equally simple. For the past thirty-plus years, Frank had performed the exact same operation on the exact same type of part, at the exact same workstation, on the exact same machine between twenty and thirty times per hour, eight to ten hours per day, and every single day since starting on the job shortly after his eighteenth birthday.

The very suggestion of such tedium might make another person run from the factory, screaming in terror while ripping out his own hair by the roots, but not Frank. For him, it was one of the most perfect jobs ever known to man. Once he had picked up the initial techniques of operating the machine as a young man, he immediately began honing his skills to make the job as mindless and stress-free as possible.

His responsibility was to take stainless steel tubes about two inches in diameter and about eighteen inches long from a part-feeding conveyor, place them into the Bore-O-Matic machine, and simultaneously counter-bore two precision holes in the ends of the tubing. As soon as the boring process was completed, he was required to inspect the diameters for proper size and surface finish requirements. Then if all of the dimensions were to specification, he would place the finished parts onto the completed product conveyor, where they would then be transported to the next subsequent workstation for the appropriate next operation in the manufacturing process.

In those early days, the company had its hourly unionized employees on an incentive plan, also known as "piece work," meaning the more parts Frank produced, the more money he could make. About ten years ago, the company switched to a straight hourly pay rate with no incentive, and Frank's job only got easier. Since he could make 100% of the required rate without breaking a sweat, his already excellent job became a perfect job.

Frank's co-workers knew about his quirks concerning change. His nickname on the shop floor was "S-Q," which stood for "Status Quo." The name was derived from the reply Frank would often give to the typical greeting. For example, if someone would walk by Frank and ask, "Hey Frank, how's it going?" he'd smile, and extend his right palm out flat and rotate it slowly a few degrees clockwise then counterclockwise and reply, "Status Quo, baby, Status Quo." This was Frank's way of saying things were going smoothly and according to plan, no hassles, no muss, no fuss.

Neither did Frank like experiencing change in his personal life. Shortly after starting at the factory, he married his high school sweetheart, Janet, who was the first and only girl he ever dated. Within a year, he purchased a small but sturdy row home along the main street of Ashton, near the top end of the town a few miles from the plant. It made perfect sense to Frank as he didn't ever plan to leave his job until retirement. He also knew he'd be faithful to Janet for as long as they lived and never do anything to endanger his marriage. That sort of thing was inviting chaos into a perfect situation. Now, almost thirty years later, he was still married to Janet, and they were still living in the same row home; status quo, baby, status quo.

When his kids were growing, Frank's company was bustling, and he was often asked to work ten hours a day, work Saturdays, and occasionally Sundays. The pay was great, as was the never-ending need for more money, so Janet never complained.

As a result, Frank was away from home most of the time the kids were growing. When he finally came home at night, after stopping by his favorite local bar for a beer or two, he would eat dinner with minimal conversation, then go into the living room and watch the news on television, followed by his favorite network programs and eventually he would fall asleep in his recliner. Janet would put the kids to bed then wake him so they could retire as well. The next day he would awaken once again and complete the exact same routine he had done the previous day; status quo, baby, status quo.

Before he knew it, the kids were grown and out of the house, leaving just himself and Janet in what he once considered a small house, but lately had seemed much too big for just the two of them. However, since he still spent so much time at work, this new change did little to affect his daily routine. Yes, as far as Frank Delveccio was concerned, he would be happy to spend the next sixteen years with life going just as it had been until the day, he turned sixty-five and retired. In fact, to prepare for the changes which retirement would bring, Frank planed on easing into the retirement mode of operation by slowing down a little bit more each year.

But sometimes life has a different plan in store for us, and it doesn't bother to warn us or ask us for our opinions regarding such changes. Nor does it care what consequences its actions may have upon us; it simply lets things happen. That's exactly what occurred a few weeks after Frank's forty-ninth birthday.

Frank had arrived as usual at his job by 6:50 on Monday morning and immediately went to his workstation at the Bore-O-Matic machine, only to find a chain secured tightly around the machine with a maintenance lockout tag affixed to it, preventing anyone from putting power to the machine.

At first, Frank thought his machine had been temporarily shut down for routine maintenance. On the rare occasions when this happened, he dealt with the minor disruption by going to an adjacent identical machine to perform his duties. But there was something about the way the chain hung around his machine, which gave Frank a strange sensation in the pit of his stomach as if the locked machine was an omen of sorts, a sign that his perfect, unchanging world might be about to experience a terrible upheaval.

He slowly raised his head and looked around the rest of the department and was shocked to see that all of the boring machines in the area had the same type of lockout chain. The entire department was shut down. Since Frank was the first man to arrive in the department that morning, he immediately headed to the supervisor's office to find out what was happening.

He knocked on the door of his boss, Clifford Johnstone's office. When he heard Cliff's voice inviting him to come in, that is exactly what he did.

"Cliff!" Frank said a bit louder and with a bit more panic in his voice than he meant to, "What the hell is goin' on back in the Bore-O-Matic area? Every damn machine has a lockout chain on it. They can't all be down for repair at the same time. What's goin' on?"

"Yes, Frank, you're absolutely right," the supervisor said cautiously, dreading the news he was going to have to pass on; he understood how Frank was about change. "Unfortunately, there ain't nothin' wrong with the machines, and they ain't down for maintenance, either. Sit down here for a minute, and let me try to explain."

Frank looked at Johnstone as if he didn't comprehend what the man was saying, then sat in Cliff's guest chair, never taking his apprehensive eyes off him.

"I don't like the way this is looking, Cliff." Frank said, "I have a sneaking suspicion you are about to deliver some really bad news."

Cliff said, "Actually, Frank, that's exactly what I have to do. You see, the boys upstairs in their infinite wisdom have decided to make a change." Frank knew by "boys upstairs" Cliff was talking about the management of the facility; those stuffed white-shirted pencil-neck bean counters; the ones he felt not only couldn't find their way around the shop floor but also probably couldn't even find their way down to the shop floor in the first place.

"What kind of change, Cliff?" Frank asked cautiously as he felt the hairs on the back of his neck stand on end. Suddenly a cold chill ran down his spine, and a pang of uncertainty gripped the pit of his stomach.

"Well," Cliff said, "They've decided to take the entire department, lock, stock, and barrel and ship it to our sister plant down south."

"But how can that possibly be?" Frank asked, hoping for a way out of this dilemma. "We've been working ten hours a day and seven days a week for the past couple of months. If we're so busy, how can the company afford to shut down production for a month or two and move everything?"

Cliff said, "Well, it's like this, Frank. We don't really have any more orders than we usually do. What the company did was put the department on overtime to build up a sufficient inventory so they could schedule the move. And before you ask, yes, I knew about it but wasn't allowed to say anything about it. I'm sorry Frank, I was just following orders. Don't take it personally ‹cause it has nothin' to do with you or anyone else around here. It is just a cost-saving measure they said they had to take to stay in business."

Frank countered angrily, "Don't you really mean to say, they're sending all of our work to a non-union shop so they can get the stuff done for slave wages?"

"Now, Frank," Cliff replied, trying to calm him down. "There's no need to get all upset about this. There ain't nothing you nor I can do about it. The decision's been made, and the machines'll be moved by the end of the week. The good news is you can jump onto one of them new computer-controlled machines that they call CNC machines that they have over there in Department 17. You have enough seniority over most of those fellas, so you will be guaranteed to stay on dayshift, and the company will be willing to train you."

"Train me? Cliff, I've been doing the same damn job for over thirty years. I'm forty-nine, and I'm looking at only sixteen years to go until I retire. I don't like having my life disrupted like this and being forced to learn some stupid new-fangled machine." Frank said angrily.

"Well, no matter what you might want, the deal is done, and the opportunity for retraining will be there." Cliff explained to Frank, "that is, of course, unless you choose to disqualify yourself and take some other job. But I guarantee you the money won't be nearly as good. And as it is, even the CNC job will be a bit less pay than you currently make, but at least you will still have a job."

Then after a bit of hesitation, Cliff said, "Or else you could always take the layoff, and you know, you could try to find another job somewhere else. I really hope you won't do that, because we can always use a dependable man like you, Frank. And as you know, jobs ain't growin' on trees around here. You just have to try to learn to be a bit more flexible to change."

Frank's face reddened with anger as he lost his temper, shouting, "I don't have to learn no such thing!" He began walking rapidly back and forth in the supervisor's cramped office, his hands balling into and out of fists repeatedly. He couldn't believe this was happening or that Cliff had been part of its planning. Cliff wasn't just Frank's supervisor but also his friend; they had been to each other's homes, knew each other's families, and had broken bread together on many occasions. He couldn't believe Cliff had participated in such a traitorous act.

Frank was a much bigger man than Cliff, and for a moment, the supervisor was afraid Frank might lose control and possibly attack him. Then thankfully, Frank said, "Look, Cliff. I just can't think about this right now. I don't know what I'm going to do. Just, just put me in for a vacation day today. I have to get out of here for a while and take some time to think about all of this."

Cliff could see Frank was extremely upset, as he knew his friend would be. In his heart, Cliff felt very bad about the decision; understanding Frank would never be willing or able to make the transition to the new computer-controlled technology. Frank was too set in his ways and too resistant to change, so he'd either end up in some lower-paying menial job or else he'd simply have to take the layoff and find some other way to earn a living until he was old enough to retire.

There was little Cliff could do for the man other than present his alternatives. And by the way Frank was behaving, Cliff thought it would be best for all concerned if he got Frank out of his office and out of the building as quickly as possible.

Frank stared at Cliff for a moment, and something strange began to happen. He imagined himself reaching across the desk, grabbing Cliff by the collar with his huge left hand and picking up the boss's letter opener with his right, then pulling Cliff onto the top of the desk where he would begin to systematically disembowel the man, allowing his hot steaming innards to flow all over the top of the desk, spilling blood and stomach contents all over the company's precious production orders. It was much more than a simple fleeting thought; it was as though he could actually see himself committing the act and enjoying it immensely. One side of Frank's mouth turned up slightly, and his eyes got a mad, sinister look about them at the thought.

Because of this new, even more terrifying look, Cliff decided now might be the best time to send Frank on his way. "I'll tell you what, Frank." Cliff said fearfully, "I think that's a great idea." He stood, walked around his desk, and gently placed his hand on Frank's shoulder, leading him out. "Why don't you take a day to relax and think about your different options? Sleep on it tonight, and in the morning, you can come back, and we can figure out where you'll best fit into the new scheme of things."

Frank didn't bother to reply; he simply turned and walked out of the office, slamming the door hard behind him. By the time he reached the main department area, the rest of the crew had already clocked in for the day and stood off to the side watching him storm out of the office, past the time clock where he punched out and went out through the exit, having never acknowledged any of them. They could immediately see by the look on his face things were no longer status quo for Frank Delveccio.

Frustrated, angered, and stressed to the point of breaking, Frank decided not to head directly home, but instead he drove to a local park where he stopped and sat in his car for an hour or two trying to make sense of everything that had happened, and attempting to relax and keep focused so he could figure out just what direction he was going to take next. At present, he had no idea what he would do. The most frustrating part was there was little he could do to stop the torrential tempest of change heading his way.

After a while, he realized what he really needed was a taste of some familiar routine, something he could count on to provide some consistency. So he decided to stop at Maxine's diner, where he often went for breakfast on Saturday mornings. He suddenly realized he hadn't been there for several months; thanks to the rigorous schedule he had been working. What he believed he needed right now was a good heaping plate of Maxine's scrambled eggs with home fries and sausage because he knew that a luscious meal was about as tried and true as he could get.

Frank pulled into the parking lot and made his way up the four stairs leading to the main entrance. In his haste, and because of all the mental distraction with which he had been dealing, Frank failed to notice a sign on the front door reading "Under new ownership, with a new and improved menu and decor." As he entered the diner, Frank stopped in his tracks. Nothing was as he remembered it; everything was different.

Gone were the old light green patterned cracked Formica tables and the high back vinyl cushioned booths, replaced by café style tables with wrought iron Italian looking chairs in a multitude of bright pastel colors. The counter was still in place, but it had been replaced with a polished granite countertop. The familiar old-style stools had been replaced with some fancy sort of high back swivel chairs with a very intricate ornate floral wrought iron pattern.

When he sat at the counter, being careful not to fall off the strange new stool, he looked at the first page of the menu and was shocked to see that all his favorite meat and egg dishes had been replaced with some strange health-conscious meals of fruits, vegetables, egg whites, and low-fat meat substitutes.

"What the hell?" Frank murmured to himself as he looked around at the diner, which was once filled with many blue-collar customers just like him. Now the patrons appeared to be more refined upscale Yuppie-types; people he didn't even knew existed in his little town.

A young effeminate-looking man approached him from behind the counter and asked, "May I take your order, sir?"

Frank looked at the thin man with a mixture of uncertainty and noticeable discomfort, asking, "What happened to Maxine and the diner?"

"Oh, this?" The young man said with a theatrical wave of his arm, "Well, Maxine retired a few months ago and sold the diner to me and my husband, Byron, and we decided to redecorate it and transform it from that horrible little ugly duckling to this magnificently lovely swan you now see before you. Don't you just love it? We haven't gotten around to giving the place a new name yet, but a new name is definitely coming soon, I assure you. Probably something floral in nature. We just have so many ideas and . . ."

The man continued talking unrelentingly and was completely oblivious to the fact that Frank was ignoring every word he was saying. As Frank contemplated his next move, he was unsure if he should just get up and leave the diner or give in to his primal urges and grab the fairy by his scrawny little neck and squeeze ever-so-tightly until his face turned purple and his eyeballs popped out of their sockets like the inside of a squashed olive.

For the briefest of moments, the thought was so real and so appealing to him that Frank imagined himself wringing the frail man's neck as his dying eyes bugged from his skull, his face turned ashen gray, his lips pale blue. Then the tiny capillary blood vessels in the man's eyes would begin to burst; petechial hemorrhaging, Frank believed it was called, remembering something from one of his television cop-shows. He envisioned both eyeballs literally popping from their sockets and dangling loosely on the man's cheeks like twin pendulums. The thought gave him great pleasure.

However, he, fortunately, chose the first option, and without another word, he rose from his stool, turned and walked from the diner, never looking back, as the frail man stopped mid-sentence, huffed loudly, and went back to work, having not the slightest clue how close he came to dying a horrible death.

Frustrated, Frank went to his car and drove to the one place he knew he could count on for consistency, the one place where nothing had changed for as long as he could remember: his favorite watering hole, Jimmy's Neighborhood Tavern. Jimmy Flannery was the owner and operator of the pub and, like Frank, hated change. Nothing inside the bar ever changed; in fact, the place looked exactly as it had the day Jimmy bought it.

Looking at his watch, Frank saw it was about 10:25 A.M.; perhaps normally a bit early for drinking, but if there was ever a day which merited a snoot-full it was today, Frank thought. He pulled into Jimmy's parking lot, surprised to see several cars already in spaces. He guessed for many people maybe it wasn't too early for serious drinking at all. He didn't even know if it was legal to sell alcohol this early, but he figured he'd stop by anyway. Jimmy was a longtime friend, and legal or not, Frank was fairly sure Jimmy would give him the drink he so desperately needed.

Frank walked through the front door and took in all of the comfortable and familiar sights, which made up Jimmy's Neighborhood Tavern. The place was dark and dimly lit with the heavy smell of cigarette smoke and spilled beer, which Frank had grown to love over the years. Looking around, he saw several local people he recognized in the bar and gave them all a courteous wave hello. If they were surprised to see Frank at the bar so early in the morning, they didn't indicate so; perhaps they were too engrossed in their own worldly problems to concern themselves with his.

He took a seat at his favorite well-worn bar stool, the cushion of which was barely held together with duct tape, peeling along the edges. Frank smoothed down the tape before sitting as he did every time he came into the bar and immediately felt somewhat better thanks to the familiarity of that one simple act.

Jimmy walked down along the bar and greeted Frank, "Hey Frank. How's it goin'? Let me guess—status quo baby, status quo. Right?"

"Nope. Sorry to say, not today, Jimmy. Everything is anything but status quo." Frank replied. "If you will get me seven and seven and make it a triple, I will tell you all about it. That is if you have the time."

"Of course, I have the time," Jimmy replied.

Jimmy knew the importance of listening to his customer's woes as all good bartenders did, so without another word, he mixed the drink, adding a fourth shot of Seagram's on the house, and got ready to hear what Frank had to say.

Frank hoisted the glass to his lips and, to Jimmy's surprise, downed half of the drink in the first swallow. "Holy hell, Frank," Jimmy said in surprise, "What can be that bad before eleven-a-m in the morning?"

"Well, Jimmy," Frank said, "It's a bit of everything. You know how I always like things to run smoothly. You know, status quo? Hello, you're the same kind of man."

"That is true, Frank." Jimmy replied, "I like things the way I like them, and I'm not much for change neither."

Frank said, "Well, I just experienced a mountain of change in the past few hours." Then Frank went on to tell Jimmy first about the upheaval at work and how he didn't have a clue what he could do about it. Then he told him about the diner and the two "la-tee-dahs" that were now running the place. Jimmy looked especially displeased about the diner.

"I heard the diner was sold." Jimmy said, "And I knew there was a lot of inside construction going on over there, but I had no idea that a couple of "those types" had taken over." He said this while doing the two-finger quote sign with both of his hands. "I tell ya what, Frank. This town's going to hell in a handbasket. It's no wonder I'm glad to be leavin'."

"Leavin'? What are you talking about, Jimmy?" Frank asked, shock in his voice. "What are you sayin', Jimmy?"

Jimmy reached out and took Frank's now empty glass without answering as if trying to temporarily avoid the discussion while also trying to find the best way to break the unpleasant news. He refilled it with Seven-up and added another four shots of Seagram's Seven. He slowly walked over and handed the glass to Frank, who hadn't taken his eyes off the bartender.

In those eyes, Jimmy saw something he couldn't quite comprehend. It was as if the fabric that held Frank's sanity together was becoming shredded and was unraveling before his very eyes. Jimmy became uneasy and was unsure if he could find the right words to explain it to Frank. It wasn't that he felt he needed to explain his decisions, or it wasn't that he felt Frank had any right to such an explanation, but he simply wanted to do so because the man looked as if he were about to lose control.

"Well, Frank. It's like this." he proceeded very cautiously, "As you know, I ain't gettin' any younger, and I've been havin' a lot of problems lately with my back and my legs; probably from all these years of standin', tendin' bar. I don't know."

Frank glared at the man with eyes that were starting to look less like those of a human and more like the eyes of a wild beast. Jimmy said, "I also got a bad case of Emphysema, not just from my own smokin' but also from breathin' in everybody else's smoke in this place. Well, Frank, the bottom line is, I sold the bar to a group of investors, what ya call a consortium, from down in the Philadelphia area. At the end of the month, I'm closin' the bar and moving out to Phoenix to live with my little girl Cindy and her husband. Since Vickie passed two years ago, they're the only family I have, and I ain't seen ‹em since the funeral." Jimmy hoped the mention of his late wife and her funeral might gain him some sympathy and ease Frank's growing anger.

Frank was an internal bubbling cauldron of growing fury, stoked even further by his inebriation. He imagined grabbing a nearby bottle of beer and breaking it over the counter, then taking the jagged edge of the bottle and grinding it deep into Jimmy's eye socket, twisting and ripping until the entire contents spilled into the bottle fragment. Next, he imagined turning the bottle around and shoving it neck first down Jimmy's throat, the jagged edge jutting out from his mouth like shark's teeth. Then he envisioned grabbing Jimmy by the back of his head and slamming his face against the bar, driving the bottle right through the man's spine as his face erupted in a mess of bloody shards.

Snapping back to reality, Frank stood and fumbled for his wallet, somehow managing to stay civil enough to remember to pay his tab. He refused to make eye contact with Jimmy, fearful the murderous vision would return and take control of him. He felt betrayed, first by the company who employed him, then by his favorite diner, now by his number one watering hole, and all in the same day.

"Hey. Don't sweat it, Frankie." Jimmy said, motioning for him to put his wallet away. "Your money is no good here today, my friend. The drinks are on me." Then with a bit of nervous laughter, he said, "Consider it my going away present to you."

But Frank was not in the mood for any such attempt at appeasement and ignored the bartender's effort as he staggered toward the exit, his broad hulking shoulders tense with anger, his hands clenched in fists, dangling at his sides. Frank left the bar, stumbled across the parking lot, and collapsed down into the front seat of his car, and for the first time in more years than he could remember, he felt like crying.

He was not only drunk but was physically, mentally, and emotionally exhausted by all that had happened to him. Ironically, for most people, the changes Frank was confronting would be thought of as simply something to be dealt with, a part of life, but not for Frank. In his perfect world, such seemingly minor changes were monumental. To him, it was as if the entire universe was plotting against him; and for the first time, he began to think that perhaps it was.

He put his head back against the headrest and sat silently for a few minutes, contemplating his next move, and before he realized it, he had fallen into a deep sleep. Immediately, Frank began having a series of bizarre and horrifying dreams, perhaps influenced by the stress of the day, or more likely by the large amount of booze he had consumed over such a small amount of time. But whatever the reason, the nightmares were absolutely horrible, and he couldn't seem to wake from the deep sleep. He saw scenes of terrible violence, of victims with their eyes being torn from their skulls, and of large birds feasting on the tender bloody organs.

Many other horrid unrelated images passed quickly through the nightmare landscape in his mind, spinning and swirling like a whirlwind of revulsion, until eventually, the storm seemed to fade back into the distance, and one solid image began to take shape. As he slept, Frank saw the form of a woman emerge from the swirling mass of twisting gruesome illusion and slowly walk toward him. In the background, the images continued to swirl and blur together as the woman came more clearly into focus.

She was a tall, dark-complexioned woman with an incredibly voluptuous body. She wore a skin-tight blood-red long-sleeved dress, which exposed her shoulders and upper arms, clinging to her like a second skin and accentuating her large full breasts. Frank began to feel lust rising inside of him for this woman, which was exciting considering the circumstances. That was until his eyes slowly followed the curves of her body upward as silky red material continued up from her ample cleavage, where it was wrapped sensuously around her long thin neck. When his eyes reached the area where her face should have been, he was immediately halted; as likewise was the sexual arousal he had been experiencing. He could see nothing beyond her chin and full lips because her face was covered with some sort of peculiar mask, resembling a type of outlandish ancient pagan headdress.

The piece the woman wore was some sort of skull-like mask with two long curved horns protruding from the top of the head. It appeared to be constructed of actual bone, not any sort of plastic or latex type material typical of most Halloween masks. Frank couldn't see the woman's eyes through the mask but instead stared into the two large blank sockets, which seemed to contain a blackness darker than night.

Suddenly, Frank was filled with intense terror, understanding something was very wrong with the woman who stood before him. He wanted to speak, to ask who she was and what she might want with him, but he was unable to utter a word.

As he watched in fear, the woman parted her lips and quietly said two simple words, "Status quo."

Frank didn't understand what she was trying to tell him. He tried once again to speak and found he was now able to do so and asked, "Wa . . . what are you saying?"

The woman's lips curved slightly upward in a sly, knowing smile, and she repeated the same two words. "Status quo." She didn't speak for a few seconds, then said, "I can help you. I can show you how to get back to status quo."

Finally, Frank believed he understood exactly what the woman was trying to tell him. She somehow knew how his life had been changed and how his routine had been so drastically disrupted during the past several hours. Apparently, from what she had said, this strange woman had been sent to help him.

Again, she spoke, "Frank. I know how you like things to be, and it is very unfair that so much has changed for you this day. The bad news is you haven't yet experienced all of the changes, which you'll face today. There are still more drastic changes to come than even those which you have faced so far. I understand you won't be able to handle these changes on your own. The good news is you won't have to. I'll be here to help you."

"More changes?" Frank said with fear, "I don't think I can handle any more changes today."

"Well, that's exactly what I've been trying to tell you, Frank." She said, "And that's precisely why I'm here. I'm to be your guide, to help you get through the disruptions you will face during this day of great transformation."

"What do you mean by day of great transformation?" Frank asked.

She explained, "Today, your life is going to change and to change drastically, with a great upheaval to the normal routine you crave so desperately. I'm here to lead you through the turmoil and help direct your actions in a way that will guarantee your return to a state in which you will once again be comfortable; to return you to your permanent status quo."

Frank felt some relief for the first time at the mention of returning to such a state and asked his guide, "What should I do? How will I know when you will come to help me?"

She replied, "When the time is right, simply think of me, then look for me. I'll be there to show you the way."

"But . . . but . . ." Frank tried to ask, having many more questions for the strange woman. However, before he could ask even one of his questions, she began to fade back into the swirling mass of colors, which the dream had suddenly become.

Frank awoke with a start, hearing the blare of a car horn. Sitting up, he saw he was still in his automobile but was covered in a cold sweat. He looked out the window and saw the source of the noise; it was someone stopped outside of a nearby apartment building close to the bar, apparently trying to get the attention of someone inside.

He looked at his wristwatch and saw it was after 1:00 P.M. Although his head felt a slight bit clearer, thanks to the almost two-hour nap, Frank could still feel the effects of the whiskey and knew he still had enough of a buzz, so he probably shouldn't be driving. Nonetheless, he decided it was time to head home to tell Janet of his situation, so he started up his car, left the bar's parking lot, and began weaving his way up the steep hill, which was Centre Street, heading for his home.

When he arrived at his row house, he noticed his favorite curb-side parking space was gone, and another car was parked in its place, directly behind his wife's car. Parking spaces were at a premium on Centre Street, not to mention virtually every street in town, but since his house wasn't in the downtown business area and was, for the most part, residential, he was usually able to find the same spot available. In his opinion, there was little reason for anyone to be parked in his spot at 1:00 P.M.

Maybe because he was supposed to be at work, someone visiting a neighbor decided to use the spot. In the meantime, he had to deal with the frustration of going about a block and a half further up the hill until he could find a parking place or perhaps two spaces, sufficiently large enough so that he could get his car situated safely in his current less-than-sober condition.

Frank parked his car as close to parallel as he could do and ended up with the front tire two feet away from the curb and the back tire squeezed tightly against it. Then he practically fell out of his car, staggering down the sidewalk, still feeling the effects of the alcohol.

"Holy crap!" Frank said aloud with a drunken slur, "One in the afternoon, and I'm hammered. Wow! That has to be a first for me."

When he got to his house, he glanced over at the car occupying his spot, and for a moment, there seemed to be something familiar about it, but in his condition, he pushed the thought aside. He fumbled for his house key and used it to open the front door. As he did, he tried to think of the right words to explain to his wife, Janet, the reason he was three-sheets-to-the-wind in the middle of the day. She knew how he was about change, and he felt certain she'd understand. As he quietly entered the house and was just about to call her name, he heard strange moaning noises coming from upstairs.

"What the hell?" Frank mumbled to himself. At first, he was unsure what the sound had been, then realization found its way through the drunken fog, and then he knew immediately what the sound was and, more importantly, what it meant. He knew it was Janet; he recognized the pleasurable moaning; the same sounds he had been responsible for stimulating countless times during the past thirty years. But now it was apparent someone else was in the driver's seat and was responsible for her making that sound, a sound which once brought him so much satisfaction but now sounded like the cackle of an ugly old crone.

And as if his day hadn't been bad enough so far, he now realized his life had just become as cliché as a bad country-western song. He had a brief flashback to the dream where the strange woman told him there were more terrible changes in his future. Then he suddenly recalled the car parked in his space; he remembered he did know that car; it belonged to Janet's old classmate and Ashton resident, Will Preston. That was Will's car out there in his spot, and that meant that Will was also upstairs parking his other car in what was supposed to be Frank's garage, so to speak.

Frank could feel the anger growing fiercer within him by the second. He knew what this all meant and understood what he would face if he went upstairs. He didn't know what to do. As his rage grew, he noticed something materializing out of thin air over by the closet under the stairs. After a second or two, the strange woman in the red dress from his dream stood right in front of the door. Her sensuous mouth curled up in another devious smile, and without saying a word, she slowly waved her left hand in the direction of the closet, and Frank understood instantly what she was suggesting. And he liked it; yes, he liked the idea very much.

He staggered clumsily over to the closet, reached inside, and pulled out the loaded twelve-gauge shotgun he kept there originally for Janet to use if she ever needed to protect herself from an intruder. But now its purpose would be for something quite different indeed. Looking back at the woman in red, Frank saw her nod her head with confirmation, indicating that he was doing exactly as she had suggested. As the woman's head nodded, Frank saw a small black spider crawl from underneath the woman's bone mask and walk down toward the corner of her mouth. Without hesitation, the woman's serpent-like tongue flew out of her parted lips and latched onto the creature, pulling it quickly inside her mouth. As Frank watched, she swallowed the creature and gave a pleasurable smile. Then she mouthed the words "status quo," and Frank understood what he must do next.

Running like a wild man, gun at the ready, Frank charged up the stairs and burst through the bedroom door as a startled and panic-stricken Will Patton fell off of Janet onto the floor next to the bed; the same bed which Frank and his wife had shared for almost thirty years; she same sheets he had slept on the night before.

"Hey, Will." Frank said cheerfully and matter-of-factly, "How's it hangin'? Oops. Bad choice of words, I suppose. I hope you realize that you are parked in my favorite spot?" Frank didn't know if Janet or Will could appreciate the double entendre in his bizarre statement, but he didn't care because he found it hilarious. Frank uttered a weird flat maniacal laugh.

Preston was terrified to the point of being unable to speak, which was probably for the best as nothing he could say would help to appease the man standing over him with the flaming eyes of a wild animal, and the shotgun pointed directly at Will's crotch.

"Now, Frank," Janet pleaded, her throat thick with tears and fear. "Don't do anything rash. I can explain everything."

Frank replied, "No need, Janet, my sweet. This picture is worth much more than a thousand words." Frank saw something move in the right corner of the room as the strange woman in red appeared and nodded in his direction, indicating what he had to do.

"What are you looking at, Frank?" Janet asked, wondering why her husband was staring into an empty corner of the room. Preston decided to take the opportunity to make a break for it but never got the chance.

Without another word and without taking his eyes off the woman in red, Frank's pulled the trigger on the shotgun and, with a thunderous boom, sent the man's genitals and half of his insides splattering against the floor and back wall of the bedroom. Janet screamed uncontrollably, pulling the covers up to her neck as if they might somehow protect her from the madman who had once been her husband.

Preston slumped to the floor, screaming in agony as he bled uncontrollably, death now only a few moments away. Frank still held his gaze toward the empty corner of the room where only he could see his invisible guest, and once again, the woman in red nodded approvingly. Without a moment's hesitation and again without looking, Frank raised and aimed his shotgun, pointing it at Janet. She opened her mouth to either scream or plead for her life but never got the opportunity. Frank calmly pulled the trigger once again, and with another explosive blast, Janet's head became a mass of splattered pulp decorating the bone-white headboard of the bed like a work of modern art. The woman in red nodded once again and mouthed the words "status quo."

Frank knew what he must do next. He decided he would first start with Jimmy at the bar, then the diner's new owners, and finally his boss at work. Each of them had caused a disruption in his life, and each would die in turn. He believed if he took care of them, then everything would be back to normal once again.

As Frank walked out the front door of his row home and stepped out onto the pavement, he was surprised to see the town's two police cars parked in front of his home at odd angles, lights flashing. Then he realized one of his neighbors must have known about Will Patton and Janet, probably her best friend Gail, who lived just two doors away. The nosey bitch must have seen him come home early and called the police anticipating trouble. That meant they probably got there just in time to hear the screaming and shooting.

From behind the rear of the closest police car, Frank saw Ashton police chief, Max Seiler, pointing his service revolver directly at him. Just a few feet in front and to the left of Frank, he saw the strange woman in red standing with her skull mask. She looked at the many police officers and the crowd of onlookers, all of whom seemed to be watching the events unfold in hungry anticipation. None of them seemed to be looking at the woman, however.

"Hey, Max." Frank shouted, waving nonchalantly, "I suppose you've probably figured out what just happened in there."

Chief Seiler heisted for a moment, and then in an effort not to have the scene escalate further, he said as calmly as possible, "Yep, Frank. I believe I did, at that."

Seiler understood this was already an unbelievably horrible mess, which had the potential to end in even more bloodshed, but he knew he'd do whatever he had to do to end it quickly. "I'll tell you what, Frank. Why don't you just put down that shotgun, and we can talk about all of this."

Frank looked toward the woman in red and asked, "What should I do?" but she didn't seem to offer any suggestion. Some of the cops turned to see who Frank was speaking to but, of course, saw no one. Seiler shouted, "Frank. I think the best thing you could do right about now would be to drop your weapon and lie down face first on the ground."

Again, Frank looked at the woman for direction. From the patrol cars' vantage point, he appeared to be actively involved in a conversation with no one. The police all watched in confusion, as after a few moments, Frank nodded at the empty air as if he understood something.

Frank shouted out to the police, "She told me I should do what you said, so I'm going to lay down now." The police looked at each other uncertain what was happening, realizing the man must be completely out of his mind. With that, Frank put down his shotgun and lay face down on the pavement while police officers swarmed around him, securing him in handcuffs.

///

Frank awoke once again in the small six by ten-foot room and slowly sat up on his small cot-like bed, allowing his body to wake up enough to greet another day. He looked around at the plain tan walls and the small stainless-steel sink and toilet in the corner. Frank lived in this same room for almost six years, and nothing about it ever changed.

It looked exactly like it had looked the very first day he arrived at Summit Ridge Sanitarium. The door to his room had a wire-reinforced glass window with a small round vented opening beneath it for speaking. At the base of the door was a small slot, which was used to provide meals three times a day.

After a few moments, Frank saw a guard appear at the small window. He believed the man's name was Sam. "How's it goin' Frank?" The guard asked cheerfully as he did every morning at 8:00 A.M. on the dot. The woman with the skull mask sitting in the corner of his room smiled at Frank with satisfaction then nodded.

Frank looked up at the guard with a smile and lifted his right arm, holding his hand out horizontally, then slowly rotating it first clockwise, then counter-clockwise. Then with a visible contentment most people could only hope to achieve in life, Frank said, "Status Quo Baby, Status Quo."

AS PER YOUR REQUEST

The email was so mysterious that Jesse was certain it had to be some type of scam or perhaps a phishing scheme. Yet there was something about it, which made him feel it might be something he should consider more closely. Then again, what did he know? He was still hungover from yet another party he had attended the night before and knew he wasn't exactly thinking as clearly as he should be.

He decided he'd better proceed cautiously. He'd recently completed an internet security course at his job and knew the risk involved with such emails. He was certain that simply opening it as he had already done wouldn't cause his computer any problems, but opening attachments or clicking on hyperlinks might, and there were two such hyperlinks in the email.

The email had been sent to his attention, Jesse Franks, and had come from an email address he didn't recognize, "ProbSolvr@DeadLink.com." He had no idea who this person was or why they had sent him the strange email. He had also never heard of a web provider known as DeadLink.com. The main text of the email read simply, "We met recently, and you made a request. That request has been granted."

"What a strange email." Jesse thought. He couldn't recall making any sort of request of anyone. He looked down at the first hyperlink. Above the mysterious link was a line that read, "As per YOUR REQUEST. Click this link to see the RESULTS YOU REQUIRED."

Jesse knew this was a critical juncture. If there was anything potentially malicious embedded in the email and he clicked the link, his
computer might be flooded with viruses and rendered useless. They
might also be able to ascertain all of his personal information and perhaps steal his identity. But even though he didn't recognize the sender's
email address or couldn't recall making any request whatsoever, his
curiosity was beginning to get the better of him.

He recalled from his web security training he could highlight a
link then copy and paste it into a search engine to see if it was a legitimate link. He decided rather than copy the entire link, he'd simply
enter "DeadLink" into Google and see what happened. The result was
about 222,000 hits, and they all seemed to be for a variety of software
programs whose purpose was to find and report dead hyperlinks on
the Internet. He never did find a listing for DeadLink.com. Next, he
decided to type in www.DeadLink.com directly into his Google search
bar and once again couldn't find such a web site, but only got a bunch
of hits the same as before for reporting dead hyperlinks. He sat and
stared at the hyperlink in his email.

Then he recalled reading about websites that couldn't be found
by traditional search engines. He believed they were part of what was
known as the "deep web." He had known a bit about it from watching
the now canceled CSI Cyber show on television, but other than that,
he had no experience with such things. He had also heard some urban
legends at work about the deep web. From what he could recall, the
deep web was supposed to be hidden from most search engines and
was a place of untraceable, often illegal websites. Jesse had heard things
about drug dealing, prostitution, child pornography, and worse. He
had recalled from his training to stay away from such places, as often
the owners of these websites could back trace and find the actual physical location of anyone who chose to come to their website.

He wondered if that was the case with the first link, which he
continued to stare at inquisitively. Reluctantly, he let his cursor hover
over the link for a long while, not sure if he should click it or not. Jesse
looked at the second link, which was almost identical to the first but

with a few different characters. Above the second link was a message, "DO NOT click this link UNTIL you have completed the instructions shown to you after clicking the LINK ABOVE."

He wished he could recall what, if anything, he had requested of anyone he had recently met. He thought back to several recent parties he had attended. He had ended up drunk at most of them. In fact, he was more often than not drunk these days since having recently learned that his wife had filed for divorce and had moved in with her lover. Thank goodness, the couple hadn't had any kids yet; this separation was hard enough for him to deal with. He let his cursor hover for another indecisive moment, and then with a deep breath, he threw caution to the wind and clicked on the hyperlink.

Suddenly, the screen filled with what appeared to be a video file with a right arrow in a circle in the center of the black, blank screen. Jesse knew from experience he needed to click the arrow to play the video. After another moment of slight hesitation, he let his cursor hover over the arrow and clicked. The video began to play.

A dark foreboding organ melody, awash with deep bass notes, began to play as the camera filming the scene glided down a shadowy stone hallway and approached a large wooden door. As the door pushed inward with an eerie groan, the music died down to a faint background sound. The view beyond the door was that of a dark room lit only by a scattering of candlelight. Despite the lack of illumination, Jesse was able to see far more than he had wanted to see. In the center of the room were two large wooden chairs cemented into heavy concrete footers sunk into a mostly dirt basement-type floor. The chairs resembled pictures Jesse had seen of old electric chairs used in executions and were complete with leg, arm, and head straps. Then, to his horror, he saw secured to one chair bound, gagged and completely naked his estranged wife Janice, and in the other, equally naked and helpless, was her lover Charles.

As he stared on in horror, a foggy memory suddenly flashed into his mind. He had been at a party a week earlier and, of course, was drunk. An odd-looking man had struck up a conversation with him.

He couldn't recall the man's name or even what he looked like, but he believed he had been dressed in all black and might have had dark hair as well. Jessie recalled how he had been ranting and raving about his estranged wife and her lover in his drunken stupor. He said he had a good mind to track them down and kill them both. Then he recalled the strange man saying something to the effect that he would take care of them for ten thousand dollars.

Jesse was certain the man had been joking and had replied, "Believe me, it would be well worth it. And I'd be more than happy to pay for it." Then he had proceeded to get fall-down, blind drunk, and had forgotten the entire encounter. Now the memory had suddenly returned. Had the stranger been serious after all? Was that who had filmed this video? Jesse broke out in a cold sweat, and his stomach lurched.

He watched as the camera approached the bound couple, who were doing their best to cry out for help despite their gagged mouths. Their teary eyes were uncovered and bulged with terror as the figure carrying the camera approached. As it got closer, Jesse saw a long sharp knife come into the field of vision, and when the camera zoomed in on his wife's face, he heard a familiar voice, which he immediately recognized as being that of the stranger from the party.

"Hello, Janice. I hope you and Charles are quite comfortable. You both are here at the request of your husband Jesse, as am I." The voice said with a disturbingly calm and calculating tone.

Jesse suddenly found himself shouting angrily at the computer monitor, "No! Oh, my God! No!"

The glimmering blade slid underneath Janice's cloth gag, and Jesse heard her scream out in a muffled cry of pain as it dug a crimson furrow in her cheek, and blood began to run down the edge of the blade. With a quick yank, the gag fell from her mouth, and Janice screamed in agony as her eyes bugged out from her face.

"Please, please!" She screamed in desperation, "Whatever he's paying you, whatever Jesse is offering you, we'll double it! I swear! Please just let us go."

"Oh. I'm so sorry, Janice." The voice said, "You see. I'm a man of my word, and I've already promised Jesse. In fact, he'll be watching this video sometime after we're finished, so make sure you do your best to scream as loudly as possible. I want to make sure he gets his money's worth."

"Jesse!" She screamed, looking right into the camera, "You bastard! How could you let someone do this to me?"

Next, the camera pulled back as the man placed it on a solid surface, freeing up his hands for the job he was about to complete. As the man entered the picture, Jesse could see he was dressed completely in black from head to toe, and his face was hidden from view by a black hood. He next sliced through Charles' gag, so Jesse assumed he could also hear Charles' screams of pain. Suddenly three other people dressed similarly to the first man entered the screen, each of them armed with long sharp blades.

During the next hour of the video recording, the group of assailants began to systematically slice and fillet the couple in ways that were far beyond Jesse's most horrible imaginings. The group made sure to keep the two prisoners alive as long as was possible before finally slitting both of their throats and letting them bleed to death as their screams faded into unintelligible liquid gurgling sounds.

Then a message popped up on the screen, reading, "We've done as you requested. Now you have exactly one hour to wire the sum of ten thousand dollars to the bank account, which you will find along with further instructions in the second link of the email. You most definitely don't want to be late."

Suddenly the screen went blank, and Jesse returned to the email where the second link awaited his reply. He looked at the clock on his computer monitor and realized with great anxiety not only was he just responsible for causing the death of two people, but he didn't have the ten thousand dollars necessary to pay for the horrible service which had just been performed on his behalf.

An hour later, he sat staring at the clock on his computer monitor. Suddenly a message window popped up on his monitor, stating,

"You're late. We warned you." A moment later, his front door exploded inward as several people dressed in black, wearing black hoods burst into his living room, and he knew they had found him. What was worse, he knew what would come next.

THE REDEMPTION OF RALPH

"Redemption is not perfection. The redeemed
must realize their imperfections."
—JOHN PIPER

She felt the cold tiled kitchen floor against the exposed portion of her back. Her attacker was strong and had already managed to pull up her shirt and pull down her panties. He held a knife to her throat and pinned her down with his weight. As revolting as the thought of being raped was, She hoped the maniac would stop there. Through a curtain of tears, she saw he had a faraway look in his insane eyes, void of all compassion. She was helpless to do anything, even to scream as the man's weight on her chest made it almost impossible to breathe.

Then suddenly, her attacker stopped, as if frozen. He looked at something across the kitchen and out of her field of vision. A look of utter terror was painted across the attacker's face as the knife fell from his hand and clanged against the floor. He grabbed at his chest with both hands. She saw his lips moving silently as his eyes bulged impossibly out of his head. A moment later, his face became ashen, and his lips turned dusky blue. Finally, he fell sideways, crashing to the floor in a dead heap.

/ / /

"What in the world was that supposed to be?" The angry voice of the one who called himself Peter bellowed from deep within the billowing white clouds, as Ralph reluctantly floated ever closer. "You call that redeeming yourself?"

Ralph was confused, "You told me to find a way to help that girl. That's what I did."

"No, Ralph. That's not what you did. You may have saved her from being assaulted by that maniac, but you let yourself be seen in your spirit form, and in the process, you scared her attacker to death. YOU KILLED HIM RALPH! What part of redeeming yourself says it's okay to kill somebody?"

"Honestly, Peter. I never meant for him to drop dead. I just wanted to scare him away. How was I supposed to know he had a bad ticker?"

Peter confided, "I'm going to be honest with you here, Ralph. I wasn't in favor of giving you a shot at redemption at all. But those in power above me seem to think there's something about you worth saving. Frankly, I don't see it. You're pretty much a mess, Ralph."

Suddenly someone floated past Ralph and stood in front of the pearly gates. Ralph recognized him as the would-be rapist who had just had the heart attack. The man looked back a Ralph with sudden, surprised recognition.

He shouted, "Hey! It's you; you're that ghost! You did this to me."

"Yeah, well, sorry about that. My bad. I only meant to, you know, I honestly had no idea you'd keel over."

"Me either. I'm usually much better than that. Then again, I ain't ever seen a ghost before. You look a lot less scary here with all the clouds and crap. What is this place?"

"It's Heaven. Well, not exactly. Heaven is on the other side of those gates."

"So, what you doing out here?" The man asked.

"Trying to win my way in there. They seem to think I got a chance at redemption."

The man thought for a moment then said, "I'm pretty sure scaring me to death ain't a very good way to win favor with the halo and harp crowd. Speaking of which, what do I gotta do to get in the joint?"

Peter looked down and said to Ralph, "Can you excuse me for a minute, Ralph?" Then he looked down at the new arrival with angry eyes and shouted, "Seriously? You think you've got any chance whatsoever of getting in here? From what my ledger says, you've broken every commandment on the slabs; multiple times."

The man replied, "Say, why shouldn't I get the same shot old Ralph here is getting? I'm sure we can work something out, maybe a loophole. Waddya say, Pal?"

Peter rolled his eyes and conceded, "You, my sad and deranged unfortunate, are what we call irredeemable."

"Really? No chance at all?" He countered.

"Nope. No chance whatsoever. Here's the way it is. You get to go to Hell, go directly to Hell, do not pass go, do not collect two hundred dollars. Capish?"

"Wow." The man said, "That's really harsh!"

"Yes. I suppose it is." Peter replied with a sly smile as he raised his hand in a semi-circular motion.

Suddenly from somewhere behind the man, the atmosphere seemed to ripple as a long, black slit opened in the billowing clouds, and a sulfurous stench poured from the opening, which was now rimmed with burning embers. It looked to Ralph as if someone had cut a slit in the air then set it ablaze.

Long and fleshy tentacles began to snake out of the opening and wrap themselves around the man. As they came in contact with his spiritual body, the flesh began to melt away from his bones. He screamed in agony as the long flapping arms pulled him ever closer to the void. Swarms of countless spider-like flaming insects poured from the gap and began feasting on the man's tortured body.

Ralph couldn't comprehend how this non-corporal thing was able to experience the same sort of tortures as if it had been comprised of flesh and blood. The agony the rapist was suffering was completely real. The wailing man was pulled ever further into the slit, and as he passed the glowing rim of the opening, his remaining flesh was flayed in rolling ribbons from his bones. A moment later, the opening pinched closed, and all signs of its existence were gone.

"What was that?" Ralph asked in astonishment.

"Peter replied, "That, Ralph, was Hell. That is, it was one of the portals to Hell. Think of that as Hell's express elevator. That poor soul will have an eternity to experience things much more agonizing than what you just witnessed. And by the way, Ralph, if you can't come up with some way to redeem yourself, you'll be joining him."

Ralph realized he was in real trouble. He had heard stories of Hell and the relentless tortures, but seeing it up close and personal was an entirely different matter.

"Um, okay. I get it. I need to make things right. So what do I do now? How can I make up for all the bad things I did when I was alive?"

Peter replied, "I have another opportunity for you; perhaps your last chance. Do you remember a woman you pretended to be in love with? The woman whose life savings you managed to swindle from her?"

"Do you mean Doris? Okay, I'll admit it. I faked being in love with her to get her money. Then I skipped town and left her penniless. I never really loved her, but . . ."

"But what?" Peter questioned, "And be very careful here, Ralph. I expect complete honesty."

"But I actually did like Doris a lot, and it's probably the only time in my miserable life that I felt ashamed over what I'd done. It's a bit embarrassing to say so, but it's the truth."

"That's good to hear, Ralph. It's a start. Perhaps it was that guilty feeling that made the boys upstairs feel you might be saved."

"So, how do I go about making up for the wrong I did to Doris? I'm a spirit now, not a human. There's not much I can do to help redeem myself in this form."

"I might have a way. It's a bit unorthodox and could prove to be a bit risky. But it might be worth the danger."

"Danger?" Ralph asked, "How can there be any danger to me? I'm already dead. What else do I have to fear? Other than maybe . . ." His voice trailed off as he cautiously looked behind him as if anticipating that portal to Hell to reopen.

"Ralph, you've already seen what awaits those who are sent to Hell."

"Yeah. But if I redeem myself, I won't have to worry about that. Right?"

"Yes, of course. But here's where things get a bit sticky." Peter explained, "What I'm proposing is something which will allow you to do whatever is necessary to undo the bad you've done."

Ralph gulped and said, "You keep mentioning risk and danger. Maybe this idea of yours isn't a very good one after all."

"Well, you may be right. But think about it this way, Ralph, what do you have to lose? If you don't find redemption, then you're doomed to the tortures of Hell. All things considered, even with the risk, you don't have any choice."

"Point taken. So, what's this plan of yours?"

Peter expounded, "I know you're familiar with the earthly location known as Las Vegas."

"Sin City? Of course, I know all about Vegas. If I had a dollar for every dollar I blew in Vegas, well I'd have . . . actually, I wouldn't have squat because I'd probably lose it all over again."

"Here's what I have in mind for you, Ralph. I've come up with a plan to send you to Las Vegas to win money, a lot of money."

"Oh yeah! Now you're talking, Peter."

"Easy there, high roller. You're dead. You have no need for money. This money is all for Doris, who is currently employed as a maid for one of the less desirable no-name hotels in a bad part of town."

"Okay, so what's the plan? How do I start making money? For Doris, of course."

"I'll send you back down to Earth, to Las Vegas, with a gift for winning. You'll have a six earth-hour window of time to win as much money as possible. After that time is up, you'll cash in your earnings and take all the money to Doris. I'll arrange for you to find her hotel as well. When that's all finished, you should have gone a great distance toward redeeming yourself."

"Hey, wait a minute here. I assume this 'gift for winning' will be given to me by you. Is that correct?"

"Yes, of course. I'll provide you with the right sort of help for you to win and win big."

"But wouldn't that be, you know, cheating and stealing from the casinos? And isn't stealing a sin?"

"Well, yes, which is one reason why I'm doing this on my own without approval from up the line. This is just going to be between you and me."

"You said one reason. What's the other?"

"The other is the risky part. As you may not be aware, your earthly remains were disposed of, cremated, so you no longer have a body to return to."

Ralph noted, "That's probably a good thing because Doris would likely kill me as soon as she saw me."

"But of course, you need to occupy a human body. As a result, I had to find you another one."

"Another body?"

"Yes. As it happens, a gentleman just died, and you're going to take over his body for a short time."

"So I'll be alive again, right?

"Wrong. You'll never be alive again, Ralph. You'll be a disembodied spirit operating a corpse. You'll have no heartbeat, no pulse, nothing. You'll be a puppeteer operating from inside a hunk of decaying flesh and bone."

"Since I'm already dead, I can't be killed, right? Is it like I'm invincible?"

"Not so fast, Ralph. Here's the risky part. Once I put you inside that body, the forces from Hell will know about it. They won't be able to touch you as long as your body remains usable. However . . ."

"However, what?" Ralph asked.

"If somehow your temporary body is, for lack of a better term, killed, then the dark forces will come for you and drag you into the bowels of Hell for eternity."

"Oh." Ralph replied uncertainly, "I guess this is the place where I should ask what constitutes ‹dead' when it comes to a reanimated corpse; a shot to the head like in a zombie movie?"

"Well yes, actually that would do it. So would decapitation, or falling from a high building, being crushed by a heavy object, or blown to smithereens in an explosion. Anything that would render the host body incapable of sustaining your spirit would be an end-game situation. The instant that happened, the demons of Hell will know, and they'll come for your soul."

"But if I don't try this, they're going to come for me anyway, so I suppose we might as well get this show on the road."

"So be it," Peter said with a commanding voice.

A split-second later, Ralph awoke in an alley next to a trash dumpster. The area was shadowed in darkness, yet he could see the glow of lights from the casinos and hotels seeping into the alley from the strip. He stood up and noticed he was a bit unsteady on his feet. He was at first having difficulty getting this strange body to follow his commands.

However, in a surprisingly short time, Ralph was able to master the body's physical movements, although he moved a bit awkwardly. Then he realized this strange gate might actually benefit him. If he kept a cocktail in one hand at all times, the casino personal would simply assume he had too much to drink. In fact, they'd probably like that and consider him an easy mark. That could only work to his advantage.

He stumbled into the first of what would be many casinos that evening, and at each one, the story was the same; he won big. At one point during the evening, he had actually gone into a luggage shop and bought himself a carry-on piece with wheels and a telescoping handle to hold his winnings. He kept his eye on the time, planning on allowing an hour buffer so he could deliver his winnings to Doris at the flea-bag hotel where she worked.

Now that he realized he would be able to make her life a lot easier, he actually started to feel good about himself. He sadly comprehended that if he had known helping someone else could make him feel so good, he might have done more when he was alive. But then again, who was he kidding? He was no good in life, and now he was just trying to make up for lost time and keep himself from the fires of Hell.

After the last casino, with his luggage swollen with money, Ralph stumbled down to the hotel where he knew he'd find Doris. She was just ending her shift and was walking out to the parking lot, to her beat-up old sedan. Ralph cautiously approached her.

"Are you Doris Casey?" He asked, pretending not to recognize her.

Doris looked up at him with the sort of distrust of strangers common in the world and said, "Excuse me. I don't believe I know you." She was reaching into her purse, likely for a can of mace or pepper spray.

"My name is Charles Bentley." He lied, making the name up on the fly. "I was an acquaintance of someone you knew once; a man named Ralph Gibson."

"That no-good-for-nothing bastard. If I could get my hands on him, I'd strangle him dead."

Ralph felt as if he had a lump in his dead throat and replied, "Well, Ma'am. I'm afraid that won't be necessary, as Mr. Gibson passed away some time ago."

"Good riddance to bad rubbish." She said angrily, "So what are you doing here? Did he tell you I was a sucker, an easy mark just waiting to be fleeced again? Because if that's your plan, I can just as easily strangle you in his place."

Ralph decided this conversation wasn't going the way he had hoped it would, so he figured he'd better cut to the chase. "Ms. Casey. Please hear me out. Ralph did tell me about what he had done to you, and in his will, he left you all the money he had stolen from you and more. This suitcase is full of the cash Ralph asked me to bring to you." He unzipped the top of the suitcase to give her a look at the money. Her eyes practically jumped out of her head at the sight.

"This is all for you, Ms. Casey. Ralph felt very bad about how he treated you, and his dying wish was to make amends for the wrong he had done. He didn't expect your forgiveness, neither do I, but I hope you'll accept this cash on his behalf."

"Oh, my goodness!" She exclaimed. "I don't know what to say."

Suddenly a gravelly voice called from a dark corner of the parking lot. "How's about you don't say anything. How's about you both put your hands in the air and give me that loot."

Ralph turned and saw a stranger dressed in dark clothing, brandishing a gun and walking toward them. The man must have followed him from the last casino and now was going to rob them. He couldn't allow that to happen, not when he was so close to completing his task.

The man pointed the gun at Doris and insisted, "You, Buddy, back away from the suitcase, and maybe I won't put a hole through your little girlfriend here."

Ralph had seen characters like this one many times in his life, and he knew that no matter what he or Doris did, the man was going to kill them both. They had seen his face. They could identify him, which meant he couldn't afford to let them live, especially not with a suitcase full of money just waiting to be taken. Ralph thought about trying to rush the man but knew if he did, his temporary body might be damaged, and then the demons from Hell would come for him. But he couldn't just let the criminal kill Doris. Ralph truly cared about what happened to her, and now he finally had a chance to make up for his past sins.

He saw the man's finger tightening on the trigger and knew Doris was about to die. With no more thought about the consequences, Ralph rushed the robber just as the gun fired. The bullet entered through the bottom of Ralph's neck and exited up through the top of his head in a shower of blood, bone, and brains. His body collapsed to the ground. Ralph knew instantly this was one of the unrecoverable wounds Peter spoke of, and as if to accentuate this fact, he could suddenly smell the rank odor of sulfur.

A thin fiery red slit opened up in the air in front of him, and he saw dozens of thin crimson fleshy tentacles working their way out of the gash and heading straight for him. As they got near, he could feel the unbearable heat, and he knew he had failed. He was going to Hell. Then suddenly, he felt himself being lifted out of the body and slowly floating upward. The Hell-spawned tentacles reached for him but couldn't touch him. Then he heard a horrifying scream and saw the would-be murderer being flayed alive by the horrifying appendages from Hell. Just as the scene faded from sight, he saw Doris grabbing the suitcase and throwing it into her car before speeding safely away.

///

"It appears my little experiment was a success." Peter said, "You've won your redemption, Ralph."

"But how can that be? All I did was win a bunch of money and give it to Doris. My motivation was pure selfishness. How does that win me absolution?"

"Think about it for a minute Ralph. I set this whole thing up knowing you would win and knowing that winning would put you into a situation where you had to make an impossible choice. Walking around Las Vegas with a suitcase full of money was just asking for trouble."

"But I don't get it."

"When you threw yourself in the path of that bullet to save Doris, you did so, knowing you'd expose your soul to be taken to Hell. Yet you did it nonetheless. That was probably the one and only selfless act you have ever committed in your entire miserable life. You saved Doris knowing full well what could happen to you."

"Oh. I guess I see. But it was the only thing I could do."

Peter looked at Ralph knowingly and said, "And it was that which won you your redemption. Welcome to Heaven, Ralph."

KILL OR BE KILLED

Edwin awoke, lying on the cold cement floor in what appeared to be a concrete and steel bunker-style basement. His head was foggy feeling, like he had been disoriented by some sort of drug. He felt something hard and cold around his left wrist. Looking down, he saw a steel manacle on his wrist attached to a long heavy black chain.

Following the chain's path, he saw it was connected to another cuff, which was around the wrist of a still sleeping man. The man was twice his size, if not larger. He was shirtless, with bulging muscles covered in prison-style tattoos, and wearing filthy, baggy orange pants. His head was shaved, and his scalp likewise adorned with a myriad of black and white symbols.

An accountant by profession, Edwin was the man's exact opposite, with a slight build, little muscle tone, and not a single tattoo anywhere on his body. He wore wire-framed glasses that currently hung askew on his thin face, and one of the lenses was cracked, somewhat hampering his already poor vision.

He couldn't understand why he had been brought to this place or why he was now tethered to the frighteningly huge sleeping behemoth. Suddenly he heard a buzzing, crackling sound, and on a display screen across the room above a huge steel door, the words "Welcome to Kill Or Be Killed" were flashing in bright letters more than a foot tall. A moment later, a small sliding door built into the larger door lifted, and a long machete with a leather handle was slid into the room, stopping halfway between Edwin and the sleeping man.

Edwin suddenly recalled a scene from an old western movie he had seen as a boy, where a cowboy and an Indian were tied at the wrist with a bull rope, and a single knife lay in the dirt between them. The object of the challenge was for one of them to get to the knife and kill the other to survive.

"Kill or be killed." Edwin thought, and he suddenly understood what was happening. Then he looked over at the sleeping giant and saw he was starting to stir. The man-mountain was waking up! Edwin's heart leaped into this throat.

He had no idea why he had been kidnapped and forced to participate in this sick, twisted game. He was an accountant, for God's sake! He wasn't a killer or even a fighter. He was a thinker, a cerebral man. He had spent most of his childhood running away from bullies who would one day grow up to look just like the man lying on the floor. Judging by the orange prison pants the man wore, Edwin was certain most of those same bullies would have ended up in jail or dead by now.

But he suddenly realized he was faced with an impossible decision. He knew he'd be no match for the muscle-bound convict, even if he had the weapon. He was a dead man waiting to happen. However, he was determined not to die this day. Sensing he had no alternative, Edwin hurried over and grabbed the machete from the floor, dragging the heavy clanging chain along with him. Then, without taking even another moment to think, he grabbed the handle with his right hand, closed his eyes, and brought the razor-sharp edge of the blade down, across the neck of the sleeping man, all but decapitating him. The body twitched once or twice before becoming still, as a puddle of crimson pooled below the hacked stump.

As he stood panting, sick to his stomach, drenched in fear sweat, he heard a computerized recording speaking in a disembodied voice, "Welcome to Kill or Be Killed. In order to survive this challenge, you two gentlemen from radically different backgrounds will have to find a way to join forces and combine your skills."

Edwin's stomach suddenly lurched with shocked realization. A moment later, another steel door slid open, and an eight-foot-tall grizzly bear roared into the room on its hind legs, its claws slashing the air. Spittle flew from its gaping maw as Edwin recognized his fatal mistake much too late.

PROM NIGHT

"I'm sure that love exists, even infinite, eternal love."
—Kylie Minogue

"A lot of people like the idea of eternal love and eternal romance.
The notion of love that is more profound and deeper because
it is eternal is very powerful."
—James Patterson

The gymnasium-turned dance hall was cast in darkness, with the only illumination coming from a few dozen electric Chinese lanterns dangling from makeshift wires strung overhead. The theme for the annual senior prom was "Oriental Gardens," hence the reason for the Asian décor. There were also hundreds of white, yellow and green flowers, all handmade from facial tissues by the prom committee members and various volunteers. A disc jockey was spinning some of the senior class's favorite tunes, and a nice slow ballad had just begun to play.

The young man walked slowly, standing nervously in front of a pretty girl sitting alone with her head cast downward as if doing all she could to avoid making eye contact with anyone.

"Excuse me, young lady. If I may be so bold as to ask, would you do me the honor of the next dance?"

Eric Holder instantly knew he had screwed up and sounded like a complete nerd. But now that the offer had been made, it was too late to take it back or to change his blatantly lame approach. If he was to be honest with himself, he actually was a nerd after all. In fact, this had been the first dance he had ever attended in his twelve years of school, and he had absolutely no experience when it came to dealing with the opposite sex.

The girl he had so pathetically asked to dance was Ginny Patterson. Since elementary school, Eric had secretly been crazy about Ginny but had never had the courage to approach her before, or heaven forbid, ask her on a date. He doubted she even knew he was alive. It had taken him all evening to work up the nerve to even talk to her now, and after all of that, he sounded like a complete doofus. He had no idea how to dance and realized he would probably make a fool out of himself if she was even willing to agree to dance with him. Then again, he probably already made an idiot of himself with that pathetic request.

"Me? Are you asking me to dance, Eric?"

Eric was dumbfounded. He pushed up his horn-rimmed glasses, which were sliding down his nose as always, and thought, "Holy crap! She knows my name! How can someone as gorgeous as Ginny know my name?"

"Um, yes. If you'd like to, that is. To be honest, I really don't know how to dance very well. But, I mean, if you don't want to, I'll understand."

The equally shy girl looked at Eric, with eyes reflecting great appreciation behind her cat's eye spectacles and said, "I'd love to dance with you, Eric, but I have to warn you that I don't know how to dance very well either."

"Then I guess we'll have to fumble through this together." He replied, sounding much more confident than he actually was feeling.

Moments later, the couple was out on the dance floor, engaged in some sort of slow back and forth motion that might vaguely resemble dancing to someone from another planet that had never seen dancing before. But none of that seemed to matter to Ginny or Eric. They both knew something incredible had just happened, as they stared into each other's eyes and talked as comfortably as old friends who had known each other for years. The rest of the world had disappeared for them, and as far as they knew, they were floating inches above the floor of the gymnasium floor on billowing clouds.

"You dance very well, Eric."

"So do you, Ginny," Eric said, his heart thudding inside his chest. After a time, he asked, "So um, how did you get here tonight? Did your Dad drop you off?"

"No. I hitched a ride with Penny Andrews and her boyfriend, Brad. But to tell you the truth, I don't think Brad liked having me tagging along. You know, being the third wheel and all."

"Yeah, I get it. Um, I drove my Dad's car tonight. I can't believe he let me have it. Do you think it would be okay with Penny if I took you home? I mean, if you'd want me to, that is."

Ginny seemed to think for a moment, and Eric was worried that he had been too forward and that she might turn down the offer. However, to his relief, she didn't.

"Yes. You can take me home, Eric. I'm sure Penny won't mind, and I know Brad will love the idea."

"What about your parents?"

"They won't know who dropped me off and as long as I'm home by midnight. I won't be in any trouble."

Eric suddenly realized the dance was over at eleven, which would give them an hour alone together before she had to be home. His heart skipped a beat with the anticipation of maybe actually getting his first kiss.

For the remainder of the evening, the two danced in the same slow, embraced cadence for every single song, whether it was an up-tempo, moderate or slow tune. They would rock slowly back and forth, staring into each other's eyes and talking like the soul mates they suddenly realized they were. They were both astonished how all of this could have possibly happened so quickly, but at the same time, thrilled by the feeling.

The other students went about their business, completely ignoring the obviously lovesick couple as they danced on. But neither Eric nor Ginny cared. Being considered odd-balls all of their lives, they were accustomed to being ignored, and now that they had found each other, nothing else mattered.

When the last song finished and the lights of the gymnasium were turned back on, signaling the end of the prom, the young couple turned and walked slowly hand-in-hand toward the door and out into the night, unaware that they would once again face what they had faced and forgotten dozens of times before.

///

"This was where it happened. Right down the road after the senior prom." A dark-haired student said to his date and their friends.

"Jimmy. Seriously? Why did you have to bring that up?" His girl-friend asked. "It's so sad and so tragic."

"Yeah, yeah. I know. But it's, you know, history too."

"History, schmistory Jimmy! You never cared about history in high school, so why now? And why is it every single year, somebody has to bring up Eric and Ginny? It's always the same thing; Eric and Ginny, Eric and Ginny, blah, blah frickin' blah!"

"Jeeze, Sandy! No need to go off all nuclear and bite my head off." Jimmy argued. "It's just that this is one of the most famous stories to ever come out of our nothing high school in the nothing town, is all."

Another girl chimed in, "Yeah, Sandy. Lighten up a bit. Everybody talks about them at prom time. It's like a tradition. You know, it's just the way it is."

"Well, somebody ought to change that tradition." Sandy retorted. "Because frankly, I'm sick of hearing the morbid story of two teenagers who met, fell in love, then tragically died in a car accident all in the same night."

"But it's so romantic," The other girl argued.

"And you forgot to mention the best part of the story, Sandy." Jimmy prompted, "You forgot to mention how every year on prom night, the ghosts of Eric and Ginny return to reenact their fateful night. And how sometimes if the lighting is just right, you can still see them dancing to a slow song only they can hear."

Then a cold chill seemed to collectively radiate throughout the group as they warily looked around the dance floor, hoping not to see what they feared they might see.

SPITTING IMAGE

"Wow, he sure is a hungry little fella." Nurse Wanda Erickson said as she entered the hospital room to find her patient breastfeeding the newborn. Wanda had just started her shift early that morning, and as such, had missed the birth.

The new mother, Cindy Archway, was one of the most strikingly beautiful women Wanda had ever seen. There was something cherubic, almost angelic, about Cindy's face. Even after having given birth just a few hours earlier, the woman looked radiantly stunning. Although Wanda was quite attractive herself, she honestly had never seen a creature as ethereally glowing with beauty as Cindy. She found it amazing and couldn't wait to see her child with a gorgeous mother like that. The baby was destined to be a beauty.

However, since the baby was nursing, all Wanda could see from across the room was the back of the child's wrinkled, bald head poking out of the top of its blanket. She resisted the urge to go closer, as that might be taken as an invasion of her patient's privacy.

"My name is Nurse Erickson, Mrs. Archway, but you can call me Wanda."

"And please, by all means, call me Cindy."

The nurse gave Cindy's chart a cursory glance, noticing the light blue color of the blanket, and said, "Congratulations. I see you had a little boy."

"Yes, I did. We had thought for a time he might have been a girl, but just before the birth, the heartbeat was well in the boy zone."

Wanda loved babies, especially newborns, which was why she had chosen to work in the maternity ward. She never tired of seeing that special bond form between mother and baby. During her thirteen years on the job, she had learned quite a lot and believed she had developed something of a sixth sense regarding both mother and baby's health and well-being.

Unfortunately, to Wanda's surprise, she suddenly realized that her sixth sense was on high alert. For some unknown reason, she felt something was very wrong with the baby; yet the image before her told a completely different story. It was that of a beautiful contented mother feeding her precious newborn. So why in the world did she feel that something was wrong? Perhaps it was the way the boy was lying; she didn't know. But despite the calm, serene look of love on the mother's face, Wanda was certain something was drastically wrong.

"Is everything all right, Mrs. Arch . . . I mean Cindy?" The nurse asked nervously.

"Oh, yes. Most certainly." The mother replied as if in a state of ecstasy. "Everything is perfect. I have my beautiful baby boy and my wonderful handsome husband. Who could possibly ask for more?"

Yet despite the woman's reply, the nurse couldn't shake the strange, unpleasant sensation and decided to try to make some small talk with the hopes that the feeling would pass. "Your little boy; um, what did you name him?"

"We called him Charles Jr. after his daddy. It's the most amazing thing. Even though he's so tiny and new, little Charlie is the spitting image of his father. It's really quite incredible."

"Uh, yeah. That's probably a lot more common than you realize." Wanda said, feeling the need to reply in some way. Her strange nervous perception seemed to be getting worse rather than subsiding, "Um, is your husband here? I wasn't here when you were admitted and haven't met him yet."

"Yes. He was here with me all night. He just left a few seconds ago. He went down to the cafeteria to get some breakfast. It was a long night for both of us. He should be back shortly."

Cindy looked lovingly down at her baby boy and spoke to him in baby talk, "Is you all finished with your num nums, my beautiful wittle sweetie? Do you need a wittle baby burpie?"

With that, she lifted the baby over her shoulder and began to gently pat his back. He was still wrapped tightly in that light blue receiving blanket, and from where she stood, Wanda could still only see the top of his head. After a few seconds, the child let loose with a loud, echoing belch that would have put a drunken longshoreman to shame.

"Oh my." Cindy said lovingly, "My little fella even burps like his Daddy. Isn't that just precious?"

Wanda was taken aback not only by the volume, tone, and intensity of the newborn's belch but the way his mother seemed to take it all in stride. She imagined the woman's husband letting such a belch rip at the dinner table and was quite disturbed if not completely nauseated by the image.

Just then, the receiving blanket slipped down, and for the first time, Wanda learned that her initial fears were justified. She noticed that the baby's head was horribly misshapen, looking like a huge pink peanut, with thin wisps of hair covering it sporadically in places. From her years of experience, she knew there was no way this baby could be what was considered normal. There had to be some sort of brain damage associated with such a malformed skull.

Then, to Wanda's shock and horror, Cindy turned the child around to give her a better view of the baby. A scream caught in her throat, and she was unable to speak. In fact, for a moment, she felt she might not be able to breathe. The child was the most hideous creature she had ever seen.

Besides the deformed appearance of its bizarrely shaped head, the baby's face was horrifying. It had two large, overhanging Neanderthal-like brows; one more than two inches higher than the other. Under the right brow, a huge oversized eyeball jutted outward and seemed to move constantly back and forth as if scanning the room, while under the left brow, the eye socket was practically closed and sloped downward, revealing a barely visible grey-filmed eyeball. The child's nose was twisted off to the right, with a pushed-up front revealing two huge misshapen nostrils. Its mouth was shaped like a sideways teardrop with the large side hanging down to the right. A thin stream of milky-colored drool trickled from the corner. Wanda wanted to shriek at the horrifying sight but somehow managed to muster enough professional willpower to hold back. To her astonishment, her face mustn't have shown the disgust she was feeling because Cindy didn't even seem to notice Wanda's revulsion.

"Isn't he just the sweetest little thing you ever did see?" Cindy asked, beaming with pride. She rubbed her lovely tiny nose against the child's misshapen thing and cooed. "Let's rub noses like the Eskimoses."

"Um, yes, yes. He really is something," Wanda replied lamely.

"Would you like to hold him?" Cindy inquired. This sent an immediate cold chill racing down the nurse's spine. There was no way in Hell she ever wanted to hold that revolting monstrosity. Just seeing the pitiful beast was enough to give her nightmares for months.

"Uh, no. I mean, sorry. I can't. I have to go to see another patient. You can have the, the little angel all to yourself."

Again, Cindy didn't seem to notice Wanda's distress. "No problem, Wanda. That's fine with me. I just didn't want to come across as being too possessive and keeping little Charlie all to myself."

The repugnant baby-thing turned and let go with yet another of its loud, repulsive belches, and a rank stench floated across the room, accosting Wanda's senses. It was revolting, like the reek of a dead creature that had been fermenting on the side of a road for days in the hot August sun. It took all of Wanda's strength not to vomit.

"Oh my!" Cindy exclaimed, "That sure was a loud one, wittle Charlie."

"Well," Wanda said, trying desperately to keep a business-like tone to her voice. I'd better be going." She couldn't wait to get away from that heinous child as quickly as possible. She understood a mother's love, as she was a mother herself, but she was certain if her child had looked so vile, she would have to acknowledge it at least.

Wanda tore her eyes away from the writhing baby-thing and turned to walk out the door. As she did, she bumped into someone in the doorway and had to step back to regain her balance.

"Oh, Charles, you're back." Cindy said from her bed, "This is Nurse Wanda. And look, little Charlie's awake. He just finished nursing."

Wanda stood and stared in shocked silence, her mouth agape. Standing in the doorway was an adult version of the dreadfully ugly baby she had just seen. Same overhanging brow; same bulbous eye; same deformed skull and twisted mouth. The troll stood just a bit over five feet tall and was every bit as hideous as his spawn had been. He smiled an abnormal smile awash with yellowed, crooked teeth, stuck out a gnarled hand, and slurred, "Niish to meet you, Ma'am. I'm Charlesh Alchway."

Reluctantly, Wanda stuck out her hand and grasped the claw-like appendage that served for his hand. It was clammy, and his touch made her nauseous. She had always heard that love was blind, but this had obviously taken that expression to an entirely new level.

She had no idea what it was about this ugly creature that the beautiful Cindy found so appealing. He might have a great personality, or maybe he was rich, but the thought of sharing a bed with something so revolting was beyond Wanda's comprehension. God knew it took all of Wanda's strength just to remain civil and not turn away in disgust.

But despite her shock and misunderstanding, there one thing Wanda did know for certain, and that was that little Charlie was most definitely the spitting image of his father.

THE DRAIN

Ever since Andrew walked into the revolting bathroom, he had a strange feeling something wasn't right. The odd sensation was more than just the uneasy feeling he received from the deplorable condition of the filthy place, with its drab dark red graffiti-covered walls, peeling yellowed ceiling paint, or the rust and urine-stained porcelain troughs. It was even more than the disgusting, vile puddles of God-only-knew-what surrounding the urinals or the stinking reek of the unflushed toilets.

It was as if a fog had begun to settle over his mind, creating an almost dreamlike state. Andrew had been drunk many times before and was fairly certain that that wasn't his current problem, as he hadn't had all that much to drink since arriving at the night club only an hour ago.

He stood washing his hands at a grubby sink, wondering if he would have been better off, not bothering to wash at all, considering the bathroom's unsanitary conditions. This was all Reilly's fault. It was his stupid idea to come to this bar in the first place.

Reilly James was one of Andrew's friends. Although maybe friend was too strong a word. Andrew had actually only recently met Reilly through one of his other friends. Reilly had sort of inserted himself into Andrew's life. "Glom onto" was a more accurate description of the way Reilly had become somehow attached to Andrew. Reilly saw himself as a combination Goth-Punk Rocker type of character, but

Andrew just thought he was an oddball. All things considered, most of Andrew's friends were oddballs in one way or another.

Just before coming into the bathroom, Andrew had been having a discussion with Reilly and several of Reilly's freaky friends about extra-terrestrials. At least, they were trying to but had found it very difficult because of the deafening noise of the God-awful band of mutants who were screaming from the stage. Reilly and his cohorts were apparently believers in UFOs, aliens, Area 51, government alien cover-ups, and the rest of that sort of crap, but Andrew didn't buy into any of it. In his opinion, if he couldn't see, hear, touch, taste, or smell something, it simply didn't exist. And that was the whole enchilada as far as he was concerned.

As his hands drip-dried because there were no paper towels, Andrew made up his mind that he would beat feet and get out of this dump as quickly as possible. Screw Reilly and his conspiracy theorist anarchist buddies, with their innumerable tats and body piercings. This filthy place had pushed him over the edge. He was going to make like a baby and head out.

In fact, he knew he needed to get out into the fresh air to clear his head of this strange dreamy feeling he was suddenly experiencing. He was starting to wonder if maybe one of those weirdoes had slipped him something, but he was certain his drink had never left his sight, and he had downed it quickly, maybe too quickly, now that he thought about it.

That was when Andrew heard a distant scraping sound. It was barely audible over the muffled thumping drums and thundering bass seeping through the concrete walls. He turned around and looked in the direction from which he thought the noise had come. He noticed what appeared to be a drain on the floor.

The grade of the concrete sloped slightly downward toward the opening. Andrew was momentarily grossed out by the thoughts of what all might have flowed down from the disgusting floor. He noticed that a typical thick metal plate didn't cover the drain but instead had a sort of makeshift mesh grate. Probably one of the freaks who frequented this

Hell-hole must have ripped off the old one. Andrew saw the screening was fastened at four locations with screws. It was rusted, torn in places, and coated with some horrible, filthy slime.

Murky water was splashing up through the small holes in the grate, leaving small puddles and dark stains on the worn concrete surrounding the drain. Andrew looked closer and saw what he thought at first might be a lizard or a frog gripping the screening from inside the drain, as water continued to splash up behind it, raising its body and pressing it tightly against the screen's metal surface.

Andrew bent down to see if the creature was still alive and perhaps in distress, even though he wasn't thrilled with the idea of getting any closer to the foul-smelling drain. He had a penknife in his pocket equipped with a screwdriver blade that, if necessary, might be used to remove the screening. Andrew shivered with disgust at the thought. Then he saw the creature move slightly as he reluctantly kneeled to get a closer look. The thing was alive. The strange sensation he was experiencing inside his head suddenly became stronger.

Then to his horror, Andrew saw that the tiny hands gripping the wire mesh were not reptilian as he had assumed but appeared to be almost human, or at least human-like. They had long thin fingers, with knuckle joints and miniature long fingernails. The sensation inside Andrew's head grew even stronger, and he began to feel as if someone were trying to speak to him through his mind.

Andrew suddenly realized the creature in the drain was actually a small man of sorts, no more than seven or eight inches tall. The miniature humanoid was naked and hairless, and when its face rose to look through the screen, Andrew noticed its eyes were not human but were bulging and fly-like, with thousands of facets. It did, however, appear to have a humanoid nose, ears, and lips. It opened its mouth wide and let out a silent scream of terror that reverberated inside Andrew's mind like an ear-piercing howl. It was then he saw numerous rows of tiny, razor-sharp teeth inside the thing's open maw.

Then, another thought suddenly appeared in his mind, and Andrew realized the creature feared for its life and was somehow calling to him desperately asking for his help. But all of this was impossible; he was sure. He didn't believe in telepathy or any of that mumbo-jumbo. But he realized somehow was actually seeing the strange creature and was really hearing its thoughts.

He couldn't explain it, but it was as real as anything he had ever experienced in his life. And now he understood there was something else in the filthy water of the drain, somewhere below the creature. And this tiny man was terrified of whatever it was. The stench coming up from the drain was unlike anything Andrew had ever smelled before. The thing clinging to the screen kept turning to look back down into the murk while alternately looking up at Andrew, still sending its mental pleas for help.

Without taking any more time to try to rationalize what he was witnessing, Andrew took his penknife from his pocket, pulled out the screwdriver blade, and began to loosen the screws. As he managed almost to unscrew the first of four screws, he heard the creature in the drain begin to scream louder inside his skull. Then it thrashed about as if something had grabbed it. Whatever was in the black water below began to pull the terrified creature down into the murk. Andrew could see the screening strain as the creature struggled to hold on. He quickly switched to his knife blade and began to cut at the screen. He could see the creature's right hand still holding desperately onto the screen.

He managed to cut a section of the screen and bend it backward. Against his better judgment, he was about to reach down into the slimy liquid to try to grab the poor creature when he noticed that the section of bent screening now held the severed arm of the tiny creature. It had apparently been ripped from its body by whatever had pulled it down to its death. The voice he had heard inside his head was now gone, but the strange feeling was still there and actually seemed to be growing stronger once again.

He decided his best bet now was to stand up and get the hell out of this terrible place, but when he tried to do so, he realized he couldn't move. Somehow, he had become paralyzed as if every muscle in his body had suddenly become useless. He was still bent over, looking down into the drain through the ripped open screening.

Andrew saw something coming up slowly from the blackness of the opening. At first, he thought it might be the remains of the tiny creature floating up to the surface, but he was wrong. The foul stench of the water inside had suddenly grown even more revolting, and Andrew saw something black, shiny, and slime-covered slowly coming up out of the darkness of the drain.

As it reached the concrete, it seemed to flatten out like some sort of gelatinous, oily substance and began to inch its way toward him. In his mind, Andrew began to see visions of distant planets and unknown galaxies, things he seldom, if ever thought of before. And there was another thought, much stronger than the others; the thought of an insatiable hunger about to be satisfied.

He saw the black slime crawling up onto his hand and covering all of his fingers. He heard a sizzling sound and could smell something burning, realizing suddenly that it was his own bubbling flesh. At that same instant, he felt incredible pain surging up his arm and throughout his body. He wanted to scream but was unable to raise as much as a whimper. He saw the liquefied flesh of his hand drip from his now exposed bones like candlewax. His bones began to smolder, then smoke, and were turning to dust before his eyes.

The black sludge was now creeping up both of his arms and slowly dissolving him inch by agonizing inch. In between the mental screams of his own pain, he sensed the complete satisfaction of whatever sort of unimaginable alien horror was devouring him alive. Yes, he realized it was an alien creature, something from another world. Reilly and his stupid friends had been right after all. But it no longer mattered, since within a few short minutes, the pain was gone, the creature was gone, and Andrew was gone.

///

"Yo, Andy!" A voice shouted from the doorway. It was Reilly, looking for his new friend.

He glanced around the disgusting bathroom and exclaimed. "Damn, this place is a toilet." Then he chuckled, realizing the irony of what he had just said.

As he closed the door to leave, he said, "Man, I would have sworn I saw him come in here. I wonder where the hell he got to."

SURVIVOR

"Oh, I'm a survivor. My whole life has been surviving."
—EDDIE BRACKEN

"Loneliness is my least favorite thing about life. The thing that
I'm most worried about is just being alone without anybody
to care for or someone who will care for me."
—ANNE HATHAWAY

The old man sat on the cool concrete bench, staring down at his feet.
He was wearing canvas sneakers and no socks. He could see his bare
ankles and realized he was in shorts, which seemed right for such a
warm day, but he couldn't recall putting them on or even driving the
thirty miles required to sit here alone. Yet here he was. It surprised him
at how young his legs still looked for a man of seventy-five years old.
Maybe they were a bit thinner and not as tan as perhaps they should
be, but all in all, not too bad for an old guy.

The bench was one of the dozens scattered about the walkways
of the outdoor shopping center. This particular place had been constructed to resemble an old-time small town, with street lights, brick
walkways, ornate storefronts, and the whole deal. It claimed to be
an outlet center for many high-end manufacturers, although Henry
doubted the prices reflected the discounts one would expect in a true

outlet center. The place was far too grand and the overhead expenses obviously too high to assure such discounts. He knew this shopping center well and knew they specialized in women's clothing since about ninety-nine percent of the stores were of that variety. That was why Maggie had loved it so much.

During moments of solitude in a place such as this, Henry often contemplated how uncertain and perhaps fickle the world was regarding shopping practices. When he was a boy in the 1940s, everyone did their shopping in small towns. Then, as the years passed and people moved out to the sprawling suburbs, suddenly malls and shopping centers began to pop up, and small-town businesses began to die away. Then, in the early part of the twenty-first century, these new types of shopping centers began to appear, which resembled small towns, only they weren't really small towns because no one actually lived there.

Maggie had always hated it when Henry mentioned things like that. She'd call him an old fuddy-duddy, saying he had to accept the changes that life brought and move on. This particular shopping center had been one of Maggie's favorites. In fact, the bench where he was presently sitting was the same one where he often sat, people-watching as he waited for Maggie to complete her shopping. Usually, he'd go to one of the snack kiosks and buy a soft pretzel and a soda so he could nibble while he passed the time. And how the time had passed, much quicker than he had realized. He shook his head of thin grey hair in sad resolution and stared down at the ground. All around him, he could hear the people moving about, laughing, talking, looking down at their cell phones, and shopping. But he didn't feel like people-watching today. He didn't know if he ever would again.

No, Henry realized that wasn't true. He wished to God it were true, but he knew the exact opposite would be his reality at some point in the future. And that thought bothered him more than words could ever express. It would be like trying to describe the hollow, empty feeling in the center of his chest where his heart used to be. Henry was a survivor. He both understood and hated that about himself. He didn't want to survive, he didn't want to live, yet he knew he would because that was who he was.

In his early years, Henry had made it through a devastating divorce that for a time he was certain was going to kill him. He foolishly believed at the age of thirty-three that his life was over, and he'd never find another woman to love. He was convinced he was destined to be alone forever. The pain and loneliness had become so great that at one low point, he had even had a passing thought of ending it all, anything to make the pain stop. That was when he learned he truly was a survivor, and pain or no pain, he didn't have it in him to simply give up. A few years later, he met his beloved Maggie, and after a year of dating, they were married. Henry soon learned what it really meant to love and to be loved in return.

Maggie had been the one true love of his life, and over the past thirty-five years, she had become much more than that; she had become part of him. When they had taken their wedding vows, the minister had told them they were no longer individuals, but a new single entity formed from their mutual love. And that was what they had become.

Then a year ago, Maggie became sick. He could still hear that single word the doctor had spoken echoing in his brain. "Cancer." Then a month ago, after a year of suffering, Maggie died. And now here he sat in the middle of what was once her favorite shopping center staring at his feet and wanting nothing more than to die and be with her once again. But he knew he wouldn't die because like it or not, he was a survivor. He was alone and wanted nothing more than to be alone for the rest of his life until it was time to join his precious Maggie.

He missed her more than he could ever put into words, but he wasn't afraid of being alone. He was, by nature, a solitary sort of person. He and Maggie would often sit together for hours, not needing to say anything for long periods of time, just content to be together. As a result, Henry would gladly spend what remaining years he had sitting alone and remembering all the wonderful times he and Maggie had shared. However, what he feared the most was just the opposite.

He knew well the expression "time heals all wounds," and that saying terrified him. He didn't want his wounds to heal, he didn't want the world to be right again, ever, and more than anything, he wanted it all to end. But simply wishing it wouldn't make it happen. He knew someday he'd wake up and realize that was the day he would begin to start rebuilding his life over again. He dreaded that day. He feared someday he might very possibly fall in love again and maybe even remarry, and that thought sickened him. How could he possibly do such a thing to the memory of his beloved Maggie? During their years of marriage, he had never once even been tempted to cheat on her, and the idea of starting over with someone new someday was more than he could bear.

So why was he here? Why did he unconsciously drive thirty miles to come to Maggie's favorite shopping center? And now what was he supposed to do? Should he continue to just sit and do nothing? All day? Should he go back home? To what? His house was an empty echoing shell of what it had once been. Then he realized it didn't matter what he did. Nothing mattered to him anymore. He was like a rudderless raft, adrift in a gigantic ocean with no land in sight. Maggie had been that rudder, and now she was gone. He was just floating aimlessly through life now. What little remained of his broken heart ached with incredible sorrow. God, how he missed his Maggie.

Then he felt something strange, as if he was being watched. He lifted his head, looking out through the crowd of shoppers, and he saw her. It was Maggie, his Maggie, standing in the morning sun smiling at him. And it wasn't the gaunt skeleton of a wife who had been ravaged by that dreaded disease, but it was Maggie as she had appeared before she became ill. She was happy, healthy, and smiling at him.

Suddenly all of the shoppers seemed to vanish, leaving only Henry on his bench and his wonderful wife standing down the lane waiting for him. It had always been like that for Henry. When Maggie entered the room and smiled at him, everyone else seemed to vanish. Yet how could this be? How could his Maggie be here? He didn't know, didn't understand, and didn't care. All that mattered was that she was here.

Henry stood up from his bench and began walking toward his wife. The empty hole where his heart had been begun to fill with joy, the same joy he had always experienced when he looked into his loving wife's beautiful eyes. Moments later, he was in her arms again, feeling the mutual love flowing between them like before, and nothing else mattered.

Then he heard a commotion coming from behind him and turned to see a crowd of people gathered around the bench where he had been sitting. Some had looks of worry on their faces. One woman had a cell phone to her ear and was speaking frantically into the thing. He couldn't hear what she was saying, but he could tell she was frightened. A space opened between the crowd, and Henry saw his own body slumped, apparently lifeless on the bench.

"Yes." Henry thought, "Good. Now I can be with Maggie again at last."

He suddenly heard the sound of an approaching siren. He saw an electric golf cart of sorts painted white with bright red crosses and the words "Rescue Unit" stenciled on its doors.

"No." Henry shouted to the unhearing rescue workers who were already attending to his body, trying to resuscitate him, "Don't save me. Please."

He turned to look at his beautiful wife and, to his horror, saw that her smile had vanished, replaced by a look of heartbreaking sadness. She was moving, floating away from him. Then he realized it wasn't her who was moving, but it was he who was floating backward toward his body.

"No." He screamed. "Please, no." He didn't want to go back. He wanted to stay with his Maggie.

Henry opened his eyes and looked into the faces of the two rescue workers who had just brought him back from the dead. What had they done? Saved his life? No, they had saved him from nothing.

He heard one of the workers say to the other, "Thank goodness this old guy is such a fighter. He's a real survivor."

Henry turned his head to look out at the place where Maggie had been, but she was gone. The hollow, empty feeling had returned, and with sad resignation, he realized both he and the rescue workers were right; he was a survivor.

THE GATEWAY

"Explanation separates us from astonishment, which is the only
gateway to the incomprehensible."
—EUGENE IONESCO

"The mind is its own place and in itself, can make a Heaven of
Hell, a Hell of Heaven."
—JOHN MILTON

It appeared to be a gateway of sorts, comprised of an incredible rectangular arch-like framework made from enormous trees' trunks. There
were two vertical columns about six feet around rising perhaps forty
feet in the air, supporting a massive cross member which spanned the
twenty-foot wide opening between the two vertical columns. At first,
Salazar thought the two verticals had been sunken deep into the earth,
but he was mistaken. They were actually two huge trees rooted in the
ground, and only the uppermost branches remained. These branches
had grown around and, in some places, had actually fused into the
huge cross member holding it securely in place. He had no idea how
the massive trunk had gotten forty feet in the air because the thing had
to weigh tons.

Salazar wondered what the purpose of this opening had been, and more importantly, why he was now standing in front of it. He did not know how he had gotten to this place. He was a man of countless phobias, and being lost in strange and unfamiliar surroundings was just one of them. Fortunately, this was not his worst fear, but it was well into the top ten.

He couldn't see beyond the opening, as there was a bright luminescent haze blocking his view. He suddenly had a feeling of déjà vu, as if what was happening to him, or at least something similar had happened to him before, yet he couldn't remember a single detail.

Since all around him was nothing but darkness, he felt compelled to step closer and see what lay beyond the opening. One of his other fears was fear of the dark. As a result, the blackness on three sides of him became very upsetting, making the luminescent fog, although ominous, seem at least slightly more inviting. He took a step forward to look more closely at the huge tree on the right side of the gateway. It wasn't comprised of rough bark as he'd expected but seemed to be made of something of a very smooth texture. Salazar reached out cautiously with his right hand and let his palm gently rest against the strange surface.

An icy chill instantly raced down his spine as he realized what he was touching felt like human flesh, not warm and living flesh, but what he suspected cold and dead flesh might feel like. He had never touched a corpse in his life, as he had an aversion to both dead bodies as well as funeral homes in general. Yet he instinctively sensed what he was feeling would be very much akin to dead human flesh.

Again, he experienced a slight familiarity, but nothing he could pinpoint. As his fingers rested against the surface, he felt something moving. Looking closer at the fleshy bark, he saw it beginning to pulsate, and for the first time, he could see something crawling below the undulating skin.

He wanted to pull his hand away in disgust but was transfixed by what he was seeing. On the tree's fleshy surface above where his hand was positioned, letters began to slowly rise from the undulating skin. These letters first formed words, which became a cryptic phrase that somehow seemed familiar to him. It read, "As it is, it was and ever will be, again and again for eternity."

"What a bizarre message." Salazar thought in confusion. He realized it was actually a poem of sorts, or perhaps just a line from some work he had read once years earlier. Maybe it had been something biblical. He couldn't recall.

After a moment, he noticed an area between his thumb and forefinger, where the fleshy surface was beginning to expand outward. A small hole appeared in the skin, and the head of a worm-like insect with a tiny, sharp mandible poked out of the opening. Salazar had not only a fear of worms and insects but revulsion for the creatures as well. Before he had a chance to pull away, the thing's horrible pincers grasped onto the flap of skin between his fingers and bit down hard. An unbelievable bolt of pain shot from his hand up to his arm and seemed to explode inside his brain.

Salazar finally pulled his hand away in disgust and backed away from the tree, shaking his hand wildly, trying to get the accursed thing off. He reached over with his left hand and grabbed the creature by its squirming hind end. Knowing somehow that the thing was just a second away from burrowing into his flesh, Salazar yanked the thing away from his hand, tearing out a chunk of skin in the process. Then he threw the thing far into the bank of mist and heard the thing screaming as if in agony as it flew.

He instinctively put the wounded area into his mouth, expecting to sense the coppery taste of his blood but instead coming away with the tang of something vile, repugnant, and unidentifiable. He spat the putrid substance onto the ground. Although he couldn't see the surface, he was standing on because of the penetrating mist swirling about his feet, he would have sworn he heard his own spittle squealing and scurrying away as the insect had done. He worried that the substance might be some sort of venom that would shut down his ability to breathe.

Suffocating was probably one of Salazar's greatest fears, next to the fear of heights and fear of drowning.

Salazar began to wonder. Was he asleep and having some sort of horrendous nightmare? He didn't believe this to be the case, but then again, who really knows they're dreaming, when in fact, they are? The fiery pain he felt in his hand, which was now shooting up his left arm, was certainly real enough. And it didn't seem to be subsiding. If anything, it felt as if it might be getting worse.

In his clouded mind, he was still uncertain whether he should try to pass into the glowing gateway. He was afraid of what might await him in the fog, but the blackness surrounding him was unnerving. Then he suddenly heard a deep guttural growling noise coming from behind him. He could not see anything, but he could hear deep breathing, and the unremitting growling was now getting ever closer. It sounded huge and just as dangerous. He was terrified of wild animals, and after what he had just experienced with the strange maggot-like creature, he didn't want to confront whatever might be approaching from behind.

Then he heard a rumble and felt the ground beneath his feet began to quake. To his shock, Salazar saw that both trees were somehow impossibly moving closer together, pushing up mounds of dirt before them. He looked down and saw the roots had begun to move like dozens of thin creeping legs. He glanced up and saw the massive cross member was coming rapidly downward. If he stayed where he was, he would be crushed.

Seeing no other alternative, he jumped through the gateway and into the mysterious vapor, losing his footing and falling onto the thankfully soft soil. He rolled, trying to protect his aching left arm. Then he stood up, dusted himself off as best he could, then began to walk deeper into the mist. After a few steps, he found himself completely engulfed in the strange fog. He no longer heard the menacing growling behind him. Looking back, he couldn't see the gateway, just more of the glowing mist. It was as if passing through the entrance, which he thought had been just a few feet behind him, had somehow put him into a place, somewhere perhaps miles from where he had previously been. He understood this instinctively but couldn't comprehend how that could be possible. Again, there was that faint sense of familiarity.

He noticed that his skin immediately began to tingle, as the strange haze seemed to cling to his flesh like a glove of moisture. He felt it on his hand, arms, and face. He noticed the fiery feeling had left his hand and arm, but a dull pain remained. Then he could feel the strange stinging from the fog on his legs and chest as well. Salazar reached down to touch his shirt and was shocked to discover he was completely naked. He knew he had just been fully clothed a second earlier when he dusted himself off, but now he was as naked as the day he was born. His entire body was tingling, feeling as if the mist was working its way through every pore in his body, crawling deep inside him. He thought about the maggot-creature and shuddered with disgust. Was this strange fog just another form of living thing trying to work its way inside him?

He began to walk slowly and reluctantly forward, deeper into the luminescent fog, not because he wanted to do so but because he felt as if he were being drawn inward for some unknown purpose. He looked down and couldn't see his feet since everything from his chest down was shrouded by the mist.

Salazar suddenly felt a shortness of breath and discovered that the air felt thick, hot, and heavy, making deep breathing almost impossible. Was this caused by the density of the fog, or had that strange mist actually entered his body, surrounded his lungs, and begun to suffocate him? He could feel his panic beginning to rise. There was a disgusting stench to the place now, something dank and fishy, perhaps even sulfurous and rotten. His panic piqued as he suddenly realized he could no longer breathe at all. He felt like a drowning man fearful of taking a deep breath, knowing his lungs would fill with the vile liquid air.

Finally, realizing his lungs were burning for oxygen, he had no alternative. His fear of suffocating was now more real than it had ever been. He opened his mouth, expecting to be smothered by the soupy atmosphere, but to his surprise, he was suddenly able to breathe once again; the air was still vile, hot, stinking, and humid, making his breathing labored, but at least he was alive.

After a few dozen arduous steps, he stopped suddenly, hearing a series of strange chittering and squealing noises like those made by small animals. A moment later, his blood turned to ice as he felt something brush past his bare ankles. It had only touched him for a millisecond, but in that brief moment, Salazar got a very good idea of what the thing might have been. He had felt stiff, fiery hot bristly hairs, which simultaneously felt impossibly slimy with moisture, likely from the fog. He couldn't comprehend how something could feel so hot yet still feel as if it had been coated with a thick liquid. His ankles began to burn as his hand had done earlier, then the pain began to climb up his legs. Soon it had spread throughout his entire body, and his brain felt as if it were boiling inside his skull. Then, just a quickly, the pain subsided, and his body was wracked with icy chills.

He wondered what sort of creature was capable of inflicting so much agony so quickly. From that minimal contact, he determined the creature had to be about three feet long and about ten inches tall. An image of a large flaming napalm-covered rat-like creature appeared in his mind, and he suddenly trembled from head to toe. Perhaps from fear, perhaps from the icy chill that was finally starting to subside.

He heard what sounded like dozens of these creatures and perhaps others even more revolting scurrying about the ground all around him. Images appeared in his mind of giant deformed multi-headed lizards, unbelievably long flame-spitting snakes, and spiders as large as men with the ability to shoot webbing that not only captured their prey, but which contained an acid-like substance to melt flesh from bone. He had to move on quickly. But just before he did, the words from the poem on the tree came back to him, "As it is, it was and ever will be, again and again for eternity."

He walked on a few steps more, wanting to put some distance between himself and the strange creatures, not knowing if he was actually leaving one bad situation and walking into another, but not seeing how he had any choice. Soon the strange noises died down, and he recognized they were far behind him. He suddenly felt a cool, wet crunching sensation under his feet and realized he had left the roadway and had found his way onto some surface that felt like tall cool grass. Up ahead, the light seemed brighter, and Salazar noticed the mist was blessedly dissipating. Moments later, he found himself standing in a brightly sunlit grassy meadow. Most of the pain and burning had left both his hand and his legs. He looked behind him and could see the bank of fog, which he had just passed through. For the first time since coming into this bizarre place, he felt he might be somewhere at least somewhat normal.

When he turned to look forward once again, he was shocked to see something he hadn't expected to see. Then again, in such an inexplicable world like this one, what should he really have expected to see? Standing low in the grass in front of him was a huge land tortoise, more than five feet long and four feet across, of the sort he had seen in wildlife documentaries as a kid. The thing had a massive head that was staring up at Salazar with a look that he could only be described as both curious and surprisingly intelligent. Maybe Salazar was personifying the creature based on cartoons he had seen as a child where aged creatures such as this were often portrayed as having great wisdom.

Feeling not in the least bit foolish—and why should he if he was actually dreaming anyway?—Salazar looked down at the creature and asked, "What do you want me to see?" He had no idea where that question had come from or why he thought the tortoise had wanted him to see something. He just had a strange sort of understanding appear in his mind, which told him that was why the tortoise was there.

The ancient tortoise looked up at him, and suddenly inside his mind, Salazar heard an old raspy voice say, "As it is, it was and ever will be, again and again for eternity." Then it slowly pulled its head, legs, and tail into the shell. For a moment, Salazar thought nothing else would happen.

Then impossibly, the top half of the tortoise's massive shell became transparent as if it had been constructed of a glass dome of some sort. Inside, Salazar could see perhaps a dozen baby tortoises milling about.

These little ones were without the benefit of shells, just small pink crawling creatures with tiny tortoise heads and beaks.

At first, Salazar thought them quite cute until he looked closer and saw what the creatures were feeding on. There, in the center of the transparent shell, was a kitten. It was obviously dead and flyblown with hundreds of maggots crawling about its ripped-open stomach. The tiny tortoises were taking turns tearing off chunks of flesh, fur, and innards and devouring them raw. In his mind, Salazar heard high pitch chittering noises similar to what he had heard in the fog. Salazar couldn't remember ever reading about turtles being anything but herbivores, and as such, was revolted by the sight. Moments later, the transparency disappeared, and the shell returned to normal; the huge tortoise poked out its head and feet, then turned and started to walk slowly away.

In shock, Salazar stumbled backward in the meadow a few steps until suddenly, the ground behind him opened up, and he fell into a massive sinkhole. His arms and legs flailed uselessly in the air as he tried desperately to grasp onto something to stop his inevitable fall. He had always feared falling to his death, but instead of slamming against the solid ground and dying, he landed with a splash in a deep pool of ice-cold water.

As he sank deeper into the water, Salazar struggled to swim upward. He realized not only was he now fully clothed once again, but he was bundled in several layers of shirts, pants, and heavy coats, all of which had become sodden with water. The additional weight was pulling him further downward with every passing second. Once more, he could feel his lungs burning with the need to breathe, but unlike the thick atmosphere, this was icy water, and he knew if he attempted to breathe, he would most definitely drown.

Just when he knew he wouldn't be able to hold his breath for another second, Salazar landed on the hard floor of the water hole with a thud, pushing all of the remaining air from his lungs. To his shock, he looked about him and saw he was no longer underwater, but was sitting on the floor of a large room, perhaps thirty feet square. He was once again wearing his original clothing, none of which was wet or even the slightest bit damp. This dream was getting stranger all the time, and he wished he could wake himself up.

He looked about the room and saw it wasn't so much a room as it was a large elevator with two doors, typical of such a device, positioned at what he assumed to be the front. However, there were no buttons to select any desired floor, nor were there any lights to identify floor location. He felt a slight motion, and the elevator began to move. By the downward pressure he was feeling, Salazar believed he was moving up at an incredibly rapid rate.

The elevator seemed to go on forever until finally, it stopped. Salazar stood clumsily on wobbly legs. Before the doors opened, a message began to scroll across a light bar, which had just appeared above the door. The message said, "As it is, it was and ever will be, again and again for eternity." It was the same message he had been receiving since coming to this strange place. The doors slowly began to open, revealing nothing but complete blackness outside. He knew there was no way he was going to step out into that blackness.

At the same time, the wall behind Salazar began to move forward, pushing against his back and forcing him out through the doors into the black void. He had no idea what awaited him out there, but his fear of heights and falling into open space was running rampant. The back wall pushed him ever closer to the black void beyond the doorway. Before he realized it, he was standing out in the darkness. To his surprise, he appeared to be on solid ground.

He took about five apprehensive steps forward with his hands extended out in front of him to feel in the blackness for any obstructions. A few steps later, his hand touched something cold and solid, forcing him to stop. He looked back over his shoulder and saw no sign of the elevator behind him. All that surrounded him was more blackness.

Suddenly the area around him was illuminated with blinding white light, and Salazar raised his hands to protect his eyes. Slowly, he removed his hands and was instantly paralyzed with terror. He found himself standing on a circle of ground no more than twelve inches in diameter, atop a cropping of stone that had to be several hundred feet above the ground. He didn't want to look down but had no choice. All around him was a vast canyon of immeasurable size, with hundreds of similar outcrops far below him. The ground behind him had fallen away, leaving him stranded.

But even if he hadn't been too terrified to move, these outcroppings were too far away to do him any good. To make matters worse, giant pillars of flames suddenly began to spring up all around him, and Salazar could hear the moans and wails of what sounded like a million tortured souls, all writhing in agony somewhere deep within those flames.

Then he understood. This was Hell, his own personal version of Hell. He was about to be forced to join the ranks of the tortured dead. He had thought he led a good life, but apparently, he hadn't. At the instant of this understanding, the pain in his legs returned with a vengeance. The phrase, the poem, suddenly flashed into his mind again, "As it is, it was and ever will be, again and again for eternity." Then he lost his balance, teetered for a moment, then fell down, down into the scorching flames.

He opened his eyes and saw what appeared to be a gateway of sorts, comprised of an incredible rectangular arch-like framework made from the trunks of enormous trees. He had a feeling of déjà vu as if what was happening to him or something very similar, or perhaps a slightly different version of events might have happened to him before, yet he couldn't recall.

WALLFLOWER

The teenage girl stared at her aunt with growing fury. The room was in silence, save for the antique grandfather clock's ticking in the adjacent hall.

Then, unable to hold her anger any longer, the girl shouted, "I don't care what you say. I'm not going to any stupid dance!"

Her Aunt Doris returned her hateful stare and with equal venom and insisted, "Admit it, Daisy. We both know it's way beyond the time for you to get out there and introduce yourself to the world. You're sixteen years old now, young lady, almost seventeen, for God's sake. What's the matter with you, anyway?"

Daisy Lynn Durfmann and her aunt were arguing yet again. This time the argument was about Daisy's attending the upcoming "Welcome Spring" gala at her high school. More often than not, the two headstrong women found themselves at each other's throats regularly, although even at the best of times, their relationship had never been a good one.

Despite her confrontational attitude around her aunt, in public, Daisy was a shy and introverted young woman with very few friends. Until this point in her young life, Daisy had never attended a single school dance and didn't intend to do so now. The idea of being at a dance with boys was beyond her comprehension.

Being timid by nature, Daisy could always be counted on to say whatever was expected of her in public, but in the privacy of her mind, her thoughts often told a different story. Daisy suspected she might have inherited this trait from her mother, although she couldn't remember her mother. Both of her parents had been killed in a head-on collision when she was only a toddler. The child had somehow managed to survive the wreck, and her unmarried Aunt Doris had been saddled with the responsibility of raising the young girl.

Doris was an odd sort of woman in her own right, wavering between kindly aunt and demented she-devil. During the early years when she had been raising Daisy, it wasn't uncommon for Doris to verbally berate and even physically abuse the child. And young Daisy never understood what she had done to deserve such treatment. On any random day, Doris could be kind and caring one minute and then a raving lunatic the next. Daisy learned early on, not to trust her aunt. And each year, her hatred for the woman grew.

Apparently, today Doris was in one of her "kindly aunt" moods and was attempting to get on Daisy's good side but failing miserably. This was because, unknown to Doris, Daisy had a very special secret and knew a lot more than her aunt realized.

"But Daisy. You can be such a pretty girl when you let yourself be. You just have to take a little time to fix yourself up." Doris said.

However, what Doris thought was, *"No matter how hard you try, you'll never be as pretty as your mother was at your age. Damn her for dying and dumping you on me. Although I have to admit she may have been better looking than I was, the boys loved me more because I knew how to make them happy. I wasn't as stuck up as she was. And you have no right to be so picky yourself, girly. You're practically flat-chested, you're round-shouldered and look so depressed and sullen most of the time like you have the weight of the world bearing down on you. I don't know what's wrong with you."*

"Look, Daisy. Why not let me buy you a nice dress? You can take off your glasses, put on a little makeup, and we can even do something special with your hair."

"Easy for me to say. Sheesh! I may have to fork out some serious cash if I'm going to successfully turn this homely little cave troll into something even the ugliest of boys would give a second glance. I'll certainly have my work cut out for me."

In truth, Daisy really was a pretty girl on those rare occasions when she appeared happy and smiling. She had a natural, wholesome loveliness, which even didn't need makeup under the right circumstances. But she never wore any expression close to happy around her aunt. To make matters worse, for the past several months, Daisy had fallen into an extremely dark place mentally. As a result, she now did everything she could to play down her looks and keep boys disinterested in her.

The fact was, she wasn't flat-chested at all and had quite an ample bosom, but she wore clothing that hid that feature. She likewise wore her hair long and straight with absolutely no style whatsoever. She only bothered to wash it every two days or so, and as a result, it appeared greasy most of the time. Her glasses were thick and unfashionable, and she went out of her way to find dresses that did nothing to flatter her figure. Daisy walked through the halls at school with her head down, and her books clutched tightly to her chest in order to avoid eye contact with any of her fellow students.

She enjoyed being alone with her thoughts and her books. And despite her aunt's constant suggestions to the contrary, Daisy was never lonely. She had her stories and her imagination. She also had a special gift, which neither her aunt nor anyone else knew anything about. It had only appeared several months earlier. However, the insights this gift provided were a double-edged sword and were largely responsible for her sullen moods.

"No, Aunt Doris. My dresses are fine. My hair is fine. I'm fine. I don't like makeup, and I don't want to go to any stupid dance! I'm not like you, Aunt Doris. I'm not some sort of social butterfly."

Daisy thought, *"No, I'm absolutely not like you, Doris. And if I can help it, I'll never be like you. Because I don't want to ever be you. You go to the hairdresser every week and change your hairstyle and color each time. For God's sake, Doris! You're in your mid-forties, and you still dress like a*

*wild teenager. You change your men as often as your hair color and have
never had any long term relationships work out for you."*

"But Daisy. You need to go out and meet some boys. You need to
get out there and start dating."

*"No, Doris. I don't need to date at all, and you need to date one hell of
a lot less. How many different 'uncles' did I have growing up, Doris? How
many different men lived here with us at one time or another before you
eventually threw each of them out? Did you think I was an idiot? Did you
think I wouldn't notice; that I couldn't figure out what was going on? For
the love of God, Doris, how could I possibly have so many uncles? Do you
really think I was that stupid?"*

"I just don't have any interest in dating." Daisy said, "There aren't
any boys that I know who I'd want to date or who would want to date
me."

"But surely there must be some boy you fancy at school, Daisy;
maybe just one."

*"Is that what you call it, Doris? Fancy? Do I have a fancy for a boy? Is
that what you called it back when you were my age and when you spread
your legs for all those boys who had their way with you, then dumped you
like garbage? My, yes, I'll just bet that was quite a fancy."*

"No, Aunt Doris. There's not a single one I care for. Besides, Miss
Newman, our church youth group leader, says teenage boys are evil
tools of Satan."

"That sounds exactly like something 'No-Man Newman' would
say. Why do you even listen to that wicked old maid, Daisy?"

Doris thought, *"Old maid, hell. That ancient dried-up old sow is a
diesel dyke if I ever saw one. She's probably got her sights set on Daisy and
all the other girls as well."*

"Don't you dare accuse Miss Newman's of being a lesbian, Aunt
Doris, because she's not."

"What, Daisy? What was that you said? I never said anything about
her being a lesbian. Why would you think I said that?"

*"You may not have said it, Doris, but you thought it. And I heard
every single word. I always do now, every word you think, clear as a bell.*

But I slipped up there for a moment, didn't I? I don't want you to know my little secret. I'd better play the timid little girl you expect me to be so you don't get too suspicious."

"Um, no. You called her 'No-man Newman' and um, I assumed you meant, I mean, I could tell by your expression that was what you were thinking."

"Don't you dare put words in my mouth, Daisy Lynn Durfmann. I never would say such a thing."

"Alright, Aunt Doris. I won't." Daisy said, feigning contrition.

"But I don't need to put words in your mouth, do I? Because you've already thought those words, and I can hear what you're thinking. You might want to keep things close to the vest, but I hear the truth."

Daisy decided it would be better to let things stand where they were for the time being. These arguments always seemed to escalate on the verge of going out of control, and with her feeling abnormally angry of late, it was probably best to just walk away from this encounter before things got really bad. So Daisy sat down on the sofa and began reading a paperback.

Doris looked strangely at her niece and suddenly felt an icy chill race down her spine as gooseflesh crept along her arms. Had she been imaging things? Had it just been a coincidence? Or did Daisy actually just read her thoughts? Daisy was always a strange girl, and it wouldn't surprise Doris if she did have such a freakish ability.

She thought back to her sister, Daisy's mother. Back to her teen years when her body began to change, and her hormones were running rampant. Hadn't there been a time when she thought her sister might be able to hear what other people were thinking? Or had she just imagined that too? Had her sister just been perceptive of facial movements, voice inflections, and body language?

She recalled a few incidents that might have been construed as a bit strange. And since Doris had wanted to be the popular girl in school, she made sure she did everything she could to suppress any rumors about her sister's peculiarities.

Maybe Daisy had recently discovered her own hidden ability. And maybe her gift was much stronger than her mother's had ever been. She looked down distrustfully at her niece. She didn't need any sort of freakish stuff like this to come between them. As things were, they argued almost every day.

Doris had stopped pretending to love the girl long ago and was just trying to have some sort of peaceful coexistence until the day the wretched creature would graduate and hopefully move away. Doris knew she could no longer get away with smacking the girl around, not since that time a year ago, when Daisy struck back harder than Doris would have imagined possible.

At the moment, Daisy seemed to be absorbed in her book and was no longer paying any attention to Doris. But Doris had a strange feeling Daisy was "listening." Sometimes, Doris felt that Daisy might hate her as much as Doris despised Daisy, perhaps enough to do her harm someday. The girl never said such things aloud; still, there was something. Maybe Doris actually had a bit of her sister's special incite. She decided to try an experiment to see if she could get a response from the odd girl.

"Can you hear me, Daisy?"

The girl remained silently reading her book, not giving the slightest hint that she might have heard Doris' thoughts.

"Thank goodness you can't, Daisy. I don't know what I'd have to do you if I truly believed you could read my mind. I can't imagine living in the same house with some sort of freak monitoring my every thought. And I'd have to worry about what you already discovered about my personal life, especially when my men friends come over. I don't think I could live with knowing you were eavesdropping on my most intimate thoughts. I'd have to do something."

Daisy flinched ever so slightly, but it went unnoticed. She continued to pretend to read her book.

"I just don't understand, Daisy, why you can't be more normal, like me. But that shouldn't surprise me, should it? You've been weird, different

since birth. Sometimes you make me so angry that I wish your mother had aborted you, or maybe even suffocated you at birth and tossed your tiny body in a dumpster. Yes, that probably would have been better. God knows my life would have been a lot easier."

Daisy was growing angrier by the second and struggled not to let her anger show. She couldn't believe what her Aunt was thinking. She didn't ask for this ability; it just showed up. But now that it was here, she was both disturbed yet thankful. She now knew things about what her Aunt felt about her, things she would have never previously imagined were possible. Did she really just think she wished her mother had killed her at birth? That was unimaginable.

"I'm going to keep my eye on you, Daisy, and you better hope I never see any more signs of you trying to read my mind, you disgusting little freak. Because if I do, then I'm going to do what your mother should have done when you were a baby. I'm going to take a pillow, sneak into your bedroom, and put it over your face while you're sleeping. Then you won't be able to invade my mind any longer."

Daisy's grip tightened on the book as she fought the urge to hurl it at her Aunt's face. She imagined the pleasure she would have knocking the woman's eye out of her skull. Then her Aunt Doris's horrible murderous thoughts would be gone forever.

"What a ridiculous idea it was for me to suggest you go to the dance. Who would want to dance with such a pathetic creature? You'd probably sit on the sidelines in your frumpy dress, hands folded, head down, hoping no boy would pay any attention to you. Well, you wouldn't have to worry about that, because no self-respecting boy in his right mind would ever notice you. You're not beautiful, Daisy, not the ingénue I'd hoped you'd turn out to be. You're nothing but a pitiful, ugly wallflower."

Doris had enough of this for one day. She angrily hurried past Daisy like a stubborn toddler, as she usually did when they quarreled. But this time, as she got to the place where Daisy sat, she didn't notice the girl deliberately stick her leg out. Doris tripped over the outstretched limb and felt herself losing her balance.

Soon she was falling helplessly in slow motion, unable to stop her steady descent. As she fell, she saw Daisy sitting on the sofa, smiling a hideous smile, and she understood her niece really had just heard her thoughts. And what was worse, Doris had meant every word of what she had thought, and Daisy knew that too. Then the side of Doris's head struck the coffee table, and seconds after a bolt of agonizing pain shot through her skull, there was nothing more.

Daisy slowly stood, walking casually around the corpse of her aunt. She thought, rather than said, "Hum. I can't seem to hear you anymore, Aunt Doris. Can you hear me? Are you receiving my thoughts in whatever corner of Hell you now reside? Daisy to Aunt Doris. Come in, Aunt Doris." But there was only silence.

I'M NO VICTIM

"I don't want to be a victim."
CARRIE FISHER

It was black, so black; a darkness blacker than Sharon had ever imagined was possible. Although she had just opened her eyes, she felt like they were still tightly closed. Her head felt foggy; her brain was muddled. She was trying to determine where she was and what her current situation might be. The air around her felt dank and smelled musty with the scent of mildewed cloth.

She was able to determine that her hands had been bound tightly together behind her back, and when she tried to move her legs, she could tell they were tied at the ankles. She licked her dry and cracked lips and was glad to discover she was not gagged. She wiggled her eyebrows to try to sense if she had been blind-folded, and thankfully she had not been. She tried to shout for help, but all that came out was a small, dry, and raspy sound. Obviously, it had been a long time since she had a drink. Upon that understanding, she suddenly realized how thirsty she was.

"What I wouldn't give for some water right about now." She thought.

She could tell she was lying on her side in a slightly curled position. She could feel some sort of cloth material pressing against the side of her face. Where the hell was she, and why was she here? The last thing she recalled was walking out of her apartment on her way to work that morning. That was when it happened. Someone had come up behind her and placed his hand with a rag in it across her mouth. There was a strange medicinal smell, and that was when everything went black.

So someone had obviously drugged and kidnapped her, then tied her up and put her in this place, whatever place this might be. But why would anyone do such a thing to her? She was no one special. She was just a normal woman with a boring office job that she went to dutifully every day. Why would someone want to victimize her?

"I'm no victim." Sharon declared. And she meant it.

Although, like most people, Sharon never expected to find herself in such a situation. She understood what sort of violent world she lived in and had taken precautions to defend herself against any such attacks.

She had even attended a survivalist ten-week class, where, in addition to self-defense techniques, she had learned to get herself out of many different situations. The classes' mantra was "I'm No Victim." And even though Sharon had no idea why she had ended up in this condition, she was determined to find a way to get herself free. Her initial confusion and fear at discovering her captivity had been replaced by determination and anger.

Sharon struggled to try to wriggle free from her bindings but found the effort useless; the ropes held. She tried to lift her head and banged it against something metallic. A sharp bolt of pain shot through her skull, and she had to wait for several minutes for the pain to subside.

"Okay. So I'm obviously tied up in a metal box of some kind." She said to herself, being grateful she wasn't claustrophobic. That would have made things a lot more difficult.

She slowly moved her feet back and forth, trying to determine the dimensions of her prison. She could only move about a foot behind her until she came in contact with an obstruction of some sort. When she stretched her legs downward, it only took a few inches until her toes felt a solid surface. However, when she wiggled her legs forward, she was able to move about two feet before touching something.

In her mind, Sharon took all of these dimensions into consideration, along with the metallic surface she had bumped her head against, the soft cloth feeling against her cheek, as well as the musty smell of the place, and determined she must be inside the trunk of a car. She lifted and dropped her feet and could feel the floor vibrate beneath them.

"The wheel well. Yes, I'm definitely inside the trunk of a car."

Sharon swallowed a few more times, and when he felt her throat was moist enough, she shouted for help again. She expected her voice to have a bit of an echo to it but was surprised to hear a deadened quality to her shouting. She didn't know what that might mean, but there was little she could do about it at this point anyway.

Sharon also understood the car was obviously not in motion because if it had been, not only would she have felt it, but the rear lights would have been on. Even if it were daytime, the lights would have lit every time the driver pressed on his brake pedal. And it was as dark as a tomb inside this trunk, a realization which sent a cold chill down her spine. That was when she remembered something fundamental from one of her survival classes.

Her self-defense instructor had said, "Often when women are kidnapped, they're placed in the trunk of the attacker's car for transportation. If you ever find yourself locked in the trunk of a car, you should try to locate and knock out one of the rear lights. If your hands are free, you can stick one out through the hole and signal for help. If not, you can at least damage the light, and maybe if you're lucky, you can attract a police officer's attention. Cars get pulled over all the time for broken tail lights."

That was just the sort of sound advice she needed now. If she could maneuver her feet over to where the tail light should be and could get enough momentum, she might be able to knock out the light. At the very least, it would allow some fresh air to enter the musty chamber, and as her instructor suggested, maybe when the car was back on the road, a cop would notice the damaged light and come to investigate.

Sharon felt along the wall below her feet, and she wriggled them closer to the location of where she thought the taillights might be. Using the tips of her toes, she felt about, gently tapping surfaces while imagining the inside of a trunk in her mind. She hoped she would be able to determine when she found the location of the tail light. As she recalled, the lights were usually protected on the inside by some sort of plastic covering, which should be easy to compare to the trunk's hard metal surface. If she could knock off that protective hood, she should be able to knock off the outer light covering, or at the very least, damage the light bulb. Although a damaged light might not help her until later, she hoped to break the plastic to get some fresh air in the confined space. She felt her foot come in contact with something hollow, which moved when she pressed her foot against it.

"I'm no victim!" She shouted as she bent her knees, and with all her might, slammed the bottom of her feet against the plastic hood. She felt it easily give way and fall off somewhere in the trunk. Then she slowly maneuvered her feet over to where she believed the light was located and inched them into the opening made when the cover was destroyed. Then she felt it; the plastic outside covering of the tail light.

"Nobody does this to me and gets away with it." She said through gritted teeth as she jammed her feet into the opening, repeatedly striking the covering until, at last, she felt it break off.

Her momentary elation at her success was short-lived, however, as she felt the rush of icy cold water flowing in from the opening and soaking her legs. That was when she realized why the air in the trunk had been so musty and why when she shouted, her voice had seemed muffled. She was in the trunk of a car, but that car was underwater. It was then she realized she had been wrong. No matter how much she wanted to believe otherwise, she was a victim after all.

www.ingramcontent.com/pod-product-compliance
Lightning Source LLC
Chambersburg PA
CBHW030520020726
47494CB00004B/1177